# witch window

## A *Murder on Skis* Mystery

Other **Murder on Skis** Mysteries
by Phil Bayly:

**Murder on Skis**

**Loving Lucy**

**Back Dirt**

# witch window

## A *Murder on Skis* Mystery

# Phil Bayly

# witch window

## A *Murder on Skis* Mystery

©2022 by **Phil Bayly**

# WWW.MURDERONSKIS.COM

ISBN: 978-1-60571-634-3

Cover Design: Carolyn Bayly & Debbi Wraga
Alexey Novikov / Dreamstime.com
John Alberton, Nataliia Nesterenko & William Sherman /
istockphoto.com
Author Photo: Carolyn Bayly

Printed in the United States of America

This is dedicated to my wife, Carolyn, whose patience seems to be a bottomless well. And to the brave folk from Vermont who helped found this great nation. They were of all colors and all genders. They all deserve their due.

"Fame is a vapor, popularity an accident, and riches take wings. Only one thing endures and that is character."
—Horace Greeley

"I've outgrown arrogance. It didn't prove to be very useful."
—Sipp Ives, Police Chief

# 1

It was a leap of faith. He hurled himself down a steep pitch. She gulped and followed. They pedaled furiously to get up an equally steep ascent on the other side. It meant leaning forward and sticking their noses even closer to the packed dirt they did not want to impact with their faces.

It reminded them of the half-pipe where they met over the winter. That was on snowboards. Now they were pushing the pace on mountain bikes. Both of these toned athletes believed that scary fun was the best fun.

Clearing that obstacle, they propelled themselves down a narrow corridor. Purple phlox and cattails bordering both sides of the path were a blur. The wild trail barely provided room for them. Leaves and branches slapped their arms and legs as they sped by.

The fragrance of the flowers and the warm sun greeting their faces made them miss the winter less. They were happy to shake off the chill.

The intensity of the color around them, especially the green grass and budding leaves, was a blazing distraction. They had to admit that it was something they missed during the coldest, darkest days of winter.

The single track they followed entered wetlands. Only thick wild hedges of marsh plants like swamp smartweed and horehound separated them from the water.

Attuned to the possibility of taking a tumble, the bikers only stole a glance at a blue heron, and then a great egret, standing at attention in the shallow water as they raced past.

The riders re-entered the woods. The path beneath their bikes became grass instead of hardpack. It was such a unique place to mountain bike. They were loving it.

Finally, they stopped at a spot where the trail was slightly wider. It had plenty of sunshine and they needed to catch their breath. They drank from the metal water bottles carried in harnesses on their bike frames.

They stood in the full sun, knowing that in the shadow of the forest there were clusters of mosquitos that, now that the riders could be caught, would love to have them for lunch.

The young man and woman straddled their bikes and took time to survey their surroundings. The man also surveyed the woman's bare legs, strong and appealing. She watched him and admired his tan arms. They smiled at each other.

The forest they had entered was a mixture of tall trees and dead logs, the remainder of trees knocked over in a tornado a few years before. They spied a bald eagle swooping overhead, scanning the nearby Mohawk River for fish.

"Let's see if I can impress you with a factoid, if I can get it right," the man said with a shy grin. "The bald eagle became the symbol of the United States because our forefathers were inspired by the Iroquois Indians who used to roam these woods. The bald eagle was the Iroquois' symbol too.

"The United States' official emblem of the bald eagle holds thirteen arrows, for each of the original thirteen states. The Iroquois' eagle held six arrows, for each of the nations belonging to the Iroquois Confederacy."

She made a face. He was disappointed to think his story had missed its mark.

"Do you smell that?" she asked.

"It always gets a little smelly this time of year," he told her. "This marsh floods every spring when the snow melts and the river rises. Then when the water recedes, dead stuff decays and smells like, well, dead stuff."

"The smell is disgusting," she told him.

"It *is* worse than I remember," he admitted.

They were on their first date that didn't involve carrying a snowboard. They were both curious to see if this would work away from snow, if it could thrive doing everyday stuff like going to the movies or lunch or doing laundry.

After a February of showing up at the mountain alone and hoping to bump into the other, in March they decided to take turns driving and rode to the mountain together. April was awesome, but winter ended.

He finally asked her out on the kind of date that didn't require wearing layers of fleece, polyester and goggles. This date.

He was kind of a bad boy. She was drawn to him. He was different than the other boys she had dated. He was wild, bordering on reckless. She believed that it was going to be a great summer.

Their bike ride had started on the other side of an old Erie Canal bridge. Their trip roughly followed the historic canal itself. The famous ditch still held water within its stone container. The canal bottom was shallow, filled with silt. And the water was mostly stagnant. It was choked with pondweed and water chestnut.

"Okay, that smell is going to gag me," she proclaimed. She squeezed her water bottle back into its harness and placed her foot on a bike pedal, preparing to push off.

But *he* dismounted from his bike and carefully laid it down. Intently, he took a few steps through the tall grass to the edge of where the ground looked like a drained swamp.

"Look out for ticks," she warned. He pushed deeper into the brush and disappeared beyond a grove of trees.

"Where are you going?" she asked. He didn't answer.

It occurred to her that he was looking for a spot where they could conceal themselves in the forest and take their relationship to another level. She liked the idea of that and pulled her tee shirt over her head, revealing her sports bra.

But the longer he was gone, she started to grow uneasy at the thought of being left alone on the remote path. It was sort of creepy. She looked over both shoulders to be sure no one was sneaking up behind her. Assured there was not another soul in sight, that bothered her too.

She didn't know her companion well enough to call him her boyfriend. And now she asked herself how well she really knew him.

He reappeared, lifting his knees high to clear the brush and walked back toward her. His smile was gone. It was replaced by a sour gaze, aimed in her direction. Her heart began to beat a little faster. She regretted pulling her shirt off. He began to frighten her.

"I saw you bring your phone. Give it to me," he commanded with a serious tone. He held out his large hand. She hesitated. That phone was her only lifeline. Was she willing to hand it over to him? Did she have reason to be frightened of him? Her next decision felt like it could determine, literally, if she lived or died.

She was strong and thought that, normally, she could take care of herself. But he was stronger. And any chance of escaping on her bike had already passed. He was only a few feet from her.

He still had that strange look on his face. He seemed to stare straight through her. He continued to hold out his hand. She unzipped a pocket on her shorts, reached in and paused a moment. Then she handed him her phone.

He saw the uncertainty on her face. It bordered on terror, he thought.

"Sorry," he said. "I didn't mean to freak you out. Stay here."

He gave her an assuring smile and glanced at her sports bra before turning back toward the field. She closed her eyes and let out a breath. A sense of calm returned. Scary fun was a turn-on. She looked at his muscular back pressing against his tee shirt. It was wet with sweat. He held the phone up to his ear.

"9-1-1?" she heard him say into the phone. "I think we just found a body."

# 2

"What the hell is he wearing?" the coroner asked.

"Has he been here since Halloween?"

"I think it's ski clothing," Investigator Foot said as he swept a mosquito away from his face.

"Ski clothing? What do you mean 'ski clothing?'"

"Isn't that what it looks like to you?" the sheriff's investigator asked the coroner.

"This is golfing weather," the coroner said. "Ski season is over."

"Except in Vermont. Killington will be open for a few more weeks," the investigator informed him. "We'll check with them, once we figure out who we're looking at."

The coroner looked down at the corpse and slapped a mosquito that had landed on his hand. Blood indicated the critter had just finished lunch.

The dead man was still face-down on the ground. The investigator noticed stubs of new grass growing up around the corpse.

The dispatcher who took the 9-1-1 call had contacted the Saratoga County Sheriff's Office in Upstate New York.

"Two mountain bikers report finding a body in Vischer Ferry Preserve," the dispatcher said. She was asked where the body was located.

"In a field, off a trail connected to the old Erie Canal. Not the towpath. He said it's on a grass trail leading away from the old canal bridge."

"I know which one she means," Investigator John Foot said from his desk. He had gone for rides on the same trail.

After the investigator and two deputies arrived at the scene and got a look, they called the sheriff. The sheriff instructed them to call the county coroner and get more deputies out there.

The body would remain where it was until someone who outranked Investigator Foot said it was time to move it. The sheriff was on his way. Until then, deputies would walk the field looking for evidence. They found none.

When the sheriff showed up, Investigator Foot reported that they found the victim face-down, his nose planted in the hardened mud.

The arms of the deceased were above his head, bent at the elbows, as though the last thing he had been told was "Stick 'em up." His legs extended straight below his torso. They weren't twisted or broken.

His fingers had been chewed away by either coyotes, fox, rodents or all of the above. His face likely wouldn't be a pretty sight either. That would wait until they rolled him over.

"The coroner says that he's probably been lying here for a while," the investigator said to the sheriff.

Following the briefing, the sheriff put Investigator Foot in charge and departed for something else requiring a sheriff.

The coroner had been nearby when he received the call, having lunch at the Vischer Ferry General Store. It occupied a building erected one hundred and fifty years ago, built on the foundation of a store built one hundred years before that.

"They have great food," the coroner said as he worked on a fried egg sandwich. Foot had marveled, over the years, that the coroner's appetite wasn't altered at all by the close proximity of a rotting corpse.

"My God," uttered the coroner.

"What?" the investigator asked as his eyes scanned the crime scene.

"This is a latte with caramel sea salt," the coroner said with reverence. He held a large paper cup before his eyes. "Unbelievable."

"Unbelievable," Investigator Foot muttered to himself.

"Go around the sessile-fruited arrowhead," the coroner instructed the deputies, his voice raised as he chewed. He pointed out a deer path the deputies could take to approach the body from the biking path. "And watch the northern blue violets."

The coroner, it turned out, was also a lover of wildflowers and leafy things. Vischer Ferry Preserve's seven hundred acres was one of his favorite places to hike.

"He's got a flower fetish," one deputy said to another, who was bewildered by the coroner's instructions.

The spot where the corpse was discovered by the two bike riders was a large field with matted ground cover. Leafy tree groves were sprouting in the field and starting to connect with each other.

The field was adjacent to the towpath from the original Erie Canal. The canal had been cut from dirt and rock in 1825. The towpath was a primitive road running alongside the canal, allowing oxen, horsepower or manpower to pull a barge along the way.

The crowd of law officers was standing in the general location where a colonial village was once settled in 1672. It was called Forts Ferry. There had been a barge there that was used to cross the Mohawk. George Washington is believed to have used the ferry at least once.

Before that, First Natives grew corn in the field. There were no trees then. And the Indigenous people called the spot Canastigione. It meant "corn flats."

Investigator Foot speculated that the colonial village had not been abandoned. He figured that its citizens were all devoured by mosquitos. He swiped at another one as it landed on his neck.

"Can I just start shooting them?" a deputy asked in frustration as he swatted at a mosquito caught plunging her proboscis into his vein. He received sympathetic commentary from the other law enforcers who were busy fending off their own feeding swarm.

Investigator Foot spoke with the man and woman who found the body. They seemed interested in being so close to a crime scene. Foot detected that they were also interested in seeing each other close-up. There was a lot of touching, he noticed.

Finished with his sandwich, the heavy-set coroner lit a cigar. It was his experience that mosquitos didn't like cigar smoke. Offered a cigar of his own, Investigator Foot joined the coroner, just in case he was right.

Sheriff's Investigator John Foot was the namesake of his sixth great-grandfather. The elder was a Hessian soldier, coming from Germany to fight alongside the British in the Revolutionary War. Johannes Caspar Fuss didn't care if the Americans separated from the homeland or not. Fuss fought for money.

He was captured by the Americans at the Battle of Saratoga, less than thirty miles from where his sixth great-grandson was currently standing.

Following the American victory at Saratoga, many of the Hessian prisoners of war were marched south through Claverack.

There were few American sentries guarding the German prisoners. This was because the Americans needed their own able-bodied soldiers elsewhere.

The Americans even hoped that some of the Germans would escape and disappear into the countryside. Then they would sit out the war rather than rejoin the British fighting force.

But Johannes Caspar Fuss came to the New World to make money fighting. And it turned out that he wasn't particular about who he fought for.

The Americans were desperate for professional soldiers, and Johannes Fuss accepted an invitation, while in Claverack, to join the American Continental Army. For money. He fought under his new name, John Foot.

Saratoga County was historic soil. The man dressed in strange clothing, now lying in the mud, wasn't the first violent death to happen here.

"Did you identify him yet?" the coroner asked.

"No," replied Investigator Foot. "There's nothing in his pockets except a tube that probably was lip balm, and some faded currency."

"Is anyone missing?"

"Any missing skiers? No."

"Roll him over," the investigator said. The deputies complied.

"You're right," the coroner said to the investigator. "It does look like ski clothing."

They both stared in wonder. The dead man wore a jacket that was once a luminescent green. It was now dirty and the color was faded. The fabric was torn. He also wore black nylon overalls, a black helmet and one unbuckled gray ski boot on his left foot.

"Are we to presume," the coroner asked, "he once had a matching ski boot?"

"They usually sell them in pairs," Investigator Foot responded.

"A lot of people cross-country ski in this preserve over the winter," a deputy offered.

"But those aren't cross-country ski boots. They're alpine boots," the investigator noted. The deputy nodded his head in agreement.

They looked around them. Shadows were getting longer and the best light of the day had passed. But they could see that the ground was flat in every direction.

"There's no ..." the coroner began to comment.

"No downhill ski area within thirty miles of us? No," said the investigator, reading the coroner's mind. "It's unlikely that this is a skiing accident."

"Well, how did he end up here?"

# 3

I t was the same dream.

JC Snow saw a medieval warrior being carried out of the forest. He was lying on a large shield. He was unmoving, dead. The shield bearing the corpse was being carried by fellow warriors.

Their garments were brilliant in the sun. Yellows and blues and reds. They wore armor protecting their arms, heads and torsos. A dog followed behind the procession. Somehow, JC knew that the dog belonged to the man on the shield.

JC woke up after that scene, just as he always woke up after seeing it. He didn't know who the dead warrior was or how he died. He had no idea what the recurring dream was about, only that it would come again.

He often had trouble sleeping in the middle of the night. Almost without fail, he awoke between the hours of two and four in the morning.

Studies of the human mind suggested those were the hours people usually saw ghosts. Those particular hours, between two and four, had come to be known as "The Witching Hours."

Psychologists explained most ghostly sightings as a trick of science. Those hours corresponded with the time that the human body peaked in its allotment of melatonin. It was something that helped control circadian rhythms when we fell asleep and when we woke up.

JC rose from bed and sat for a moment. He let his feet hit the floor without depending on them to bear his weight. That would wait until his feet were on speaking terms with his brain.

He had fallen back asleep after his vision of medieval knights, as he usually did. It was probably the best night of sleep he had since his knee surgery.

"It was just a scope," he'd tell people who were concerned about his fifth knee operation. It was arthroscopic knee surgery, to cut away more tissue that was tearing. X-rays of his knees, lately, had looked like seaweed deep down on a dark ocean floor.

That had been five days ago. One crutch lay on the floor next to his bedside table. Easy to find if he needed it in the dark of night.

The orthopedic surgeon had told him to stay on the crutch for a week, until JC was to return to the doctor's office for a follow-up visit.

The knee throbbed. It was time for the day's first application of ice and dose of ibuprofen. He'd never filled the prescription he was given for stronger medication. He wasn't a fan of the stronger stuff. He got used to the pain and the Advil and ice kept the swelling down.

He grabbed the crutch and made his way across his Larimer Square apartment in Denver, Colorado. He needed to go to the bathroom.

JC looked into the mirror. He had thick dark hair and a mustache. He was still fairly tone for a man in his mid-thirties. He was athletic but he vowed to get to the gym more. He was due to begin physical therapy on his knee, anyway.

He felt that his body was starting to betray him. Another doctor said that his metabolism was changing. Said doctor informed JC that he could no longer consume every food or drink that looked attractive to him.

"You were lucky," the doctor said. "Many of us learn this at a much earlier age. We had to start watching our diet while you were still practicing gluttony without paying any real price. Now, you have been enrolled in our reality. Consider this a warm welcome." The doctor smirked for a moment. Then he said, "Drink less, eat less. You'll be fine."

JC looked in the mirror at the reflection of the scar on his left shoulder. That surgery was some years ago. It honored his body of work playing high school football and some college rugby. Now he would have another scar across his knee celebrating his fixation on ski racing.

He looked at his mustache. He wondered about shaving it. He'd had it since college. He wasn't certain what he'd look like without it. But if he was serious about pursuing this opening for an anchor job at his television station, it was probably the sage thing to do.

The news director hadn't asked him to shave it. No one in management had even suggested it would enhance his chance for the anchor job. But JC added up the number of news anchors on TV who wore a mustache and he came up with: zero.

After brushing his teeth, he and his crutch made their way to the kitchen. The crutch was made of some lightweight alloy. He was sorry they hadn't provided him with crutches made of wood. He thought wood had more character.

He'd injured his knee in the last ski race of the season. He fell and got up. His race was over for the day, but his knee wasn't doing a lot of complaining. So, he'd gone skiing for a few more hours with friends who had also raced.

The next morning, the knee was blown up to the size of a squishy softball. "Crap," he'd said.

He ignored it for a couple of months. He'd go for a run but it would swell again. So, he fell into a routine of running, then swelling, then icing. All the while, he thought the knee would get better with time. It didn't.

He finally visited a friend who was an orthopedist and was told that he'd torn something.

"It looks like seaweed," he told the orthopedic surgeon when shown an image of his knee on the inside.

"Yes," the doctor agreed, "and it's getting caught on things every time you bend your knee."

"What can we do to get this behind us?" JC asked his orthopedic friend.

"Surgery," was the answer provided by the surgeon.

Following surgery, there would be physical therapy and then a lot of mountain biking. That would define the end of JC's summer and autumn. He hoped to be ready for ski season.

His life was made a little easier because at work, he suddenly found himself behind a desk pushing a pencil. That's how he facetiously described the job of being a news anchor.

He was temporarily anchoring the early evening weekday news. JC found it easier, with one good leg, to work at the anchor desk. When he was a field reporter, something he truly loved, his job entailed running after stories up and down the Front Range of Colorado. Reporting required a lot of literal legwork.

It was blind luck that there was an anchor seat to place him in. The anchor who had been holding down the evening weekday newscast had notified his employers that he accepted a similar job in California.

So, when JC returned to work after surgery, he was escorted to the anchor desk and told to sit there. He would be the centerpiece for the early evening news for a while. Days later, he was told that it was going well and he was being considered for that anchor job on a permanent basis.

It wasn't something JC had pursued. He liked reporting. No, he *loved* reporting. He loved the legwork. He loved being the first one to find something or figure something out. He loved solving mysteries.

But there were corrupting influences making him wonder if he wanted to *win* that anchor job. First of all, he'd make a lot more money.

"If you're an anchor," a friend told him, "you could afford that weekend home in Red Feather Lakes."

"Tell me, how can money be both evil and awesome at the same time?" JC had responded. He could see himself on the porch of the remote cabin in Red Feather Lakes, watching the sun go down as a moose slowly walked across the meadow.

JC was told there would be competition for the anchor job. There would be applicants from outside the television station and there would be a formidable rival from within.

Sam Brown was that rival. He was presently the anchor of the evening news on the weekend. He was everything television wanted from an anchor. He was more than handsome, he was stunning. And he was charming.

JC believed there was such a thing as "TV charm." He wished that he had it. Sam Brown had an abundance of it.

Sam's shortcoming, among those acquainted with him in the newsroom, was that he wasn't very smart. But on television, he read the news off the teleprompter not only like he knew what he was talking about, but that he knew something more that he wasn't ready to tell us. Maybe he thought we weren't ready for the whole truth.

JC thought Sam was miles ahead of him as an anchor. Was this really even a competition? Or was the newsroom's management just saying it was, for appearances?

That was the question JC put to the news director, Pat Perilla.

"JC, anchoring isn't all about good looks and charm," Perilla told him. "If it was, you wouldn't win. But you're a hell of a journalist. And I sleep better at night knowing my show is in the capable hands of a good journalist, like you."

"Thank you," JC responded.

"And our consultant makes another good point," the news director added. "The audience loves you. When you go on these road trips and take two weeks to solve a murder in New York or Montana, viewers tune in every single night. They don't want to miss your update. And maybe if you were anchoring every night, those same viewers would tune in every night. Not for two weeks at a time, but night after night, year after year."

JC had carved out a niche in the newsroom. He was their best reporter. And if there was an intriguing story on the other side of the country that interested Colorado viewers, especially a mystery that needed to be solved, JC was dispatched there. It provided responsible information and absorbing entertainment. It was TV magic.

"The downside of making you the anchor," Perilla cautioned, "is that you are probably the only one who can pull off those road trips." JC had already been pulled aside by a middle manager who told him *that* was why he was definitely *not* going to get the anchor job.

JC hadn't decided if he wanted the anchor job. More money meant more ... a lot of things.

But he'd become a journalist to ferret out the stories that weren't being told, and to tell the rest of the stories the right way. He labored to give his viewers honest, raw data. He wasn't going to tell viewers what to think or who to vote for. He was going to provide them with information allowing them to make their own decisions about who was right and what was wrong.

He knew that he could also do that as an anchor. In fact, he had ideas about how to do it better than anchors were doing it now.

But as a reporter, he was on the front lines. He was the one rolling around in the mud, the blood and the beer. He *loved* being the one rolling around in the mud, the blood and the beer

JC took a seat at his kitchen table and leaned his crutch against an exposed brick wall. He opened his laptop to check his mail. He saw an email from Shara. She had been sending messages for about a week. This one said, "When can we talk?"

He heard the metallic scrape of a key fitting into the lock on the door to his apartment from the hallway. He heard the door open and shut, just out of his view. He closed his laptop.

And then he saw Robin, who brought him a kiss on the lips, a cappuccino and a breakfast crêpe.

# 4

" A s you like to say, this doesn't pass the smell test,"
an old friend had told JC.

For the rest of the time JC was out on the water, he was
thinking about his friend's assessment.

JC and Robin had been looking to get out of his
apartment. After spending five days on a crutch or on the
couch, he was going stir-crazy. They thought of going
mountain biking, but his doctor objected.

"Mountain biking will be good exercise," the orthopedic
surgeon said. "But, if you lose your balance and put your foot
down to catch yourself, you'll probably destroy all my
beautiful work."

So, they decided to kayak on the South Platte River, rolling through the city limits of Denver and its suburbs. Robin insisted on being the one to put the kayaks on the car and the one to pull them down. She insisted on doing the heavy lifting, because JC had been told by his doctor to stay home and rest.

"My leg can rest in a kayak as readily as it can rest on my couch," he told Robin as he justified defying "doctor's orders."

They put in at the Prince Street Bridge. There were plenty of places near the water to eat, when they came back upriver.

As they paddled beside one another, JC couldn't help but appreciate what a beautiful woman Robin was. The red curls in her hair waved in the wind. Her fit arms had no problem moving the water. And her smile sometimes made his pulse race.

She had a nurturing manner that made his life easier. It wasn't that she lived to please him, but she made it feel that way. She could put his mind at ease, years after he came to know that his mind would frequently torment him.

He thought that she loved him. And he felt guilty for questioning whether he wanted to love her. He'd been in love before, and it nearly crushed him.

He had fallen in love during college in Fort Collins. Then Shara left him. She moved to New York City and married someone else. He'd won Shara back when he found her living alone in Montana. But the long distance between Montana and Colorado broke them again.

Shara resurfaced when her engagement to another man unraveled. But JC couldn't shake the shadow of their damaged past, and by then, he'd met Robin.

Shara had been emailing him again. He hadn't told Robin. He didn't know what to tell her. He wasn't certain what to tell Shara.

A cool breeze was gently blowing over the water on a hot day. JC and Robin heard birds chirping, happy to be back for the spring. The river made a babbling sound as their kayaks cut through the water.

"Did you know that sound travels faster in salt water than fresh water?" JC asked her. His voice was raised to be heard over the chop of their paddles.

"Are you a science professor now?" she teased.

"Yes." And they paddled in content silence for a short while.

"It travels faster in the ocean than a lake," he resumed.

"This seems to be something you have to get off your chest," she said, smiling.

"Yes."

"How deep is this ocean you're talking about?" she asked. He looked at her, disbelieving. How could he answer that? She was laughing at him, now.

"Are you testing me or torturing me?" he asked.

"Both."

"I was nice enough to share this with you," he told her with a grin. "And now you think that you've stumped me, don't you?"

"Yes," she laughed.

"Sound is faster at lower depths, no matter how much lower. Lower is faster than higher," he pronounced in a triumphant tone.

That's when JC's phone rang.

"Oh, I'm sorry, Robin. There's no time for further questions," he declared. He was relieved, knowing he would be unable to answer her next inquiry. He had exhausted his entire catalogue of facts regarding sound and water.

"Take the call," she said. "We'll drift for a while."

They pulled their paddles across their kayaks and each extended a hand to attach themselves to the other's craft.

"JC," the voice on the phone said, "I need your help. No one else gives a crap."

The voice belonged to Davey Kay, JC's best friend from childhood. They played high school football together in Upstate New York.

Skiing and college lured JC to Colorado, but he'd always stayed in touch with Davey Kay, who remained close to home in Saratoga Springs.

"What makes you think I give a crap," JC joked.

"Seriously," Davey said. "There's something wrong here and it might be right up your alley."

"You're serious?"

"I am, JC."

Davey began to tell the tale of the terrible lingering death of Josh Church.

"You remember him?" Davey asked. "He was an author. He wrote some best sellers, usually fiction about some environmental disaster."

"Yeah, like *Towering Inferno*, only the 'tower' is a tree or a cornstalk. His disasters are always set somewhere in nature," JC recalled. "One was about huge wildfires caused by climate change, right?"

"Right," Davey said. "That was one of his biggest sellers."

"Yeah, he lived in Colorado," JC recollected. "He was up in Basalt or somewhere."

"Yeah, somewhere in Colorado," Davey confirmed. "That's why I thought it was up your alley. He's famous in Colorado. What's that called?"

"A hook," JC said. "It's a hook to hang a story on. It's a reason it would be relevant to our audience in Colorado."

"You're feeling me, Bro."

"I have always enjoyed feeling you, Davey," JC joked.

"And I, you," replied the old friend.

"Did you call me to have phone sex?" JC asked.

This got a grimace from Robin, still clutching JC's kayak so they'd drift the river together. She returned to sipping from her water bottle. And JC's study of his beautiful girlfriend caused him to lose track of the conversation with Davey.

"I'm sorry, start over," JC told his friend. "I got distracted."

"Try to stay with me," Davey pleaded. "Anyway, I liked Josh. I was his tax accountant. He met a woman named Melody. She was a bookseller at a store in Aspen. Josh met her at a book signing inside the store and they fell in love. They got married, even though he was a lot older than she, and eventually they moved to Vermont. That's where Melody had grown up."

"He died earlier this year, right?" JC interjected. "We ran a story on it. He was a Colorado native who made it big."

"Yes!" Davey exclaimed. "That's the point. He died in bed in January. They called it natural causes. And I've been trying to close his books. There are volumes to go through. He was rich. But there is something wrong about all of it. I think there was some foul play."

"You think he was murdered?" JC asked. This got the attention of Robin, who couldn't help but hear the entirety of JC's end of the conversation.

"Yes, I do," Davey said.

"Do the police think he was murdered?" JC asked.

"No, they don't."

"Does his widow—Melody is it?—does *she* think he was murdered?"

"No, she doesn't," Davey acknowledged. "She was beside herself when he died. She's just trying to move on with her life. I don't blame her."

"So, *you* are the only one who thinks the famous author, Josh Church, was murdered?"

"That would be an accurate statement," Davey admitted.

Robin looked at JC. She wanted to know what Davey's answer was. JC nodded his head.

"I may be crazy for asking this," JC countered, "but why do you think he was murdered?"

"I may be crazy for admitting this," Davey responded, "but, I don't know."

Davey went on to tell JC that he'd visit with Josh Church a couple of times a year. Davey would drive to the author's home in Stonestead, Vermont, to do his taxes. But he'd always stay for the day.

"I really liked him," he said. "And when I was in the area, once or twice a year, I'd stop by and we'd go out to lunch or something. There's a great Scottish pub in the next town over."

JC's old friend told him that Melody received ample proceeds from the will signed by Josh Church. And she'd continue to reap rewards provided by considerable royalties from the books he wrote.

"Some assets went to an environmental group that Josh supported. They are called 'Vermont Stands for the Birds and Bees.'"

"V-S-B-B. Catchy," JC said sarcastically.

"Yeah. But Josh really thought they did good work. Bees are really in danger, you know."

"I agree. Did Josh and Melody have any children?" JC asked.

"No."

"Was everyone happy with the last will and testament?"

"I think so. No one filed a protest, that I'm aware of," Davey said.

"You're not giving me much to work with, my friend," JC told him.

"It just doesn't pass the smell test," Davey said.

"Wow, where did you get a hokey line like that?" JC asked.

"JC Snow," Davey told him. "That's what he says, 'It doesn't pass the smell test.'"

"Well," JC said, "I wouldn't believe that crackpot."

"Just about every time," Davey said, "he turns out to be right."

# 5

"Now what do you think?

"Now, it makes me wonder," JC told Davey Kay.

"How does it smell?" Davey asked.

"Fishy, I have to admit."

It had been over a month since they had last discussed Josh Church's death. Davey Kay had been sorting through his dead friend's financial records.

"It's like raking leaves with a salad fork," Davey said. "There's a lot of material."

"He died in bed, but you're convinced he was murdered?" JC asked.

"There's no doubt in my mind," Davey said.

With Davey's new information, JC went to the news director at his Denver television station.

"There's a famous dead guy in Vermont," JC told Pat Perilla. "He's from Colorado. Do you want me to go?"

"Yes," the news director answered. It took JC by surprise. He had expected pushback.

"Wait a minute," JC said. "You don't even know who the famous guy is."

"You're about to tell me, aren't you?"

"Yes," JC replied. "But usually I have to put on a big sales job. Maybe we argue a little. Only then do you agree. Come on, I'm a creature of habit."

"You wouldn't be here if you didn't think it was a good story, right?" Perilla was smiling. He liked having the drop on JC. It didn't happen very often.

"Besides," the news director said, "it will give us something to hang our hat on between Broncos games. I wish they'd play more. They should play every day, like baseball."

"If they played football every day, the players would die," JC answered.

"Well, that would be an interesting story too," the news director responded.

"I'll need to take a photographer," JC said, shaking off the absurd digression.

"Take Bip, if he wants to go."

"I could use a producer. It always works better when we have a producer," JC said.

"Hmm," the news director said, as though he was considering a myriad of possibilities. "We have a new producer coming to work tomorrow. He just graduated college. He's never worked a day in his life in the news business. He was actually hired as a favor to a family friend of our general manager. We could send that promising young prospect with you."

JC *thought* Perilla was joking, but the prospect of a useless newbie was too frightening.

"That's not funny," JC finally responded.

"It was to me," the news director said as a broad grin creased his face. "Take Robin."

A wave of relief came over the reporter. Robin had become the best field producer they had. And she was Robin.

JC was also grateful for the vote of confidence from his boss. He knew that he would still have to explain the story in Vermont to win ultimate approval. But Perilla had said before, their audience seemed to be drawn to the television set when JC was out of town tracking a crime.

Focus groups told the television station's management that. When the TV station demonstrated they were willing to go anywhere on the map to chase a story, it brought them credibility in the eyes of news consumers. Competing news departments in Denver rarely did it. But, Perilla told himself, they didn't have JC Snow.

"So, for a matter of formality," the news director inquired, "might I learn what this is all about? What's the story in Vermont that I'm paying for?"

"My, aren't we being nosy," JC joked.

"My wife says that to me all the time."

After telling his news director of Josh Church, and what Davey Kay had learned, the trip to Vermont received Perilla's stamp of approval.

"And JC," Perilla added, "I appreciate that you're in competition for an anchor job here. You've been doing a good job behind the anchor desk. While you're away, Sam will anchor the show. But this trip isn't going to adversely affect your chances for the job. Any questions?"

"You know that I'm torn between the job I have and the opportunity you're dangling in front of me," JC said. "At some point, I realize that I may have to stop playing in the sandbox and come sit with the adults. So, I want to stay in the competition. I appreciate your saying that traveling halfway across the country won't leave me the forgotten man."

They flew to Albany, New York, the day after Labor Day. It was the closest major airport to Stonestead, Vermont, with a direct flight from Denver.

That was followed by a two-hour drive. There weren't that many roads connecting New York to Vermont, because most Vermonters don't want them.

Vermont had the second-smallest population in the United States. Many in that population would have been delighted to have the smallest.

"I read that the governor of Vermont offered remote workers ten thousand dollars to move here," Robin said from the backseat of their rental car. "The state needs the tax revenue and wouldn't mind a few more employable people."

"I remember that," JC confirmed. "But when ten or twenty new people moved into one little town, the natives grumbled. They didn't like the idea of seeing a face they hadn't known since grade school."

JC turned on the radio and found 102.7FM. WEQX was in Manchester, Vermont. It was one of the nation's first alt-rock radio stations.

"It's legendary," JC told his friends. Further into the Green Mountains, it would be hard to pick up anything on the radio.

"No worries," JC told them. "I brought some CDs too. The Beach Boys. It's summertime and Brian Wilson is a genius. He's the Beethoven of our time. Appreciate him while we have him."

Bip was driving the rental sedan. He'd jumped at the opportunity to return to the East Coast. He'd never been there until another assignment with JC, to Upstate New York over the winter.

Bip was born and raised in Telluride. He had just celebrated his twenty-ninth birthday. JC had given him a birthday card filled with stickers from Eastern ski areas. They all had images of snowboarders. Bip's skills on a snowboard were impressive.

Robin was also eager for the trip to Vermont. The work was satisfying, and it was like going on vacation with JC. She was a mogul skier during the winter and worked to stay fit during the summer. She'd already proclaimed her intention of finding a running route during their stay in Stonestead.

The only downside they could think of, regarding this trip, was that they'd be in the heart of Vermont's Ski Country and it would be September. No skiing.

The road to Stonestead was winding and rural. They passed old colonial homes and wood-frame shacks. There were stores but no strip malls. And the stores sold maple syrup, antiques, bears cut from wood by chainsaws, and snowmobiles.

They passed an obelisk on a hilltop commemorating the Battle of Bennington, a confrontation during the Revolutionary War where General John Stark is said to have told his colonial troops to fight with ferocity, "or on this night, Molly Stark sleeps a widow."

In between grassy slopes spilling down from pine forests, there were ponds where moose were sometimes spotted. A stone had been given painted eyes and named "Indian Rock."

Grass covered the runs when they drove on Route 11 past the Bromley Ski Area. The green slopes of Stratton Mountain Resort could be seen nearby on the right. The ski area called Magic Mountain was straight ahead. The Okemo Ski Resort was only a short drive away.

"It wasn't too long ago that this was the heart of American skiing," JC told his fellow travelers. "The Rocky Mountains didn't become the dominant ski destination until the 1960s. Vail didn't open until 1962. Before that, the cover of *SKI Magazine* was usually shot in Vermont."

Approaching their destination, they spotted the Mont Vert Ski Resort towering over the trees. It was in the town of Stonestead, and provided jobs and adventure there, all year long. There was skiing and snowboarding in the winter. During the summer, they sold rides up a chairlift to mountain bikers and provided paths to follow down. The resort also had a golf course, and a ropes course allowing customers to scare themselves twenty feet above ground.

They passed an old cemetery.

"Hold your breath!" said Robin from the backseat.

"Why?" Bip asked.

"If you don't hold your breath when you pass a cemetery, the evil spirits will get in," she told him with an amused look. It was a game she said she played with her siblings, growing up.

"I thought you hold your breath so the ghosts don't get jealous because they can no longer breathe," JC offered.

"That too," she said as she took a deep breath. Bip and JC shrugged to each other and held their breaths too.

Robin had insisted that JC sit in the front passenger seat. There was more legroom. His leg still got stiff when it was immobile for too long. He'd purposely picked an aisle seat on the airplane, so he could sometimes stretch it out.

It had now been about a month since his knee surgery. He had started physical therapy and he'd come a long way, but it would be interrupted by this assignment.

The custom during a news assignment was for the news photographer to drive the car. So Bip was behind the wheel.

Bip was the youngest member of this team. JC thought he was the kind of handsome you find in Hollywood. And JC only had to look at the faces of *women* who got a glimpse of Bip to know it was an accurate assessment.

Bip spiked his hair. And its color turned lighter under the summer sun.

"Maybe that's what Bip reminds me of," JC thought to himself. "A surfer boy." But Bip wasn't a surfer, he was a skilled snowboarder.

"We can look around later," JC said as they drove into the heart of Stonestead. "Davey is meeting us. He's only still here because he knew we were coming. He'll get us up to date and then he's heading back to Saratoga."

"So, where are we heading?" Bip asked.

"The next town. A tavern in Chester called MacLaomainn's," JC told him. Davey Kay told JC on the phone that he'd chosen to meet at a Scottish pub because his old friend loved all things Scottish.

JC's blood was tartan. His grandfather was the last of the Snow family to reside in Scotland, in Fife.

"But do me a favor," Davey said on the phone, "don't wear your dress."

"It's called a kilt, wise guy."

# 6

"There's a paper trail. I just don't know where it's leading me," Davey Kay said.

It was late afternoon when JC, Robin and Bip reached MacLaomainn's Scottish Pub for their meeting with Davey.

They entered the tavern and heard the recorded music of Amy Macdonald, a Scottish folk-rock singer.

The walls of the pub were dark wood. There was a large map of Scotland to one side. And over the bar, there was a great sword the Scottish call a claymore.

There was a stag's head on another wall, above a cutlass wrapped in tartan plaid. A suit of armor stood in a corner.

David Kay was holding a table for them. He stood and gave JC a hug. Waiting to order food and drinks, Kay shared an embarrassing story from the past about his old friend, something about his underwear at the high school prom.

JC was pleased that MacLaomainn's served genuine Scottish beer. When the server arrived, a young woman with a Scottish accent, he ordered a Belhaven Black. Davey and Robin followed his lead. Bip ordered a Long Trail, brewed in Vermont.

Kay was a large man. He still had a thick upper body and bulging arms. The sport coat he was wearing looked small on him. Any jacket was probably going to look small on him.

JC told his friends that Davey was an all-league offensive lineman on their football team in high school. They were teammates.

"Was JC a good player?" Robin asked. Davey just looked at his friend with a smirk.

"I thought I was," JC told her. "The coaches rarely shared that opinion."

"Give us some adolescent dirt on JC," Robin prodded Davey Kay.

"There's so much to choose from," he told her. "Let's see. Did he tell you about when he was a boy and a family friend hoisted him up on his shoulders? I think we were playing volleyball. Little JC laughed so hard he peed down the poor man's neck. That fellow must have gone home and scrubbed his neck down to his boney vertebra."

"Oh my," Robin laughed. "He still does that, you know."

"Very nice," JC uttered as his friends laughed at his expense.

"And has he ever cooked for you?" Davey asked.

"He says he can't cook," she told him.

"That's an understatement," Davey replied. "One time, I came out to visit him in Colorado and we went skiing at

Winter Park. He got up early and made us sandwiches from some leftover chicken he said he cooked."

"At lunch, he pulled out the sandwiches he made," Davey told them. "I took one smell of mine and set it aside. I asked him, 'What year did you cook that chicken?' He was chewing away and said it was fine."

"We go back out skiing. We get about halfway up the chairlift and we're right over a mogul run," Davey told them. "And he starts throwing up. He's spewing chunks of old rancid chicken on the skiers below."

Davey was laughing so hard, the rest of the story was lost in a breathless pantomime.

"Clearly, there is no story here." JC told his giggling friends. "Perhaps we can get back to Albany and catch a plane home."

"Okay, okay, spoilsport," Davey said and took a slug of his Belhaven. "So, I told you that I was going over Josh's last tax return items. When he died, I got extensions on his taxes, so I've been up here in Vermont at Josh's house trying to figure everything out. Well, really it's Melody's house now."

"And how does she like you sitting in her house poring over the fine print?" JC asked.

"Oh, she's fine. We're friends," Davey responded. "She brings me tea and tries to answer any questions I have. I think she likes the company, our connection to Josh."

"The thing is," Davey said as he made sure they were all paying attention, "the numbers don't add up. That's why I'm going back to Saratoga Springs. I need a better adding machine." He grinned at his own antiquated reference, but he'd made his point.

"What seems to be the problem?" JC asked. "And what makes it our business?"

"Look, Josh took good care of Melody in his will. She'll never want for much," the accountant told them. "But he also wanted to take care of the charity I told you about, VSBB."

"Vermont Stands for the Birds and the Bees," JC said.

"Catchy," Bip said sarcastically. "Why couldn't they have named it 'The Bee Environmental Effort?' Then, the acronym would be 'Bee.' Or how about 'Buzz?' 'Bees Under attack by Zealous Zombies?'"

"Right," Davey continued, ignoring the tangent. "So, Josh put it in his will saying whenever he died, his last book's proceeds would go to VSBB," Davey said. "And that's what has happened, and Melody has no problem with that. Like I say, she's more than taken care of in Josh's will."

"Were they happy together?" Robin asked. "Josh and Melody, I mean, as husband and wife."

"I think they were," Davey told her, before taking another gulp of his beer. "But this isn't about her. This is about the VSBB."

"The charity?" JC interjected.

"Right," Davey confirmed. "Josh's estate still gets considerable tax benefits for making such a big charitable contribution. The more money they make, the bigger his deduction. I look after that end, Josh and Melody's end, which requires me to glance at some of the entries by the staff at VSBB."

"How big is the staff?" JC asked.

"Well, *staff* is almost overstating it," Davey replied. "There's the executive director, Benjamin Whitmore. There's Whitmore's executive assistant, Bobbi Chadwick. There's a couple of paid interns for the summer. They'll go back to college in a couple of weeks. There's an unpaid board of directors. And that's about it. The directors make the final decisions and the executive director carries them out."

The three journalists watched David Kay, waiting for the punchline.

"I'm a bean counter," Kay proceeded. "I'm seeing some strange expenses at VSBB, or expenses that would suggest someone was in two places at the same time, or expenses that aren't explained at all."

"How much money are we talking about?" JC asked. "Enough to kill someone over?"

Kay paused as the server brought them their dinner. JC had ordered a "Haggis Taster" for the table. His companions cringed a little after he explained the ingredients of the traditional Scottish dish, like a sheep stomach and the lungs of a lamb. But they promised to try some.

There was cock-a-leekie soup brought to the table, and scotch eggs. Beyond that, JC said that his friends were free to indulge in whatever they wanted on the menu. That ended up including nachos and a big Caesar salad to share.

"How much of a financial windfall could the charity realize from Josh's donation?" Davey resumed after the server departed. "Do you remember reading that Michael Jackson made more money when he was dead than the last dozen years he was alive?"

"Sure," Robin remarked. "We were all reminded how great he was. Fans had a renewed urge to own his music. Some feared it was going to disappear and some were buying albums or downloads that they'd always intended to buy but just didn't get around to it."

"Right," Davey agreed. "It doesn't always happen, but it happens in a big way sometimes. Edgar Allan Poe and Henry

David Thoreau both sold more books after they were dead than when they were alive.

"Van Gogh?" JC added.

"He lived in squalor. He sold practically nothing until after he died," Davey said.

"Now there are museums dedicated only to Van Gogh," JC said. "One of his paintings sold for one hundred million dollars."

"And Josh's last book has been a big seller since word of his death," Davey told them. "A movie is in the works. It's a disaster flick about all the ice in the world melting. Anyway, book sales and the movie deal are generating a lot of money. And it's all going to VSBB."

"And Melody's okay with that?" Bip asked.

"She seems to be," Davey said. "But that doesn't explain or legalize all these expenditures that look like someone is dipping into the cookie jar."

"Where are VSBB's offices located?" Robin asked.

"They're right here in greater Stonestead," Davey smiled. "I think Josh became fond of their charity, one cup of tea at a time. He'd bump into the executive director and his assistant at the general store or the café."

"May I get you anything else this evening?" the server approached the table and asked. "Perhaps something from our collection of single malts?"

"I'll just have tea," Davey told the young woman. "It's a fitting tribute to Josh, and I have a two-hour drive ahead of me."

"A fitting tribute to Josh?" JC asked.

"He loved tea," Davey told the table with a smile.

"So, Melody will be home tomorrow?" JC asked.

"She'll be expecting you in the morning," Davey instructed them. "She's in Burlington at a book signing. She told me she'd get back home tonight. She lives in Stonestead."

"So, if someone was stealing Josh's contributions from VSBB," JC asked, "who is our number-one suspect?"

"Well, someone within VSBB, of course," Davey said. "That could be the executive director or anyone on the board. Anyone with access to the money."

The server returned with the check for dinner.

"Did you hear the footsteps?" she asked.

"There were footsteps?" JC inquired with a smile.

"Aye," she said with her Scottish accent. "The ghost."

"The ghost?" Robin asked.

"Aye, it is a woman. Lots of people have heard her here. This building used to be a farmhouse or a store with a hayloft or an apartment upstairs. 1875, it was built. There used to be stairs going up, over there." The woman was pointing at a door in the corner.

"They were taken out," she said. "Now the stairs through that door go down to the basement."

"So, who is the ghost? Do you know?" JC asked.

"Not precisely," the server answered. "But an expert came and said the ghost is confused because we removed the only way she knows how to go upstairs."

JC gave the server his company credit card.

"They think they have lots of ghosts around here," Davey said. "It's good for tourism, I guess."

"Are you going to be okay making this drive back to Saratoga?" JC asked. "Night is falling. I don't want *you* to become a ghost."

"I've made the trip fifty times before. I'll be fine, thanks."

Davey Kay rose from the table and shook hands all around. He picked up his briefcase from beside the table and walked for the door.

Next to that large a man, the briefcase looked very small.

"Why don't we touch base next week? Sooner, if you need me," Davey said over his shoulder.

"If you come here," JC told him, "maybe I'll cook something for you."

# 7

"What are you wearing on your feet?" Robin asked.

JC looked down and smiled. They had decided to go for a walk in the cool night air after checking into their lodgings at the Flamstead Inn. There was a full moon in the sky.

"I'm wearing sandals," JC said, answering her question. "They're comfortable."

"Not the sandals," Robin said with disapproval. "You're wearing socks with your sandals. You look like a hick."

"You look like my grandparents," Bip laughed.

"Wearing socks with sandals has an honored role in the human species," JC rebutted. "Wool socks were unearthed in Egypt. They were nearly two-thousand years old. Scientists said the socks were colorful reds and blues and yellows. And they wore them with their sandals."

"I can't believe someone is going to see *me* with *you* wearing those," Robin sighed.

"Have some respect for the wisdom of our ancestors," JC advised her. "I'm really comfortable."

In their first leisurely glimpse of Stonestead, they walked down Main Street. It was quiet. The street was lined by old Victorian homes, except for a small commercial district and the town green across from their hotel.

"The town green was where livestock were fenced in for the night," JC told them. "If there was a large cattle drive, the farmer could rest for the night here and not worry about his animals wandering away."

Stonestead was the kind of place that fit Vermont's reputation for being quaint. A cable TV network recently filmed a Christmas movie in the community.

Now, a younger crowd was discovering the old town. Its population was just over three thousand and growing. There were slightly more women than men.

"I like the odds," Bip quipped.

"You don't need odds," Robin responded. "You need a security detail to keep the women away."

Many thought Stonestead was in a perfect location. There was fishing in the Williams River that flowed through town. There were five ski areas that were only a short drive away. The closest was perched at the town border, Mont Vert.

There was a Fall Festival on the Town Green in September and a Winter Festival in February.

"Are you convinced?"

JC considered Bip's question as they walked.

"Of Davey's theory or that my footwear is embarrassing?"

"Your footwear *is* embarrassing," Bip snickered. "But I was asking about Davey's belief that Josh Church was murdered.

"Something isn't right," JC answered. "And we're lucky to have an inside man looking over the numbers. Josh Church was a beloved Colorado native, so I think our audience will care about what's going on."

"Do you think he was murdered?" Bip asked.

"I haven't seen much evidence to suggest that he was," JC said, "or wasn't."

The three journalists walked past a cemetery. The shapes of the headstones, even in the dark, indicated it was an old one.

"We don't have to hold our breath, do we?" Bip asked Robin. "We're walking. It's going to take a while to get past it. I might faint." Robin granted them an exemption.

"Do you want to go in?" she asked. She made it sound like a dare.

"I'm not afraid," the two men said to each other. They exchanged a private look suggesting that maybe they were.

The footing was uneven after they entered the cemetery through an old iron gate. A bright moon provided enough light to see where they were going, though large trees cast long shadows.

They used the flashlights on their cell phones to illuminate some of the old graves. There were biblical names like Abijah and Jonas. Others had names like Omelia and Temperance and Annabel.

Many stones belonged to Revolutionary War veterans. There was also a soldier killed in the Civil War at the Battle of Gettysburg. Small flags were placed on the grave of each veteran.

"Look at this!" Robin was pointing at a stone that was so old, it was largely swallowed by a massive maple tree.

"Some people think they can see ghosts out of the corner of their eye," she said.

"Do you see any?" Bib asked with a smirk.

"If I do," she said, "I'm not telling you until he wraps his boney hands around your throat."

"Well, in that case," he responded, "I'm not going to tell you about whatever it is standing over your shoulder."

"Ha, ha," she said disbelieving, and then stole a glance over her shoulder.

"Some people believe fluoride in our drinking water blocks our ability to communicate with ghosts," JC told his companions.

"That's a real thing!" Robin blurted. "I don't mean it's really true. But I've read about it. People really believe that!"

"Are you suggesting that I report things that *aren't* real?" JC asked.

"No," she smiled. "I would never suggest that."

They decided to resume exploring Stonestead in the daylight. They departed the cemetery, crossed the street and headed for the Flamstead Inn, where they were staying.

The old hotel was built in the 1880s. It had burned down twice and twice been rebuilt.

"I'm fried," Robin said as they walked up the granite steps to the inn. "I'm going to take a shower and go to bed."

Bip and JC agreed to have a nightcap in the inn's small bar.

"Jean Claude." She was the only one who called him by his full name.

JC turned and saw Robin paused on the staircase.

"Come tuck me in later?" she asked. He recognized the look.

"I might only have time for a wee dram," the reporter said when he turned back to his photographer.

JC and Robin had separate rooms at the inn. They had kept their romance a secret from the rest of the newsroom for months. But suspicions were circulating.

The exception was Bip. He knew from the start. He was with them over the winter, on assignment in Upstate New York, when JC and Robin drew close to each other.

The couple was still careful to maintain a professional distance when in the newsroom. They didn't want it to be creepy for their co-workers. And with or without JC, Robin was on the rise as a newsroom talent. Her skills as a producer had become evident. Her intelligence and good looks drew the obvious conclusions that she might belong on the other side of the camera, as a reporter.

Wherever she was ascending to, she did not care to be accused of taking a shortcut, sleeping her way to the top.

The three journalists began the next day with breakfast at a place down the street from their hotel. It was called Molly's. Then they headed to the home of Melody Church.

She lived out of town, up a short gravel drive that disappeared into the woods. The home she had shared with Joshua Church was constructed of gray granite blocks. It looked like it had been standing for a long time and would be there for a lot longer.

"It was built in 1838 by two brothers from Scotland," Melody told JC, Bip and Robin. "You ate at MacLaomainn's last night? There's quite a Scottish influence here in

Stonestead. They were the masons who built most of the early stone buildings here. And there are *lots* of stone buildings."

The Church home was in a section of town called the "Stone District." Granite was discovered by some of the first farmers in the area when they were clearing their fields to allow plowing.

"Someone here, whose name has been lost to history, dug the first granite quarry in Vermont," Melody told them. "They used it to build the state capital in Montpelier and lots of churches and monuments. It allowed everyone here to make a living for quite a while."

"He's from Scotland," Robin said as she pointed to JC.

"Oh, where from?" Melody said with a polite smile. JC admired the way Robin could warm up a room, and get the people in it to relax. That was a good skill for a journalist to possess, he thought.

"My grandfather was in Fife," JC told her. "About halfway between Edinburgh and St. Andrews. There was family in Edinburgh too."

"My mother was born on Mull," Melody said. Her eyes were slightly more intimate since she had learned of JC's Scottish blood.

"The Isle of Mull is a beautiful place," JC said softly. Melody nodded in agreement.

The widow continued to walk JC and Robin through the house. It was clear that she liked to show it off.

"I was only twenty-five when I met Josh," Melody Church told them. "Josh was twice my age. But I was swept off my feet. I was a bookseller at a shop in Aspen and he walks in, this famous author."

"I see the pictures on your wall," Robin told her. "He was a handsome man."

"Oh, he was *so* handsome," she agreed with a smile. "He was already fifty years old when I met him, but he was still quite active. We went hiking and skiing. He was a big road biker too, back then. And he was *so* smart and fun and *famous.*"

Melody Church was now forty-eight years old. Her face was still very pretty and had few lines on it. She still wore her blonde hair long. She said that she had put on weight since she was twenty-five. But she remained a very attractive woman.

They walked into a library. It had glass doors opening to a garden. There was a large desk in the library with neat stacks of paper on it.

"Those are Josh's," Melody shared with a smile. "He was always writing. The paper wasn't stacked as neatly when he was alive. I did that. But that's where his papers belong. It makes me think he might walk through the door at any time."

JC briefly examined the books on built-in shelves dominating two walls in the library. It looked like an impressive collection of old books about Vermont. There were also shelves filled with books about nature and climate change.

"We moved here from Colorado when my mother grew ill," Melody told them. "I was born here. And Josh was a complete dear when I told him that I wanted to move back and take care of my mother."

"He loved it here in Stonestead," she said. "I hope this doesn't sound crass, but I scattered his ashes out there in the garden."

JC and Robin looked out the glass doors, almost expecting to see him there.

"It was his idea to toss his ashes there," Melody exclaimed with a grin. "He said it was where he wanted to stay forever, and he might as well help fertilize the flowers."

"That's a huge magnolia bush," Robin said, looking at a far corner of the yard.

"You should see the flowers in the spring," Melody delighted.

She opened the doors and the fragrance of the garden's blossoms breezed into the room.

"There we go," Melody laughed. "Now, Josh can join us."

Bip was in the next room, setting up lights and a tripod for his camera. They would interview Melody Church there.

"Would you like some tea?" she asked her three guests. They all accepted. JC and Robin followed her into the kitchen.

"Josh drank tea without end," she said. "He drank his first cup as soon as he rose from bed and he drank his last when it was time to head back to bed at night."

"Someone also has a taste for good wine," JC said. He had observed a shelf with only one kind of red, a Carmenet Reserve Cabernet Sauvignon. Every bottle was from 2016.

"That is more to *my* liking," Melody said with a smile. "Josh would join me for a glass at dinner. But I would drink a second glass of wine in the evenings while he turned back to drinking his tea."

It was an old house, but the kitchen had every modern comfort and amenity. JC thought that the remodeling must have cost a fortune.

"It was tricky," Melody said of the extensive facelift to the kitchen. "This is a historic district. We wanted to move the exterior wall out and make a bigger kitchen. But they wouldn't let us do that. Luckily, there was an old servants' room next to the kitchen. We took that interior wall down and that gave us all this new space."

The sink had two taps to pour water from, a smaller one and a larger one. JC attempted to make himself useful in the kitchen, so he lifted a simple copper kettle and began to fill it with water from the smaller faucet.

"Oh no," Melody interrupted. "Use the other faucet. I need to get that one fixed."

He saw water dripping on the floor from the cabinet under the sink.

"Oh no," he said, opening the cabinet. Water had sprayed over everything inside the cabinet.

"I am so sorry," JC said. He grabbed paper towels from next to the sink and dropped to his knees, pulling bottles out and wiping them dry.

Melody appeared at his side, gently turning off the water.

"Nonsense," she said. "Shame on me for not getting it repaired. I'll clean that up. It's really nothing. Come on, get up. Let's have some tea."

She set aside the copper kettle after wiping it with a cloth. Then, she reached up to a long shelf where a dozen other teakettles were squatting in a line.

"Let's use this one," she said. "It was Josh's favorite."

JC admired a nature scene painted on the side of the kettle, a bear and deer in the forest.

"As you can imagine, Josh's fanatic tea sipping extended to acquiring a good many teakettles," Melody told them. "Fans learned he was a tea drinker and they sent him kettles from all over the world. There are boxes of them in the basement."

"They loved his books, didn't they," Robin remarked.

"He was a good man," Melody said into the camera when the interview began. "I loved him as much on our last day as I did on our first."

# 8

"Too hot," JC said. "Too humid. Give me twenty-seven degrees and sunny, any day."

"They call that winter," Bip reminded him.

"Yep."

It might have been one of the last hot days of the waning summer. The reporter and photographer were standing by their car. JC was looking up both directions of Main Street in downtown Stonestead. The small community extended only two or three blocks in either direction behind Main Street. It was long and narrow.

He had been calling the office of VSBB, but having no luck locating the executive director, Benjamin Whitmore.

"I can see almost the entirety of Stonestead standing here," JC said to Bip. "How can I not find Benjamin Whitmore?"

"Who you looking for?" a voice asked from behind JC. He turned and saw a man standing on the sidewalk.

"Sorry, I couldn't help but overhear you," the man said with a smile. "You're looking for Benjamin?"

"We are," JC told him.

"Well," the man said with an affable manner, "Ben is a busy man. This small town isn't where he finds most of our projects or donors. So, he spends a lot of days on the road."

"You said *our* projects?" JC asked.

"Not very humble, am I?" The man introduced himself as Jerry Dean. He had a face that belonged on a nice man, JC thought. It was too soon to tell if this would be the case with Jerry Dean.

He looked harmless enough. He was bald on top, with gray hair on the sides. The sleeves on his button-down shirt were rolled up.

"I'm a gentleman farmer," he told JC and Bip. "That means I own the farm, but I pay someone else to sweat. I pay them to do the work," he said with a smile. "Anyway, I'm on the board of 'Vermont Stands for the Birds and the Bees.' That's why I bothered you when I heard you mention Ben's name. I wanted to see if I could help."

"So, you're one of the decision makers?" JC asked.

"I guess so," Dean said. "But that makes me sound more important than I am. We pretty much let Ben do what he thinks best. He says he has an idea and we pretty much go along with it. He's earned that. He's turned the Birds and Bees into something special."

"Do you have the power to tell him no?" JC asked.

"Oh yes," Jerry Dean said back. "We give everything a pretty good look at our semi-annual board meetings. He has to explain things."

"You meet twice a year?"

"Yes. Three of the board members live right here in Stonestead," Dean told him. "We see each other all the time. If there was anything more urgent, we could talk it over having an ice cream cone at Molly's."

"Any idea where he is today?" JC asked.

"I don't honestly know," the man responded. "I'm sorry I'm not of more help. But he'll be back. He always comes back." Jerry Dean was smiling. He was hard not to like.

JC's phone rang and they bid farewell to Jerry Dean. JC leaned against their car, seeing that the call was coming from Robin. She'd returned to the Flamstead Inn to go for a run and then do some research on their new surroundings.

"I found some stuff," she said. "It's just background on the area, but it's interesting."

"Fire away," JC told her. Bip saw this as an opportunity to shoot some footage of downtown Stonestead. JC saw him drop to his knee to get a low-angle shot of Main Street.

"Stonestead, like Chester down the road and this part of Vermont, has technically belonged to five different countries," she said. Her enthusiasm was evident in her voice.

"So, it's part of the United States now," she continued. "Of course, it was part of the British Empire before the Revolution. France had claimed it before that. It claimed to be its own country before that. They called it the Vermont Republic. And it was known for six months as The Republic of New Connecticut."

"Do we ..." JC tried to inquire.

"Wait, I've got more," she interrupted the interruption.

"Stonestead and this area has also belonged to three states: Vermont, of course. But New York and New Hampshire also claimed it, sometimes at the same time. Cool, huh?"

"You're on fire," JC conceded with moderate enthusiasm. He was hoping to have something solid to add to his first live shot from Vermont, in about three hours.

"Want to hear more about the granite?" she asked with zeal.

"I think I hit my granite quota this morning."

"Okay, maybe this will make you happy," she told him. "An investigation is being announced tomorrow morning, by the Vermont attorney general, into VSBB."

JC snapped out of an approaching slumber.

"Say again?" he implored his producer. "How did you find that out?"

"I called the attorney general's office in Montpelier and asked. They're really friendly here. They make it kind of easy."

"And you didn't think to begin our conversation with that?" JC asked.

"I thought the stuff about Stonestead being part of five countries was pretty interesting," she told him. "I've never heard of that before. We hear about new investigations all the time."

Then he heard her laughing.

"I was getting around to it," she said, snickering. "You're so serious."

"You're trying to kill me, aren't you?" He could hear her still laughing over the phone. "Okay, are you serious about this? About the AG's investigation coming?"

"Yes," she answered. "I knew it would make your day."

JC looked up Main Street. He could see the back of Jerry Dean about a block away, walking in the other direction.

The reporter nearly sprinted to Bip Peters and told his photographer to follow him. The two men walked at a jogging pace toward Dean, determined not to lose the chance at an official statement by a VSBB board member.

They caught up with him as Main Street turned from a commercial district into a residential neighborhood. Dean was just proceeding up a walk leading to a large home, presumably *his* home.

"I don't know anything about it," Dean said to the journalists when informed of the looming investigation by the attorney general. He was almost pleading for them to believe him. "It's news to me."

"Mr. Whitmore didn't inform his own board of directors that this was coming?" JC asked with a good deal of doubt.

"No," Dean said. "We don't have another board meeting until January. We just had one last month."

"Don't you think ..." JC began to ask.

"I don't want to go on camera," Dean said. "I don't have anything to say. I'm sorry, but I don't know anything."

With that, Jerry Dean turned and walked through the front door of his house. Bip captured that on his camera, at least.

"An investigation is unfolding into a possible fraud," JC told his Denver audience that night. "The probe is looking at how a fortune, given to them by Colorado native Josh Church, was spent and possibly squandered."

It was JC's first live shot from his new Vermont assignment. He was standing on Main Street with the sun setting on the quaint village of Stonestead behind him. Vermont was different visually than his Western audience was used to seeing.

There were a few Stonestead residents watching from the sidewalk as JC spoke to his primary audience, nearly two thousand miles away and where it was two hours earlier. He felt the phone in his pocket vibrate as he was speaking with the anchors back in Denver. He had to ignore the phone call.

JC's report included the interview shot that day with Melody Church, Josh's widow. The live shot also included footage of Jerry Dean turning and walking away, saying the VSBB board of directors didn't know anything.

JC, on the other hand, didn't tell everything that he was working on. He didn't say that the crime might have led to Josh Church's murder.

# 9

"I'm paving the way for your Pulitzer Prize."

The voice on the other end of the phone was Davey Kay. That was his incoming call making JC's phone vibrate during the live shot from Stonestead. Kay was back home in Upstate New York. He said that the time difference between Vermont and Colorado had never occurred to him. He apologized if he distracted JC while he was on television.

"It happens more than you think. Besides, it's not the first time you've made my leg vibrate," JC said into the phone.

"I have some new information for you," Davey said.

"Aside from the investigation being launched by the attorney general?"

"That was me too," Davey told him. "I thought it would make your life easier. I can hand you the inside information, their investigation legitimizes your reports and you have a free hand to look into the real crime, Josh's murder."

As unwieldy as his old friend's plan sounded, it made some sense.

"But if you feed me any self-serving bullshit, my next damning scandal will be about *you*," JC said in a no-nonsense tone.

"I know. But I swear that I will only give you legit stuff. I've been looking at more paperwork that came from VSBB. The attorney general has all this stuff now, too."

"I'm serious, Davey," JC said. "I'll check every piece of information that you give me with the AG. They have to corroborate everything you say before I'll report it."

"That's fair," Davey responded. "Wow, you're grouchy when you're at work."

"Yeah, I've been told that. So, what's new?"

"This is some of the stuff I gave the AG that got their interest. By the way, do you know that they're coming to Stonestead to make the announcement tomorrow?"

"I do now. What else is new?"

"Okay, you grouch," Davey complained. "Here's one: some of the receipts I have from VSBB include trips out of the country that could be called 'business' in only the loosest sense. I mean, they were submitted as business expenses, but how many birds and bees do Vermont and Virgin Gorda have in common, anyway?"

"Was there a conference there?" JC asked.

"No," Davey replied. "And yet, the burden of this non-conference not only required Whitmore's attendance, but his assistant, Bobbi Chadwick's. It also required the purchase of two bathing suits for Ms. Chadwick and some very expensive beachside lodgings and dinners."

Davey's revelation was met with silence.

"Have you *met* Ms. Chadwick?" Davey asked.

"I haven't had the pleasure," JC said.

"Oh, and it *will* be a pleasure," Davey snickered.

"How so?"

"I think I'll let it be a surprise."


The next morning, the attorney general of the nation's fourteenth state convened a news conference in the old town hall of Stonestead.

The attorney general would officially announce its investigation into the VSBB charity, though it had already been reported in that morning's newspapers across the state and by JC Snow the prior night.

The announcement would be made by the state attorney general herself, a trip covering about one hundred and thirty miles from her office in the capital.

The value of the trip to the elected official would be justified by the attendance of newspaper reporters from Burlington, Bennington, Manchester and Brattleboro. Television cameras from Burlington and even Albany, New York, would also be there. JC would be there, because Josh Church was a cherished son of Colorado and it was his money allegedly being stolen.

The attorney general didn't care much, one way or the other, about JC's presence. Voters in Colorado couldn't re-elect her. And she'd never want to run for president because she had no desire to leave Vermont for Washington. That was Vermont for you, JC thought.

The news conference would be held upstairs in the town hall, which had been built in 1884. Town residents in 1884 had been informed that they had the money for one of two public undertakings, either building a town hall or building a monument to their soldiers lost in the Civil War. There was great debate, but they chose to build a town hall.

It was brick with a cupola on top. It was built next to the railroad tracks, because most of the bricks and building materials would be brought to Stonestead by train. Why, the town fathers asked, carry all those bricks and wood and stone over to Main Street when they could just erect the structure where the ingredients were tossed off the flatbeds?

JC had purchased one of each Vermont newspaper sold at Molly's, downtown. He looked through each of them to learn if anyone else had located Benjamin Whitmore.

They hadn't. Each article on the new investigation included a line that they could have sung in chorus: "VSBB Executive Director Benjamin Whitmore was unavailable for comment."

The attorney general's announcement proceeded as Davey Kay told JC it would go. The reporter didn't learn anything that he didn't already know.

Still, these were helpful events, JC thought. Most important, it meant that he could refer to this investigation of VSBB and not get sued by the environmental organization. The investigation had been confirmed by the AG.

He didn't view many news conferences as an exchange of information. He viewed them as events to see what the officials, in this case the attorney general, were and were not willing to share.

JC's rule at news conferences was to avoid asking questions that were truly important to him. He would wait to ask those until after the event, when he could have the newsmaker to himself, in private. They usually had let their guard down at that point, and their answers were more likely to be honest ones.

Sometimes, he'd follow the newsmaker to their car after the news conference. Sometimes, he'd wait until the next day to get some "alone time" with the newsmaker. Then, he'd seek the answers he really thought were crucial.

At the news conference in Stonestead, there were no questions from the news media inquiring about the death of Josh Church. That is what really interested JC. And that was the card he would keep concealed up his sleeve.

So, following the pre-packaged answers that the AG had rehearsed with her staff beforehand, the news conference wrapped up.

JC and the other journalists noticed two VSBB board members standing in the back of the town meeting room. JC recognized one as Jerry Dean. The other was a woman he hadn't met, named Deborah Sampson. Upon their discovery, the pair was swarmed by reporters, microphones and cameras. It was time to feed the beast.

The board members were surrounded before they could escape down the restored wooden stairs of the town hall. Reporters fired questions and mostly Jerry Dean responded with, "We don't have any comment," and "No, we haven't spoken to Benjamin. But we expect to hear from him later today."

Jerry Dean looked as though he were trying to tread water in a tidal wave. He wasn't practiced in this type of media ambush.

Deborah Sampson said nothing. Her expression never changed. But her eyes followed everything, including a curious glimpse at JC.

In turn, JC studied the two board members. They were typecast for the role of rural Vermont residents. If Jerry's mouth had stopped moving, they would have looked like the couple in the Grant Wood painting, *American Gothic.*

Deborah Sampson was thin and stern looking. Her brown hair was pulled back tightly into a ponytail that hung straight down her neck. Everything was buttoned into place, except her eyes. She took everything in with her eyes.

Bip was shooting the impromptu question-and-answer period with the pair of board members. But again, JC wasn't hearing anything that surprised him. The assurance from Jerry Dean that they expected to hear from Benjamin Whitmore later in the day probably should have been followed by, "Gulp, we hope so. Because we have no idea where he is."

# 10

"They call it a witch window."

"A which window?" Robin asked. "Like, which window is his bedroom?"

"No," JC said. "A witch window. W-i-t-c-h. Like a green woman who rides a broom at night."

Robin had pointed at the odd windows on some homes in this part of Vermont. She was riding in the backseat of the rental car being driven by Bip. She had asked them to pick her up before their next interview.

That interview was actually downstairs from the news conference they had just attended at the town hall. But it was only a ten-minute trip back to the Flamstead Inn.

"I needed to get out," she told them, after a morning of doing research on a computer inside her hotel room.

"I've never seen one of these witch windows," she told them. "They look like the contractor made a mistake."

"It is an oddity enjoyed almost exclusively by Central Vermont, for reasons not entirely clear," JC told her.

He explained that a witch window is an upper-story window on a home that is rectangular but rotated forty-five degrees. The long side, he said, parallels the slope of the roof.

"Why would they do that?" Robin asked.

"The legend goes like this," JC explained. "The windows mostly date back to homes built around here in the 1800s. People believed that witches cannot fly their broomsticks through tilted windows like that."

"Really?" Robin contributed.

"That's one of the folk tales," he told her. "Another calls them 'coffin windows.' That legend suggests that the windows were placed at a slant like that because it was easier to get a coffin out of a second-floor window than down the narrow stairs that these homes used to have."

"The windows just look like they're falling over," Bip remarked.

"They also are called 'lazy windows,'" JC told them.

"So, they believed in witches back then?" Robin asked.

"They were living in remote areas that were beautiful but kind of scary," JC said. "Many of them had a relative who was killed by Indians or the French or the British. They heard noises at night that they couldn't explain. They didn't have much of an education. They believed a lot of things. Witches probably weren't the most outrageous."

"So, witches and goblins aside," Bip said. "Does anyone really know why the windows were inserted like that?"

"Okay, Mister Practical Pants," JC said. "Nonbelievers think that when a kitchen or extra bedroom was added to the ground floor of the house, the gable may not have allowed enough room for a full window. So, this was done to maintain maximum light and ventilation on the second floor."

"Are you happy now?" Robin chirped at Bip. "Are you happy that you ruined a fun spooky story?"

"I'll sleep better," Bip declared. "If I really thought there were witches around here, I wouldn't be able to close my eyes at night."

"There are some good ghost stories they tell about Stonestead," Robin said. "Remember the footsteps they hear at MacLaomainn's?"

"Great," Bip said. "Now, I won't be able to sleep again."

Bip pulled the car into a space behind the town hall. That is where the police station was located. Town hall wasn't that large a building. The small police department filled one half of the first floor.

They entered the entrance to police headquarters and approached a woman seated at a desk behind a glass security wall.

"May I help you?" the woman asked as she looked up at them.

"Do you know any ghost stories?" Robin asked, before JC could get in a word. He gave Robin a look.

"I work for a *police* department," the woman responded to Robin. "What do you think?"

"We're here to see Chief Ives," JC told the woman, hoping to reset the topic of conversation.

"Is this about ghosts?" the woman asked with a smile.

"I hope not. He's expecting us," JC said, casting his eyes back on Robin. She lowered her head, snickering.

**witch window**: *A Murder on Skis Mystery*

"Send them in," a voice from around the corner commanded.

The woman rose from her seat behind the desk and ushered the journalists around the corner and into an office. Bip carried his camera gear.

The room was illuminated by LED lights recessed into the ceiling. There was a window behind the desk and doors opening in the other three directions. It gave the chief a view of every room in the police department, except one.

To the left, there was an office with three desks. That was for the five full-time and three part-time police officers, working three shifts. It was roughly the same size as the chief's office.

To the right, there was a holding room, with arm and leg restraints attached to a sturdy, stainless-steel bench.

The other door opened to the reception area with the glass security wall. JC was told there was a small holding cell in the basement.

The offices were cramped but they were covered with fresh paint and they were clean. The law officers did the most with what they were given.

"Welcome to my castle," said the man behind the desk. "I'm Sipp Ives, chief of police in Stonestead."

Handshakes were exchanged and introductions were made. The woman from the reception desk appeared with a third chair for their guests, but Bip declined. He preferred that small extra space for his equipment. He began setting up his tripod, lights and camera.

The closest thing to a weapon displayed in the police station, JC noted, was a pencil sharpener screwed into the wall. The chief told him that they don't get much violent crime in Stonestead.

"No need to give them any ideas," he said. "We mostly deal with drunken drivers and dumb drug mules. They think they can avoid the highway and sneak through Central Vermont without being detected. But they couldn't find their way through our county if they had a tour guide." He laughed. "They're so lost when we pull them over, I think they're relieved."

Sipp Ives was a tall and lean Black man. He had a shaved head and was probably older than he looked. He had an athletic appearance. After JC had examined the chief's biography, he guessed that Ives was around fifty. The bio on the chief said that he had been a sports star in school, growing up in Stonestead. His extended family were the only Black people in the area, then.

"I left for college," Chief Ives said. "But I came back. This is home. You know, it's ironic; studies of Pangea have determined that Vermont was once connected to Africa. Fossils found here are similar to fossils found there. So, we've been here all the while. I don't know when white folk happened along."

Chief Ives was smiling. The receptionist, who was also the chief's administrative assistant, would tell them that he loves that story. He tells it to all the newcomers.

"Now, what can I do for you?" he asked. Bip rolled his camera. The interview was underway.

"VSBB," JC said.

"I have nothing to do with that," the chief responded. "If they tell me to go to someone's house and arrest them, I will. But I'm not involved, at this time, in the investigation they announced this morning."

"Did they take you into their confidence, ask you if you'd witnessed or heard of anything odd?" JC asked.

"Of course, they did," Ives responded.

"Do you have any problem with them treading on your turf? This is your town. Benjamin Whitmore is a resident here," JC asked.

"I've outgrown arrogance. When I was a younger man, it didn't prove very useful," the chief said. "It's their investigation. I'll be there, if they need my assistance."

"Do you harbor any suspicions about the death of Joshua Church?" JC inquired. The chief gave JC a long look.

"No."

During the interview, JC learned things about Stonestead. The chief told him it was statistically one of the safest cities in the United States. Stonestead's police officers also acted as animal control officers. And Sipp Ives was the only member of the Stonestead police force who had ever investigated a murder.

When the interview was over, Robin helped Bip out to the car with his equipment. It left JC and Chief Ives alone in the small office.

"Should I?" the chief asked, sitting behind his desk. His eyes were trained on the reporter.

"Should I, what?" JC asked.

"Should I harbor any suspicions about the death of Joshua Church?"

# 11

"Do you call it a buffalo or a bison?"

"Either is okay," JC told the engineer at the live truck.

The live truck and one engineer were being loaned to the Colorado news crew during their stay in Vermont. The agreement between JC's TV station in Denver and the television station in Burlington was that JC and his crew could use the truck if they also agreed to do a live shot for Vermont viewers whenever that TV station was interested.

The truck's engineer was currently enlisting JC to resolve a debate going on in their Burlington newsroom. A herd of buffalo, or bison, had escaped a local farm up there. But some of the staff in the newsroom said the animals could only be called bison, not buffalo. They figured that JC, who must see bison daily out the window of his Denver apartment, could be the ultimate judge.

"The proper name for the species is bison," JC told the engineer, who was relaying the information over the phone to Burlington. "But as you know, they have also been called buffalo for centuries."

The engineer, named Paul Fletcher, listened to someone speaking on the phone from Burlington. Then he said, "They're saying that you can only call them bison. They say a buffalo has bigger horns, stands around in water and lives in Asia."

"Ah, they've learned to search the internet for all the answers," JC said. "You realize the city in New York is called Buffalo, not Bison. And the famous cowboy was called Buffalo Bill, not Bison Bill."

"They say it doesn't matter," Fletcher stated after hearing a response over the phone. "They say it can only be called a bison."

"The buffalo-head nickel?" JC offered. "The Buffalo Bills football team? 'Oh, give me a home where the buffalo roam?'"

"Nope, they're not budging," the engineer said as he pulled the phone away from his ear.

"Okay, this is fun but let's end it," JC declared. "Tell them to go back to their magical all-knowing internet and look up 'American Buffalo.' They've been staring at a water buffalo, an animal foreign to the United States, except in zoos."

Fletcher waited by the phone. He could hear someone hammering on the keys of their computer, and someone murmur "American buffalo." Then, he pulled the phone away from his ear to relay the message from Burlington.

"They say, 'Oh,'" Fletcher told him with a smile. "They say you win."

"By the way," JC asked, "what's the name of the farm where the bison escaped?"

The engineer relayed the question to the newsroom in Burlington and awaited an answer. Then he laughed.

"It's called the Vermont Buffalo Ranch." JC gave the engineer a thumbs-up.

With Paul Fletcher's help, JC and Bip went "live" for their Denver audience again, from downtown Stonestead. They also reported live for a TV audience in Burlington.

Their report included soundbites from the attorney general's news conference and from their interview with Police Chief Sipp Ives.

But the new headline of their story came after their broadcast to Burlington, and only about a half-hour before they were to broadcast live for Denver. Robin had reached JC on his cell phone.

"I think we have a fresh lead for your story," she told the reporter.

"I'm listening," JC responded.

"Did you start to wonder if Ben Whitmore was dead, or something creepy like that?" she asked.

"The thought did occur to me. Is he?" JC asked.

"He just told me that he isn't," Robin reported. "And he's going to hold a news conference tonight at the ski area."

"That is a significant development," JC said. "How did you find him?"

"He answered his phone when I called him," the producer told JC.

"He didn't answer when I called," JC noted.

"You're not me," she said. "I'd answer me if I called, too."

"Well, you get an 'atta-boy,'" JC responded with a smile. "When is he going to talk?"

"In an hour. So, right after your live shot to Denver."

"We can get there in time, if we postpone dinner," JC told her.

"Ah, I saved the best for last!" Robin laughed. "The news conference will be catered. We get free food!"

"Did you talk him into that?" JC teased.

"No, but I would have if he hadn't already told me."


Following JC's last live shot of the evening for the station in Denver, the news crew loaded their gear into their rental car and headed for the Mont Vert Ski Resort. Robin had walked from the Flamstead Inn to join them.

"Why is he holding the news conference at the ski resort?" JC asked his producer.

"That's where the office for VSBB is," she told him.

"That must be expensive rent," JC supposed.

"It is! I looked it up," Robin confirmed. "That's sort of the point of our story, right? VSBB seems to be operating without any budget restraint."

"Do we know how much money Josh Church gave VSBB?" JC asked.

"I found that out today, too, though Ben Whitmore wouldn't confirm it to me over the phone," Robin answered. "But I called Davey Kay. He says the Birds and the Bees have received about two million dollars so far from Josh's book sales and the movie deal. And the movie is still in pre-production. Davey says 'Hi,' by the way."

"Do we know how much of this two million dollars VSBB is spending on the bees and the birds?" JC asked. "And say 'hello' back to Davey, when you speak to him again."

"He says that he doesn't have that end of the receipts," Robin reported. "But that's a lot of money."

"Yeah, I think I just saw a bee driving a Lamborghini," Bip snickered.

They pulled their rental car, a boring sedan, into a parking place at the Mont Vert Ski Resort.

It was their first visit to the ski area since their arrival in town. JC said that he had skied there when he was growing up. But the sparkling resort village was new to him.

Chairlifts extended uphill from the village. The slopes had long, green grass on them. Occasionally, a mountain bike rider emerged from the woods and crossed a ski run.

It had a pedestrian walk made of Belgian block pavers. They led from the parking lot to the chairlifts, passing stores, restaurants and bars. Amped-up music was playing from outdoor speakers, the same that would play for skiers and snowboarders in the winter.

For the summer, the music played for the mountain bikers, hikers and those who paid for a gondola ride to the top and then back down.

About half the stores appeared to have summer-hours. The other half of the storefronts were mothballed and waiting for winter to return.

There was a clock tower and benches made from discarded skis. The Tyrolean architecture reminded visitors of winter in Vermont, but the warm air and green slopes indicated that Mont Vert was on summer break.

The busiest corner of the ski resort, right now, was down the road at the golf course. There were also tennis courts that could be lighted at night and seemed to be full. The resort made money in the summer holding high-end tennis camps with retired stars of the game.

The sun was starting to set. Mountain bikers were quitting for the day. The ski resort sold a lift pass to carry bikes up the mountain so riders could careen down the slopes like daredevils.

A tall athletic resort employee waved to JC and his crew as they made their way down the walk. He directed them into a large room with seats lined into rows. JC noticed as he passed the employee that his nametag said 'Rick."

There was a podium at the front of the room and a closed dividing door off to one side.

It was a professional setup. There was a riser for cameras in the back of the room and a mult box for TV and radio reporters to plug into so they could record remarks spoken into the single microphone at the podium. About half the seats in the room were filled.

Benjamin Whitmore emerged through a door at the side of the room near the podium. He was a handsome man, with an expression on his face that said he didn't mean to offend anyone.

JC could only liken Whitmore's hairstyle to a Beatles haircut. Old-school Beatles, before Sgt. Pepper. He wore glasses. They were a soft blue and matched Whitmore's shirt, which matched his tie. He was a well-dressed man.

Whitmore seemed relaxed as he approached the microphone. He smiled and adjusted his glasses.

"Welcome, everyone. News of our death has been greatly exaggerated," he declared, trying to paraphrase Mark Twain, with a little laugh. "I am aware of the investigation by the attorney general and I welcome it. This is nothing more than a misunderstanding."

Whitmore's prepared remarks were short. Now that the executive director had surfaced, JC thought he was telling them little. Whitmore, adjusting his eyeglasses, conveyed his belief that the investigation would be no more taxing than an afternoon of tennis.

When Whitmore said that he would take a few questions from reporters, he addressed those reporters by name. Aside from JC, the journalists were all from Vermont. Whitmore had worked hard to cultivate a positive relationship with them. He began each answer to a question with, "Thank you for asking."

Bip rolled his camera on the entire event. JC never asked a question. He didn't want to talk, he wanted to listen.

As promised by Robin, the news conference ended with the opening of the dividing door, unveiling tables of food and a bar in the next room.

"It is the end of another beautiful day in Vermont," Whitmore declared as he waved his audience toward the food and beverages. "Let's enjoy some food and drinks 'on the house.'"

He smiled like everyone in the room was his closest friend. Everyone else smiled, because there was free food and an open bar.

# 12

"Please, tell me we can eat," Robin said with desperation on her face. Bip stood at her side with hope in his eyes. It had been a long day with little time for nourishment.

The rest of the journalists had stampeded past the dividing door and into the bar. Another Vermont beer, Harpoon, was cold and compliments of Ben Whitmore.

Bip and Robin looked at JC. It was an ethical gray area to accept food and drinks from the subject of a story they were working on. But JC gave them a nod of approval. His crew had worked hard. And a hot dog and a beer was not going to change their story.

JC also thought that mingling at the impromptu soiree might help him get to know more about Whitmore, and those around him.

"Bip, throw your camera on your shoulder," JC said. "Let's try to get a word with Whitmore. Then we'll eat."

Bip already had his first bite of a hot dog in his mouth. His shoulders sank at word that his dinner would be delayed. He handed the unfinished dog to Robin and followed JC.

They found the executive director of Vermont Stands for Birds and Bees near the bar. He was shaking as many hands as he could reach, whether the other hands wanted to be shaken or not.

JC introduced himself, along with Bip and Robin, and told him they had come from Denver.

"Josh Church was a Godsend for The Birds and the Bees," Whitmore said. "His generosity will be felt for years to come. Is that what brings you here, to do an essay on his far-reaching generosity? His support of VSBB?"

"Sort of," JC responded. "But you know we were at the announcement by the attorney general today."

"Oh, that is nothing more than a squabble about accounting. It's innocent," Whitmore said with a reassuring smile. "If we've done something the tiniest bit sloppy, we'll correct the way we're doing it, I assure you. Most important, the money they're seeking is all there."

Wow, JC thought. This guy was good. Innocent or guilty, he was good.

"While it's on my mind," JC framed his next question. "Why pay for offices at the Mont Vert Ski Resort when you can get much more affordable office space a block from Main Street in Stonestead?"

"Mr. Snow," Whitmore said with the tone of a teacher speaking to a pupil, "raising money is critical to saving the lives of the birds and the bees. And the money walks down this pedestrian path every winter. They're spending a good deal of cash for a day's entertainment on the ski mountain. They almost feel guilty about it. And they *would* feel guilty if they refused our solicitations, so they don't. We raise a lot of money by being on the main drag at Mont Vert."

"The attorney general says she is concerned about how you're spending that money," JC probed. "A beachfront condo at Virgin Gorda, for example."

"Mr. Snow—it's ironic that I'm talking to someone named Snow at a ski area, by the way," Whitmore said. "Mr. Snow, there are bees that are endangered everywhere. Did you know that there are even bees in the Arctic Circle? One in four bee species in the United States is at risk of extinction."

JC did not dispute the executive director's premise for saving bees from annihilation. But his explanation did not address how VSBB was spending Josh Church's money.

"It was good meeting you, Mr. Snow, Bip—Robin is it?" Whitmore gently terminated the interview when a woman appeared from nowhere, touched his elbow and whispered something in his ear.

Whitmore headed for the exit. The woman remained behind to put Whitmore's papers in a briefcase and tidy up the podium. The eyes of men in the room migrated in her direction.

She was a stunning brunette. Not just pretty, and even more than beautiful. She was captivating. JC thought she might be the most beautiful woman he had ever seen in person.

That would be Bobbi Chadwick, JC thought, the assistant to the executive director of VSBB.

Her long hair spilled over her right shoulder. And she wore pearls around her neck, perhaps intended to draw attention to a low-cut black dress.

She glanced up and made eye-contact with JC. She smiled and he managed a small smile in return.

"Well, she's attractive," Robin said softly. She was standing at JC's side.

"Really? I hadn't noticed," JC responded.

"You and every man in this room are drooling over her," Robin protested. "You're all leaving spots of saliva on your ties."

"It's polite to drool," JC improvised. "In some cultures, that is the civil thing to do when you meet someone new."

"Drool?" Robin asked incredulously.

"Sure," JC told her. "In some countries, when the president of the United States visits, he is greeted at the airport by drooling dignitaries. And our president, as is the custom, drools back at them."

"Really?" Robin laughed, crossing her arms.

"That thing you're doing, crossing your arms," JC noted. "That's body language when you catch someone lying, isn't it?"

"It should be," Robin laughed.

"Yeah, you should probably trust your instincts on this one," he said as he rubbed his hand over his face.

"You see? Everything is fine," came an assuring voice from behind JC and Robin. The voice belonged to Jerry Dean. Dean's smiling face was accompanied by another man. Dean introduced him as Thomas Caryl, a fellow VSBB board member.

"So, I've met three board members," JC stated. "How many board members are there?"

"You've met all of the local ones," Dean told him. "There are two more. They live in Pennsylvania."

"How often do they get here?" JC inquired. Dean looked toward his companion.

"They really don't," Caryl told him. "The travel isn't really necessary. We're a pretty laid-back group. They always vote. They keep up with the doings and vote from Pennsylvania."

"The important thing," Dean added, "is that Benjamin has assured us that everything is fine. It's an accounting error or something and he'll get it worked out with the attorney general."

Dean and Caryl both shook the hands of the journalists and moved back into the crowd near the bar.

Bip had reclaimed his hot dog and, with Robin, had grabbed a full plate of food. Robin handed JC a plate of cheese, pigs in a blanket and salad. He looked at her and smiled. She took good care of him, and he was grateful.

"Welcome to Stonestead," a voice in a near-whisper came from JC's left. He turned and nearly choked on the pig in a blanket. It was Bobbi Chadwick.

"You came here from Denver to do a story on Josh Church?" she asked.

"Sort of," JC replied, still trying to clear his windpipe of pork and bread.

"It was such a shame about Josh. Such a nice man," Bobbi said.

JC said nothing. He was thinking that he might ask her if she knew the Heimlich maneuver.

"He was loved in Colorado," said a voice behind JC. It was Robin, who was now patting JC on the back. It was more like a slap, but she made it look like a pat.

JC was relieved to find he was able to gulp air again. He tried desperately to disguise his near-death experience from his new acquaintance.

"So, where are you from?" JC asked. It was a sure-fire way to elicit a long response. Nearly every soul on earth enjoyed talking about where they came from. And it would buy him time to clear his throat.

"Altoona, Pennsylvania!" Bobbi declared, like she was a contestant answering a game show host.

"What brought you to Vermont?" he asked.

"This job with VSBB," she replied. "And high school basketball season was over for the girls."

"You were playing high school basketball? How old are you, sixteen?" JC blurted. It caused Bobbi to laugh. JC noted that her teeth were white and perfect. Robin, he noted, looked like she was going to shove another pig in a blanket down his throat.

"No, no," Bobbi laughed. "Altoona was a great place to grow up, but I'm an adult now. But the high school girls basketball team is one of the best in the country. Everyone goes to the games, just like everyone in town is in the stands for the boys' football games."

"And when the basketball season ended," JC said, "you decided that it was too long a wait until football season. So, you left town?"

"Well, that and a bad marriage," she admitted. "I had to get away."

"You had fallen out of love with the star quarterback of the football team, who you married after high school?" JC asked.

"Sort of," Bobbi smiled with her perfect white teeth.

# 13

"**I** 've heard things more foolish than that."

"How many more?" JC responded to Sipp Ives.

"A few. Not many," Chief Ives said with a chuckle as his eyes looked at the ground.

JC had crossed paths with the police chief at Molly's. JC, Bip and Robin had just finished breakfast there.

Sipp Ives had noticed JC at the table, made eye contact and nodded his head toward the exit.

The chief chose a spot on the sidewalk where they wouldn't be overheard. JC noticed the shine on Sipp Ives' shaved head. It was a good-looking head, JC thought.

"I've been thinking about what you said," Ives told JC. "You asked me if I harbor any suspicions about the death of Josh Church."

"Do you?" JC asked.

"I've heard things more foolish than that," the chief replied. "Are we off the record?"

"Do we have to be?"

"If you want me to tell you what I'm willing to tell you."

"Then, we're off the record." JC was disappointed that he couldn't quote the chief on that night's newscast. But he had decided long ago that learning something off the record was better than not learning something at all.

"The chief medical examiner for the state, up in Burlington, is a smart man," the chief began. "I telephoned him after your visit and asked him if he maintained any specimens belonging to Joshua Church. You know, hair, blood, a liver or a kidney. I wasn't sure because Mr. Church was determined to have died of natural causes."

"And did the medical examiner keep anything?" JC asked.

"As I said, he's a smart man," the chief told JC. "So, I asked if he wouldn't take a closer look at the remains of the great author."

"So, you think his death might be the work of foul play?"

"I think," Chief Ives said, "that this new investigation by the attorney general and the timing of Mr. Church's death is a puzzle. The timing of Mr. Church's death *could* make it suspicious."

"So, the medical examiner will do a full tox workup?" JC asked.

"A complete toxicology examination," the chief concurred. "That is correct. But that is the good news. For someone in your position, the bad news is that toxicology workups take a long time. And there is a waiting list."

"Yep, they can take time. I've played this waiting game before," JC said. "Six months? Twelve months?"

"Yes," the chief responded. "But we might have something preliminary sooner than that."

"What will the M.E. be looking at?" JC asked.

"He's particularly interested in the hair," Ives said. "He told me that Mr. Church showed no outward signs of a beating, a fall, or asphyxiation. So, special attention is going to be paid to his hair. Your hair keeps a record of how much you've had to drink, what drugs you take, and perhaps what was used to poison you."

"Poison?"

"Well, he wasn't shot," the chief said. "But it's usually drugs, in cases like these."

"Who do you suspect? JC asked.

"I don't have a suspect until I know who did it. That makes my percentages very high," Chief Ives responded. "And that's *if* anyone did anything. It's the circumstances that got my attention. And there is more than one person who could benefit from the demise of Mr. Church. So, keep digging. If you find anything, let me know what you find out."

"And you'll let me know what *you* find out?" JC asked.

The chief gave the news reporter a look that said, police chiefs do not work that way.

With that, the chief turned and walked down Main Street. It was his town. He was a familiar and friendly face to nearly everyone he walked by. He greeted each one of them by name. And they returned the greeting.

"What did he say?" Bip asked, as he and Robin departed Molly's to join JC on the sidewalk.

"Everything," JC told them. "But he did it so that we can't report *anything*."

JC watched Sipp Ives disappear into the crowd.

"Let's go get some man-on-the-street interviews," JC said. "Let's see what the townspeople of Stonestead thought of their famous author."

They began on Main Street. Stonestead residents said things into the microphone like, "He was one of us. You'd never know that he was a millionaire."

"He was the most famous person I ever met," said another, "but you'd think he was a guy you went to grade school with."

JC and Bip drove to the Mont Vert resort village to gather more public opinion. Robin returned to her room at the Flamstead Inn to do research.

They parked their rental car and walked toward the center of the resort village, right around the corner from where lift tickets were sold in the winter.

A new email caused JC's phone to ping. He looked at the message as he walked. It was from Shara. It said, "I want to come see you." He closed the message and replaced the phone in his pants pocket.

He looked up to catch Bip staring at him.

"Is the name on that email who I think it is?" Bip asked with surprise.

"I didn't ask for this," JC replied with a serious tone.

"No," Bip said. "But it found you anyway."

They entered the hub of the resort village and saw a large open firepit, built from local granite. It sat in the middle of a square. Instead of flames, it was filled with colorful flowers.

JC watched a woman walk across the other side of the square, heading for the slopes. He recognized her as Melody Church.

"Melody?" he said in a voice that was raised, but not so loud as to violate the tranquility of the village.

She smiled and turned to approach them.

"I'm going for a hike," she said.

"Up there?" JC asked, looking up at the green ski runs.

"Yes," she smiled and nodded her head. "This is my routine. It's something that Josh and I used to do at least once a week. Now, I do it alone. But it makes me feel like he's nearby."

"How far do you go up?" JC inquired.

"All the way," she said. "It's beautiful up there. You know, Josh loved wildflowers and being in nature. I guess he taught me that. There are a lot of wildflowers up there."

"That's quite a hike," JC said.

"The peak is about four thousand feet. They say the vertical drop is about two thousand feet," she said with pride.

"Wow, you have my admiration," JC told her.

"You know, I watched Josh deteriorate. It made an impression on me," she said. "I figure that I'd better keep moving. You never know when you won't be able to do it anymore."

"Amen," Bip said.

"I'd better get started," Melody stated and smiled. "The hike isn't getting any shorter."

She marched toward the mountain and the two journalists resumed collecting remarks on camera from the locals about Melody's husband, Josh.

"He liked trees and flowers and stuff," one Stonestead resident said, looking at the camera. "I'd go listen to him when he was invited to talk at the bookstore, sometimes. He'd talk about nature. And then he'd always throw a big party when he had a new book come out. There was free food and wine. It was like he wanted to share his good fortune with all of us."

"He seemed to be a big deal around here," said a tall, good-looking man. He was wearing a shirt embroidered with a Mont Vert patch. His nametag said "Rick."

"You were the guy who was guiding everyone into the news conference with Benjamin Whitmore yesterday," JC said to him as he extended his hand. "I'm JC Snow. And this is Bip Peters."

"Yeah," the man smiled and shook their hands. "I thought I recognized you. I'm Rick Teller."

"What do you do here, Rick?" JC asked.

"I do anything they ask me to do," he smiled more. "I got lucky. I only moved here recently. I'm helping out with the mountain biking concession. And this winter, I'll be a lift operator."

"Where'd you move from, Rick?" JC asked.

"Altoona, Pennsylvania."

"Really?" JC responded. "Railyards, Horseshoe Curve, frozen custard at The Meadows."

"Yeah," Rick laughed. "How do you know The Meadows?"

"I've been everywhere at least once," JC smiled. "So, you must know Bobbi Chadwick?"

"No. I don't think so," Rick said after giving it some thought.

"I didn't think Altoona was that big," JC said. "I'm surprised you don't know her."

"Well, there are two high schools," Rick said, "the public school and a Catholic school. She must have gone to the other school. I probably saw her around."

"If you saw her," JC said, "you wouldn't forget her."

# 14

"Did you ever cheat on a girlfriend?"

"Never," he told Robin.

"Really?" Robin asked him.

"Really. Never," JC told her. "It's too much of a betrayal. Too much."

It was early morning in Stonestead and they were going for a walk. JC had awakened her and asked if she would go for a run with him. She reminded him that he had knee surgery roughly five weeks ago. He didn't see that as a disqualifying event. She did.

They walked in the damp of early autumn in Vermont. It was still late summer everywhere else. But a chill was starting to creep into the Green Mountains, in the morning and at night. It wasn't uncomfortable, but it was a reminder of what was coming.

From this end of the small town, they could see two church steeples hovering over the treetops. The school was between the two churches. It was a compact community. Everything was in walking distance.

"Why aren't you married?" she asked him.

"What do you mean?" he asked.

"You're thirty-five or thirty-six years old. You clearly enjoy the touch of a woman. Why aren't you married?"

"You don't know how old I am?" he mocked. He hoped that it might change the subject.

"That is not the point," she said in all seriousness. "Answer the question."

They walked by some woods. The ground was still littered with last autumn's leaves.

"Maybe I screw it up before it gets to that point," he told her.

"You didn't screw it up with Shara," Robin said. "You were in a tough position."

"I chose my job over her."

"So did she," reasoned Robin. "What about before Shara?"

"In the spirit of full disclosure, I screwed it up with Shara twice."

"Right, twice." And Robin held up two fingers. She was making light of him.

Their walk had taken them to the old cemetery. They strolled in. Leaving the pavement, they found that the grass was still moist with dew. It quickly soaked into their shoe tops.

"What about before Shara?" Robin asked.

"Let's see," JC said. "Here is my romantic history as an adult." He stuck up one finger. "I lost interest."

"She lost interest," he said as he stuck up a second finger.

"I lost interest," and he stuck up a third finger.

"She lost interest." Fourth finger.

"I never should have been interested." Thumb.

"She never should have been interested." He raised the thumb on his second hand.

Robin stopped by a large mausoleum. They were well inside the cemetery now.

"Are you going to lose interest in me?" she asked. JC stared into her eyes. He knew the time had come to make a decision.

He had given Robin his undivided attention for slightly less than a year. Their days and nights together had been unlike any relationship he ever experienced. But during all that time, he knew there was a string still attaching him to Shara and their history. It was time to make a decision. All three of them were waiting.

JC slowly pressed his body against Robin's until her back pushed against the granite wall of the mausoleum. She felt the cold stone through her jacket but she didn't object. She searched his eyes.

"No," he said. And he pressed his lips against hers, with all the passion and belief that his lips would belong there until the last day he walked this earth.

"Jean Claude," she whispered.

"Careful, you two. This isn't where you create life. This is where you end it."

JC and Robin slowly pulled away from each other and searched the cemetery for the source of the voice. It belonged to a man with long gray hair and a black goatee. He was wearing three layers of shirts. He was accustomed to the damp mornings of Vermont in September.

"Sorry," Robin said softly, looking at the man.

"I'm just giving you a hard time," the man said, smiling. "You both look like consenting adults."

JC and Robin turned to leave. Their minds were elsewhere.

"You want to see the museum?" the man asked, behind them.

They slowed and looked at each other. "Sure."

The man led them toward the large brick building next to the cemetery. He held the iron gate open for Robin.

"My name is George Earl. I'm the historian for Stonestead. This here is the old Boys' Academy. Come to think of it, it still sorta is."

He led them up five granite stairs and through the entrance. Five older men sat in folding chairs inside the only room where the lights were on. They were seated at long folding tables with dusty volumes of old chronicles in front of them.

"See? Here are the boys I was telling you about!" And George Earl laughed at his own joke. "This here is the Stonestead Historical Society Executive Committee. At least, the ones who pay dues."

"Hell, I haven't paid my dues in two years," one man snorted.

"And that," George said, "is my cheapskate brother. That's David."

The five men mumbled hellos, or just glanced up with moderate curiosity, and returned to what they were doing.

"What are you up to, gentlemen?" JC asked. A few looked up again, but they seemed accustomed to letting George do the talking.

"We're going through old records from the Williams River Hose Company. It seems like every building in Stonestead has burned down twice."

"Except the ones that have burned down three times," David Earl interrupted. The other members of the Historical Society Executive Committee mumbled in agreement.

"So, we're trying to chart all the fires that we can," George informed the journalists.

"That's pretty interesting work," JC told them. "Would you mind sharing what you have with me? It would make a nice feature story while we're here."

George sort of shrugged and looked at his committee. Most of them looked at George and sort of shrugged back.

"Sure," George said, after counting all the votes cast. "I've got an eight-page report on our results, so far. I don't have it here, but I can get it to you."

"That would be great," JC said, looking at the approving eyes of his producer. "How soon can we get it?"

"Today," George said. "Like I say, it's not here. I left it for society members to review after our last meeting. So, it's at the Williams River Hose Company. My daughter works there. She can put it in a folder for you."

"The Hose Company is our pride and joy," David Earl said. "We restored it and suckered someone into opening a nice restaurant there."

"I don't know if 'suckered' is the right word," George Earl quickly inserted. "They do a good business. And people love us for saving the historic building."

"Would you have photographs of some of the old fire scenes you're studying?" JC inquired.

"Do these mangy old men look like they have anything better to do?" George snorted. The executive committee joined in the snorting. George produced a thick folder. It was full of early-era black and white photographs of burned-out homes, businesses and barns.

"I can get these back to you sometime tomorrow," JC said. "We'll take pictures of the pictures."

"Or Monday. Either will be fine," George told him. "And I'll give my daughter a call. The restaurant opens for lunch, so you can pick up that report then."

JC and Robin said their goodbyes and walked across the street to the Flamstead Inn.

"You notice much granite around here?" JC asked as they climbed the granite stairs to the hotel's grand porch.

"I'm noticing a trend," Robin smiled. JC held the door into the inn for her. "There's lots of granite."

The Flamstead Inn had burned down twice. It was first built in the 1840s. It was rebuilt on the same foundation after a fire in the 1880s. There was another fire in 1920 and the present configuration was constructed.

There was a large stone fireplace in the lobby. One of the stones was a grapefruit-sized cannonball. It was a local historic feature.

The floor of the inn was slightly buckled in spots. The man behind the desk told JC that the inn had been abandoned about forty years ago until a new owner reopened it. The building had needed a lot of work.

JC and Robin climbed a creaking staircase and knocked on Bip's door.

"These are pictures we should videotape and return to the historical society," JC said as he handed Bip the folder. "If you do it now, just pile them up in the order you shoot them and I'll make notes later today on what we have. There's a report I'm going to pick up that will explain the pictures. In the meantime, we'll get showered."

JC walked Robin to her room. She invited him in and closed the door behind them.

"Where were we?" she asked as she pinned him against the door.

"When?"

"When we were interrupted in the cemetery," she said. They kissed.

"Shouldn't we shower and get to work?" he whispered as he pulled his lips inches from hers.

"Want to save water?" she asked as she pulled off his tee shirt.

# 15

The historic firehouse was wood painted red. The windows and trim were painted white. It was two stories tall and two towers extended above it. The tallest tower was designed to hang hoses from, to dry after being used to suppress a fire.

The Williams River Hose Company was named such because it was on the bank of the Williams River's Middle Branch. In fact, the building looked to be close to plunging into the Williams River. The riverbank had severely eroded during the hurricane of 1938.

A sign posted near the entrance of the building told visitors that restoration was aided by the Preservation Trust of Vermont. Four numbers placed on the highest tower declared the firehouse had been constructed in 1873.

The restaurant that now occupied the structure paid tribute to its history. The restaurant was called "The Williams River Hose Company."

JC entered the front door, which was on the side of the building, and walked into the lunch rush. He waited at the door until a woman approached him.

"Mr. Snow? I'm Mary McCauley. I'm George Earl's daughter."

"How did you recognize me?" JC asked out of curiosity.

"You're the only face I don't recognize," she said as her eyes scanned the dining room. "It had to be you."

"You're busy. I'm sorry to bother you," JC said. "I'll just pick up the envelope and get out of your hair."

"Thanks. It's in the waiting room. It's on a table on the far side. The report is in an envelope with your name on it. I'm sorry there are no lights on. It's a waiting room. We only need it for the dinner crowd."

JC had come alone. Robin and Bip were getting to work on shooting video of the black and white fire-scene pictures. Bip would shoot them and Robin would gather information written on the back of each photo.

Walking into the adjoining waiting room, JC stopped to allow his eyes to adjust to the light, or lack of it. The room was decorated with overstuffed couches and chairs and end tables, reminiscent of the Victorian Era when the firehouse was built.

Once he was confident that he wouldn't stumble over something he couldn't see, JC proceeded across the room. The only light was provided by what could sneak around the drawn blinds.

"Watcha looking for?" asked a voice jumping from the gray light. It startled JC a bit. He looked into a corner of the room and saw the outline of a man, seated in a chair with his legs crossed.

"Hello," JC reacted. "I didn't see you sitting there."

The man was elderly. He was dressed in a button-down shirt and corduroy pants. It was hard to tell what color they were, in the available light, but they looked pressed and orderly.

"Mary, the manager, is my granddaughter," the man said. "I'm waiting to have lunch with her and catch up."

"I'm JC Snow."

"I'm Frederick Earle."

"Earl. You're George Earl's father?"

"That's right," the man said. "But I spell my last name with an 'E.' E-A-R-L-E."

"You spell your last name differently than your son?" JC asked. "Why do ..."

"Don't ask," Frederick Earle interrupted with a wave of his hand. He smiled like he'd told the story a thousand times. "My granddaughter broke the curse. She married a man named McCauley. She has nothing to explain anymore."

JC saw the envelope on an end table by the far wall. He walked over and picked it up.

"Oh, she likes you," Frederick Earle said.

"Mary?" JC responded. "She seems very nice. I'm sure I'd like her too."

"No," scoffed Mr. Earle. "Her!" And the old man nodded his head toward a sofa next to him.

JC was puzzled. In the low light, he had missed the man's point.

"You don't see her, do you?" Mr. Earle asked. "Well, most people don't. But she likes you. She likes most handsome fellas."

JC looked from the old man to the empty sofa and back to the old man.

"You're telling me that you see someone sitting on that sofa?" JC asked.

"Oh yeah," Mr. Earle said. "Plain as I see you. Sometimes, she has a little baby with her. But not this time."

"What's her name?" JC asked. He couldn't think of anything more intelligent to say.

"Don't know. She doesn't talk much," the old man answered. "But I come and sit with her from time to time. She seems to enjoy that."

JC suspected Frederick Earle was pulling his leg. Maybe the spelling of his last name and the ghost he claimed to see were his way of having fun with tourists.

"You can see her?" JC asked.

"Yeah, I can," Frederick said. "She's mighty pretty, herself. Lavender, I think you'd call that jacket she has on. It matches a long skirt she's wearing." The old man appeared to be eyeing the invisible woman.

"She's all buttoned-up. I seen pictures of my grandmother dressed like that," the gentleman told JC. "I guess they used to call that jacket she's wearing a 'bodice.' She's got shiny dark hair. Kind of your color. Hers is pulled back."

JC caught himself staring at that side of the couch. He still couldn't see anyone but wished that he could. He still felt that Frederick Earle was having fun with him.

"Mr. Earle, it was nice meeting you." And JC turned to head for the door.

"What's *her* name?" Mr. Earle said as JC walked toward the dining room. He stopped and took a few steps back into the dark.

"You told me that you didn't know her name," JC responded.

"Not her," the man said as he nodded to the empty sofa. "*Her*," he said as he pointed behind JC, about thigh level.

JC followed the man's index finger and found he was looking at an empty space next to his leg.

"At least, I think it's a her," Mr. Earle said. "That dog been following you around long?"

JC was now convinced the old man was toying with him.

"Mr. Earle," JC said. He felt his patience growing thin. "You seem like a nice man. Please don't make me feel stupid. You've got your ghost story perfected and you're putting on a marvelous performance. But please don't make me look stupid."

"I understand your sentiments. I hear that a lot," Mr. Earle told JC. "You don't see her either, the dog? She seems to know you. Black and brown with a little white? Maybe a herding dog? She keeps nudging you to sort of change your direction. Real pretty eyes."

JC looked at the man. He had just described Picabo, a dog JC acquired after college, when Shara had left him. JC and Picabo were inseparable for five years, until she was hit by a car. She did have beautiful eyes.

"About seventy pounds?" the man asked.

"Yeah," JC said weakly, without thinking.

"I'm sorry if I shocked you," Mr. Earle said. "She followed you into the room and she was ready to follow you out. What's her name?"

"Picabo," JC said softly.

"That's it!" the old man exclaimed. "You should have seen her eyes pick up when you said her name! Like she's waiting for you to give her a command. It's the darndest thing."

"Picabo," JC repeated.

"There she goes again!" the man laughed.

JC sat down on a soft chair. Picabo was a good dog. Smart and loyal. But she tried to fight every dog she ever met, just once, to show them who was boss. Those were herding instincts.

JC thought back to the night she jumped over a fence and into traffic. He'd crossed the road with every intention of coming right back. But Picabo didn't know that. If he was going somewhere, she was determined to accompany him. She died in his arms.

"You're serious?" he asked solemnly.

"I am, son."

"And the woman, sitting on the sofa next to you?" JC asked. "Is she real?"

"Oh yes!" Mr. Earle told him. "And she's a looker. She's young and pretty. I think she likes it here. She feels safe in the firehouse."

"Are *you* real?" JC asked the man.

"So far!" the old man chuckled.

"I'm sorry, Grandpa," Mary McCauley said as she entered the room. "But the lunch rush is winding down. Why don't you grab a table and I'll join you."

Frederick Earle rose from his chair and headed for the dining room as told.

"Nice to meet you, Mr. Snow."

"Nice to meet you, Mr. Earle. Illuminating," JC answered with a small smile.

JC didn't notice he was scratching his head when Mary McCauley spoke to him.

"My grandfather has been treating you to his stories?" she asked.

"Are they real?" JC asked. "I mean, does he think they're real? The ghosts?"

"Oh yes," Mary answered. "We all do, too. His family, I mean. He says things that you just can't make up. I don't know how he does it. But I don't know how else you can explain it."

"He's told you about the woman on the sofa?" JC asked as he looked at the spot where Mr. Earle said a beautiful woman was sitting.

"If he says she's there, then she's there," Mary responded. "I quit questioning him a long time ago." She laughed at the wonder of it.

JC waved the envelope and thanked the restaurant manager for her help.

"Tell your father that I picked it up and I'll get it back to him by Monday," JC said. Then he hesitated.

"Does your grandfather really spell his last name differently than his son?" JC inquired. Mary nodded her head with a look acknowledging that it was unusual.

"Why would they ..." JC began.

"Don't ask!" Mary laughed, shooing him away.

JC emerged from the door of the restaurant and walked to his rental car. He opened the car door and climbed in. But he caught himself pausing a moment before closing the door. It was long enough for a dog to jump in and sit on the passenger seat. Just like Picabo used to do.

# 16

Two granite steps ushered visitors into Molly's. It was the town's Swiss Army knife of stores.

JC, Robin and Bip were having lunch. But while they were there, they could also mail a letter at the post office window, buy socks, purchase fruit and vegetables, select beer or energy drinks or ice cream from the cooler, pull maple syrup off the shelf and add aspirin, an apron and band-aids to their cart.

They were not going to do any of those things, but they could. They were only having lunch.

There were thick beams extending from the floor to hold up more thick beams that held up the roof. Some of the shelves were so high up they required a ladder to reach the baskets of soap, sweets, cookie cutters, candles and greeting cards up there. The ladder had wheels and was easy to use.

The journalists were going over Robin's notes about the video Bip had shot of the old fire-scene photographs. She noted a picture of smoking rubble that used to be the Flamstead Inn.

"That was in the 1880s," she said.

Bip remarked about some of the particulars he highlighted in the photos, like interesting faces and signs and fire wagons.

"Hey," Bip blurted in a voice just above a whisper. "Aren't those the two VSBB board members?" He was pointing at a table across the room.

"Jerry Dean and Deborah Sampson," JC said. The pair was chatting and eating ice cream cones. They were animated. It was the first time JC had seen Deborah Sampson smile.

"Is that a meeting or a date?" JC asked. Robin watched the pair.

"That's a date," she said.

Dean and Sampson carried on, not noticing that they were being stared at.

"So, where to, boss?" Bip finally asked.

"Let's go to Mont Vert," JC suggested. "Let's ask Ben Whitmore if he has worked out that misunderstanding with the attorney general."

"Yeah," Bip said, "misunderstanding."

The origin of the ski resort's name was as old as Vermont itself. Vert Mont was the name the French gave to the area. It meant green mountain.

By luck, rather than design, the name of the Mont Vert Ski Resort presently had plenty of marketing muscle. "Vertical" had become a battle cry for adventurous skiers and snowboarders.

"Get Vert!" the ski resort's magazine and television ads advised. In other ads, "Mont Vert" morphed into "Much Vertical." Tee shirts declared the wearer was an "INVert." Locals and frequent skiers at the mountain often just called it "Vert."

As the news team drove up the access road to the ski lodge and the VSBB office, they passed runners working hard to get up the hill. They were in full-time training mode, getting ready for the arrival of another ski and snowboard season.

"The town historian told me there used to be a couple of other ski areas in the area," JC told the others. "I think it was in the early days of skiing. One was called Pinnacle. He said that he wasn't certain the other ever had a name."

They parked their rental car in an available spot and climbed some stairs to reach the resort village. Walking down the Belgian Blocks, they passed open ski shops with deeply discounted winter gear.

They spotted Rick Teller as they were walking past. He was leaning on a four-wheel ATV. It was one of a half dozen parked there.

"Hi Rick," JC said.

"Hey man, how you doing?" he said back.

"What do they have you doing for your dollar today?" JC inquired.

"Today," Teller responded with a handsome grin, "I'm the ATV tour guide for tourists. Most of them have never been on one in their life. So, I show them how not to kill themselves on it. I tell them to follow me, and we go up the mountain. I tell them a little history about the area and the like, but mostly it's just to let them have fun piloting an ATV."

"It looks fun," Bip said as he was checking out one of the four-wheelers. Rick told him to hop on.

"Did I see you at the Hose Company?" the tall man asked JC.

"The old firehouse? You did," JC said. "I was there to pick something up."

"Yeah, I was there for lunch," Rick said. "I usually end up there at the bar, after my shift. I don't know this area very well. But when I go there, I know where the bar is and I know where the bathrooms are."

"Did you see a dog when I was there?" JC asked.

"I can't say that I did," Rick responded.

"Yeah, me neither," JC muttered.

"You meet that girl from Altoona yet?" Bip asked as he straddled the ATV.

"I don't think so," Rick responded with a smile.

"Oh, you'll remember when you meet her," Bip laughed. JC laughed too.

"Oh brother," Robin said as she rolled her eyes.

Bip reluctantly climbed off the ATV. There was work to do.

"You don't even want a short ride?" Rick asked him.

"What I want and what I need to do are sometimes different things," Bip responded, catching up with JC and Robin, who were already on the march.

Two college interns greeted them at the door of VSBB. One was named Scooter and one was named Suzy.

"Mr. Whitmore isn't here," Suzy said. "Would you like to leave a message?"

Well-trained, JC thought. It looked like they had been stuffing envelopes. The letters were probably soliciting donations, promising that the lion's share of the money would go to the birds and bees.

"How about Bobbi Chadwick?" JC asked. Robin gave him a look.

"No, I'm sorry," Scooter said. "Ms. Chadwick isn't here either."

"What was that about? Robin asked JC as they walked away from the VSBB office.

"What was what about?" JC asked.

"Were you hoping for some alone time with Bobbi?" Robin sneered. Bip didn't say anything. But he was amused by where this might be going.

"I just asked if she was there," JC answered innocently.

"Why?" Robin asked.

"I just wondered if they were together, Benjy and Bobbi," JC said. "Maybe they went shopping for bathing suits again."

JC's phone rang. It was Rocky, the assignment editor at their TV station in Denver.

"How close are you to Clifton Park, New York?" he asked.

"About two hours," JC told him, after giving it some consideration. "Why?"

"A homeless guy got picked up here in Denver at a shelter on Curtis Street. The police just told us about it. But he's being extradited back to Clifton Park. He may have already landed there."

"He'd land in Albany," JC told his assignment editor.

"Oh, so you know the lay of the land," Rocky said encouragingly. He knew that Albany was near where JC grew up.

"I do," JC confirmed. "What's he being extradited for?"

"He's going to be charged with murder," Rocky told him. "How close are you to Niskayuna, New York?

111

JC snickered. His assignment editor pronounced the name of the town like Risky-tuna.

"It's Nis-Kay-Una," JC told him. "It's an Indian name. It's about two hours away, also. It's across the river from Clifton Park."

"Can you go check it out?" Rocky asked.

"Sure," JC responded. "When?"

"Now," Rocky replied. "The arraignment is scheduled for four p.m."

"We'd have to leave right now," JC said. "We can do it, but it's going to be a rush-job."

"Hey, then it's Saturday," Rocky said. "We don't expect you to work over the weekend unless something blows up. Do this and then enjoy yourselves for two days."

JC got off the phone and delivered the news to Bip and Robin.

"You don't have to make the trip if you don't want to," JC told Robin. "Bip and I have to go."

"Maybe I'll get more done if I stay here," she said. "I can work the phones and see if I can learn anything about this arraignment. And I just got a text from Rocky. He wants me to set up a live shot for you guys at our TV affiliate in Albany."

"That settles it, then. We'll drop you off at the hotel," JC said. Then he looked at Bip. "We'd better get going if we don't want to miss court."

After dropping Robin off at the Flamstead Inn, JC told Bip to reverse the path they took to get to Stonestead from Albany International Airport. They were passing the Bromley Ski Resort when JC's phone rang. It was Robin.

"Okay, so the arraignment isn't in Clifton Park. It's in Ballston Spa?" she said with some doubt in her voice.

"That makes sense," JC told her. "That's the Saratoga County seat. Clifton Park is in Saratoga County. I know how to get there."

"And we're all set with the TV station in Albany," she said. "They don't have an extra live truck just sitting around, so you'll go live from a seat in their newsroom. They say it's a pretty good shot, with plenty of newsroom activity behind you."

"Yep, I remember what it looks like," he told her.

"And I've got a phone number for the guy in the sheriff's office who is investigating this case. I could call him, but I thought you might want to speak with him."

"I would," said JC. "Nice work, Robin. Like usual, you're going to make me look smarter."

"Thanks," she said. He could hear the smile on her face.

JC was confident that he'd get a good signal for his cell phone when they got on one of the few improved highways in Vermont, linking Manchester and Bennington. He placed a call to the Saratoga County Sheriff's Office.

"Investigator John Foot," the voice said over the phone.

JC responded by identifying himself as a television journalist from Denver and informing him that he was bringing a news photographer with him for the arraignment.

"Can I ask you a few questions? This case has only been in my hands for about an hour and a half," JC said.

"It's been in our hands a lot longer than that, and we didn't know anything more than you until we found this guy," the investigator disclosed.

"The defendant's name is Larry Gleichman?" JC asked.

"Yeah, we found him out in your neck of the woods, in a homeless shelter in Denver. On Curtis Street? You know the shelter?"

"Yeah, it's a big one," JC told the law officer. "Not bad unless it gets overcrowded, like during the Covid pandemic. What drew you to him?"

"We found a murder victim back in the spring. He was laying in a field in Clifton Park. He'd probably been there a long time, going unnoticed," the investigator said. "There hasn't been much to go on. Then his credit card shows up in Denver. Mr. Gleichman was spotted on a couple of security cameras using it."

"But why Denver?" JC asked.

"Not sure. He was back here in Niskayuna at about the time when the victim was last seen. We think Mr. Gleichman used the credit card in Niskayuna too," Foot said. "That's where the victim lived, Niskayuna. The victim's body wasn't found for a few months, so we're not sure exactly when he died. But Mr. Gleichman is the only link we've found to the victim, and it's not a good link."

"Did I read that the victim was found wearing ski gear?" JC asked.

"That's right," the investigator said. JC could hear him laughing a little. "We checked with the Killington ski area in Vermont. They were the only ski area in the East that was open that late. But there's not a trace of him there. No credit card use, nothing."

"What's the closest you can get to his date of death?" the reporter asked.

"Judging from what we can tell," John Foot said, "we think the victim last used his credit card legitimately on January fifteenth. When Mr. Gleichman used the same credit card, a day later, he was in Niskayuna. We think Gleichman fled to Denver, hoping to avoid arrest."

"And what's the victim's name?" JC asked.

"Thurston. John Thurston," the investigator said. "We couldn't identify him until his workplace called. He's divorced and he was supposed to be driving out of town on a Monday, so his absence wasn't apparent for a few days."

"Did you find a lift ticket on his jacket?" JC asked.

"That's a good question," Foot replied. "Let me look at the list."

There was quiet on the investigator's end of the line, other than some mumbling. JC believed Foot was looking over an inventory of what was found on the body.

"Nope," Foot finally said. "No lift ticket."

"Was there a zip tie?" JC asked. "Perhaps a lift ticket had once been attached to it? The zip tie is often attached to a pull tab on a zipper of the jacket."

"It's a good question," the investigator stated. "If we found a lift ticket, it might tell us where he was and when. It might even tell us where he was killed."

JC nodded silently as he listened to the law officer mumble, again looking over the inventory.

"Here it is," Foot announced. "A blue zip tie was strung through a tab on the zipper of a jacket pocket. No lift ticket though. It might have been pulled off somewhere. We'll keep an eye out for it."

"Aside from where you found Mr. Gleichman, is there any other connection to Colorado?" JC asked.

"Let me look at my notes to refresh my memory," the investigator said. "Hey, here's something you'll like. Mr. Thurston grew up in Littleton, Colorado. Is that near Denver?"

"It sure is," JC said. "It's a suburb. Is it possible that these two knew each other?"

"That's something I'm going to have to look into," Foot replied.

"Are you going to be at the arraignment?" JC asked. "Might we do an interview on camera?"

"I think the district attorney will be doing the interviews," Investigator Foot said. "I'm not sure I'm even going to be there. I'm going to go talk to Gleichman in a few minutes, though. He's in one of our holding cells. I'll ask him about that Colorado connection. That would make our lives easier."

"Well, thanks for your time, investigator," JC said.

"You bet. Thanks for the lift ticket idea. Hey, say hi to Sipp Ives for me," John Foot said. "He's a good man."

# 17

"John Thurston was stabbed to death," JC told the television camera in front of him. The manner of death was something the reporter learned by attending the arraignment of Larry Gleichman a few hours before.

JC was wearing a lapel mic clipped to his sport jacket, seated in a TV newsroom in Albany, New York. He was briefing an anchor and their viewers back in Denver on Gleichman's extradition from Colorado and his believed connection to a murder in Upstate New York.

Video images, shot earlier by Bip, showed Gleichman being walked across a courtyard. He was in restraints and had sheriff's deputies on three sides of him. The news story also included sound bites from that day with the Saratoga County district attorney.

JC reported that the defendant wasn't charged with murder at this point. He was only charged with false use of an instrument. That was legal talk for using a credit card that didn't belong to him. Thurston's credit card. It was enough to hold him in jail while prosecutors and police built the murder case against him.

The news story also included an interview with the young man and woman who found Thurston's body while they were mountain biking. The interview was shot back in May by the Albany TV station where JC was presently doing his live shot back to Denver. The Albany newsroom allowed JC and Bip to reuse the interview. It had never been seen before by Denver's viewers.

The anchor back in Denver, Sam Brown, asked JC if Gleichman and his alleged victim knew each other.

"There's no evidence of that, Sam. Not yet," JC responded. "Right now, police don't have proof that John Thurston and Larry Gleichman ever came within arm's length of each other. That, of course, would be necessary if Gleichman actually stabbed him."

"Have they found a murder weapon, JC?" the anchor asked.

"Police admit that they have not found the murder weapon, Sam. Honestly, I don't think they even know what brought the victim to the field where those mountain bikers found him."

The anchor thanked JC for his report and informed the audience that JC was in Saratoga County and would be following any new leads in the murder investigation.

The fact that JC was actually in *Albany* County at the moment and not *Saratoga* County, as Sam said he was, probably wasn't going to disturb anyone in the Denver audience.

And few viewers, outside of JC and Sam Brown, knew that the two journalists were competing to become the next permanent anchor of that very news program. JC and Sam knew it though.

"Nice job, JC." It was Sam's voice in JC's IFB. He must have picked up the phone on the news set during a commercial.

"Thanks, Sam. You too," JC said into his microphone. The mic had been patched into the phone by now, so Sam could hear him. It was an awkward situation that neither man could do anything about.

JC called Robin during the drive back to Vermont and told her that he and Bip would be back in Stonestead by ten o'clock.

"Will you be thirsty?" she asked.

"Yep. And hungry," he said. "And it's Friday!"

"Pick me up on your way to MacLaomainn's," she instructed.


"One for my friends and one for the ghost!" JC instructed the bartender in the Scottish bar.

"Which ghost?" came a voice from a table nearby. It was George Earl, the town historian. "You have to be more specific, or they'll be handing beers to about twenty spooky apparitions."

"What are we having, gents?" the bartender interrupted. He was wearing a kilt.

Robin told JC to order for her. She asked for something with a bit of a fruit taste.

"A Tempest Brave New World for the young lady," JC said, "and Old Engine Oil for me and my fine photographer." He was sticking to Scottish beers inside a Scottish tavern.

"Do you want food with that?" the bartender asked.

"Yes," JC told him. "I'll have a Lagavulin with a side order of Glenfiddich. It's Friday."

"If you want any food after that food, I'll send a server your way," the bartender smiled.

"Yes, please," Robin said. "Apparently, I'm the parent. We need to eat."

They grabbed a table under the saber wrapped in a tartan cloth. But JC stopped by the table where George Earl was sitting.

"I met your father," JC said. "He really spells his last name differently than yours?"

"Don't ask!" George laughed.

JC hesitated before leaving George Earl's table. He was searching for the right words.

"I spoke with your dad for a while," JC said. "Do you think his stories are real?"

"The ghosts? I know they are!" George said and then laughed. "I just don't know *why* they are or *how* they are. I'm the town historian, and he comes up with information that I've never heard before. Then, I do a month of research and find out he's absolutely accurate. And he's not getting it from anyone else, that's alive anyway, because no one else knows those things."

"He's your dad," JC stated. "Do you ever see things? Ghosts?"

"Never," George admitted. "And it's supposed to be handed down through generations, right? Sometimes I think I smell things. He says he smells things sometimes. But I don't know if mine isn't my imagination. It probably is."

"I'll get those pictures and the report back to you on Monday, they're great," JC said. "If I knew you would be here, I would have brought them."

"And I would have spilled beer on them," George said. "It's just as well."

JC joined Robin and Bip at their table. They sipped their beers and ordered food. JC asked for cock-a-leekie soup and haggis again.

"What were you talking with George about?" Robin asked. JC gave them both a look. He hadn't decided if he was going to tell them about his unusual encounter with Frederick Earle.

"You're not going to believe this," he said. And he proceeded to tell Robin and Bip about his encounter with George's father.

"Wait," Robin said. "The old man and his son spell their last name differently?"

"Don't ask," JC laughed.

Bip rose from the table and said he'd return shortly. He walked out the front door, pulling his phone from his pocket.

"Can I ask you a question?" Robin said.

"Uh oh," JC responded. "Sure."

"Did you ever ask anyone to marry you?"

"Don't you have any easy questions? Like did I ever murder a nun?"

"I know you killed that man in Montana," she said solemnly. "And men can't be nuns."

121

"No, he wasn't a nun," JC said. "And technically, he was more a nutcase than a man. And he was about twenty seconds from killing me."

"And Shara," Robin added.

"And Shara," JC confirmed.

Bip returned to the table and sat down as the food was served.

"Do we really have the weekend off?" the photographer asked.

"Yeah," JC told him. "As long as there isn't breaking news that Colorado viewers can't live without."

"Can I borrow the car, dad?" Bip asked.

JC gave him a look. They had only one rental car between the three of them.

"If you smash it, son, you're going to be grounded for a month," JC told him.

"I don't smash things," Bip responded with a smile. "I just spoke with Patty."

"Patty Macintyre?" JC asked. "My biggest fan?"

"Yes and no," Bip responded. "Patty did call me, but she still is not your fan. She doesn't like you."

Patty Macintyre was a snowboarder who Bip romanced last winter at the Battle Ax Ski Resort near Lake Placid, New York. JC and Bip went there to cover the arrest of her boss. It turned out that he was innocent.

It was under three hours from Stonestead to Lake Placid. Bip was hoping to visit Patty for the weekend.

JC looked at Robin for guidance. She shrugged.

"Permission granted," JC pronounced. Bip snapped off a military salute.

"She wants me there tonight," Bip said. "How long do you want to stay here?"

"Take the car and go," JC said. "It's not a long walk home, and it's a nice night." He looked at Robin for a sign that she was agreeable to that. She smiled her approval.

Bip wolfed down the last of his crab cakes and rose from the table. He pulled the car keys from his pocket.

"Don't stay out too late, you two," he said as he exited from MacLaomainn's.

JC turned to Robin and she was staring at him with a contented look.

"What?" he asked.

"We have a weekend alone in Vermont!" she said.

"Yep, we'll be able to catch up on a lot of work," he said. He laughed as she punched him in the arm.

"If you even try to resist turning this into a romantic weekend ..." she began.

"I get it," he capitulated. "I'm Just kidding. Mostly. How's this?"

He reached for a book of poems by the Scotsman Robert Burns. One of JC's favorite features at MacLaomainn's were the books stacked on the end of each table. They were books containing Scottish history, or Scottish tour guides, or Scottish poetry.

"Here's one stanza from my favorite Robby Burns poem. It's called 'Such A Parcel of Rogues in a Nation,'" JC told her. "Burns thinks that Scottish leaders sold out the country's independence in exchange for peace with the English."

And he began to read.

"O would, or I had seen the day
That treason thus could sell us,
My auld gray head had lien in clay,
Wi' Bruce and loyal Wallace!

But pith and power, till my last hour,
I'll mak' this declaration;
We've bought and sold for English gold
Such a parcel of rogues in a nation."

"I think it has to do with killing people, but that's still romantic," Robin said sweetly.

"That's me," JC agreed. "Mr. Romance." She laughed.

"That was a fine reading," a man from the next table said. He was leaning over toward JC and Robin's table to the point of nearly falling out of his chair.

"You are skiers?" the man asked.

"We are," JC told him. Robin was wearing a fleece vest with a ski brand on it.

"We only have a few months to go!" the man said. JC assumed that he was referring to the traditional opening of the season around Thanksgiving.

The man was probably in his late sixties or early seventies, JC thought. He was plump, but still enthused about putting on a pair of skis.

"I bought my first pair of skis with S&H Green Stamps," the man laughed.

A woman sitting next to the man looked around him and said hi.

"I have a new pair of skis for this year!" she said.

"What kind did you buy?" JC asked.

"Blue!" she said. "They match my outfit." The older couple laughed.

"I hear that blue skis are the best ones," JC said with a smile.

"Are you a fast skier?" the woman asked.

"He is," Robin said, rolling her eyes for emphasis.

"Well, that worries me," the woman stated. "Maybe I picked the wrong skis."

"Why? You picked them out yourself!" the man said. JC presumed that this couple was married.

"Yes, but this young man likes blue skis and he's a fast skier," she reasoned. "Maybe they'll be too fast for me."

"Don't worry," JC assured her. "I ski on two sets of skis. One is orange and one is yellow. Blue isn't quite fast enough for me."

"Well, that's a relief," the woman grinned.

JC and Robin laughed. JC loved skiers and snowboarders. It was August, and they were as enthusiastic as if they'd just stepped off the mountain in February.

"Well, we're sorry to disturb you," the man said as he pulled his chair back toward his table. "We just enjoyed your reading of Burns."

"You weren't disturbing us," JC said. "It's a pleasure to meet you both."

"Well, that's interesting," Robin said, when the two of them were alone again.

"What?" JC asked.

"When that couple was talking with us, I happened to look at the door and I saw Bobbi Chadwick walk in," Robin told him. "But I swear, she saw you and turned around. Then, a man behind her turned around. He seemed to be with her, but I'm not sure. No, I think he was with her."

"Did you get a look at him?" JC asked. "Was it Whitmore?"

"No," Robin said. "I think it was Rick Teller."

"The guy who says he doesn't know Bobbi Chadwick?" JC said.

"Yeah."

# 18

Hot coffee offset the cool Vermont morning as they sat on a second-floor porch at the inn. Each of their rooms had a door leading out to the same porch. It was furnished with wicker couches, chairs and tables.

"Why would Rick Teller lie if he knew Bobbi Chadwick?" Robin asked. She was wrapped in a blanket. JC was wearing a fleece vest with the Colorado State University brand.

"Is it possible that he looked her up after we told him someone else from Altoona was here?" JC answered.

"I thought Bobbi was Benjamin Whitmore's girlfriend," Robin offered.

"Davey says there's not much doubt about that," JC reminded her. "The expensive dinners, the trips to romantic destinations. Just the two of them. Davey figures that Whitmore is stealing from the charity to wine and dine a woman that's way out of his league."

"Guys do stupid things to impress pretty women," Robin said.

"Should I take that personally?" JC asked her.

"No, you just do stupid things," she said with a smile and patted his leg to reassure him. "And I'm not impressed at all." JC just shook his head and smiled.

"We should track down Rick and ask him if he's run into that woman from Altoona," JC suggested. "If he says no again, then we know those two are up to something."

Quiet settled in. JC and Robin watched from their porch as the world passed through Stonestead. People were walking their dogs, walking with each other, or stopping to look at the offerings of a garage sale that just opened for business.

"Look!" Robin said as she pulled her coffee cup away from her lips.

JC searched the sidewalk below.

"That's Jerry Dean and Deborah Sampson, isn't it?" Robin asked. It was.

"Are they a thing?" JC asked. "They're the farmers from *American Gothic.* How can they be a thing?

"This town has a bee in its bonnet," Robin declared.

"How many years have passed since the last human being used that expression?" JC asked. She laughed.

"Since we're talking about work," JC said. He was testing the waters. He knew that Robin wanted the weekend to be about them, not work.

"I knew you wouldn't last," she said. But she was smiling and sipped her coffee.

"I don't think I told you this," JC started. "Thurston, the stabbing victim in Saratoga County? He grew up in Littleton, Colorado."

"Really?" she said, looking at him.

"Meaning our workload just doubled," JC said. "A guy arrested in Colorado for a murder near here and a murder victim who was born and raised in suburban Denver."

"What brought him East?" she asked.

"He went to Union College in Schenectady," he told her.

"I tell you what," Robin negotiated, "we'll work today if you'll let us play tomorrow."

"That sounds like a good deal," he told her.

They passed the day working on their computers on the porch. Thurston, they found, had some business dealings with VSBB. His bank loaned them money.

"Did you know that Paul McCartney ate lunch right down the road from here?" Robin asked, still staring at her computer.

"In Stonestead?" JC asked.

"No, in a town called Peru."

"That's a great town, Peru. It's right down the road from the Bromley ski area," JC told her.

"I know!" she told him. "I'm reading a newspaper article that says he went skiing at Bromley with friends, wearing a mask so that he wouldn't be recognized. Then, they had lunch at a general store in Peru. It's called JJ Hapgood's."

"I've been there," JC told her. "It's a really cool store. It's like an old general store."

"Can we go there?" she asked.

"Sure," he said. "But we have to wait until Bip returns with the car." She frowned.

They passed more time quietly, collecting information that might be useful to their assignments.

"Did you know that they used to ship apples from this area to Boston?" Robin informed him. "It was a big business. There was one called the 'Blue Wolfgang.' They said it was as big as a cannonball."

The day passed this way. They took a break for lunch at a café down the street. Then they returned to the porch and their laptops.

"Do you play the bagpipes?" Robin asked without looking up from her computer. But then she did, expecting an answer.

"I cannot cook and it does not appear that I can play the bagpipes," he said. "I know that I should be able to play them because I have Scottish blood. But I can't even play the little instrument that you have to become good at before you can advance to being a bad bagpipe player."

"What's that called," she asked, "a bagless pipe?"

"No," he said, noting that she was amusing herself. "It's called a chanter. It has eight notes. I can only play six of them."

"You can't cook and you can't play the bagpipes," she smirked. "You're not good at very many things."

"I will paraphrase Edison," he responded. "I haven't failed. I just found ten thousand things that I'm no good at."

"Well," she said. "You're not good at taking a romantic day off with your girlfriend."

"I will add that to the list," he smiled.

Robin thought about the day ahead. She had seen a grill in the backyard of their inn.

"Do you want to grill dinner?" she asked.

"I haven't grilled outdoors in years," he said. "Don't like it that much."

"You cook over an open fire when we go camping. Why would you not like cooking on a grill?" she asked.

"Mosquitos, for one."

"If there are mosquitos," she said, "You can go outside to cook and then bring it inside to eat."

"That makes even less sense," he told her. "You go outside, where despite the mosquitos, it's lovely. Then you cook something on an inferior device and bring it inside where there is a perfectly suitable oven?"

"A grill is not inferior," she insisted.

"A grill only cooks three kinds of food," he persisted. "Lightly burned, moderately burned and badly burned."

"What about camping and cooking over an open fire?"

"That's different," he insisted. "Camping is fun. And when you camp, you eat to survive. Everything tastes good when you camp."

"You have a genetic defect," she told him. "You have no cooking instincts whatsoever."

"If it's a genetic disorder, then it must be inherited," he said. "I'm not to blame."

"How did your ancestors survive, if they couldn't cook?" Robin asked.

"They probably invented the microwave oven," he grinned.

When Robin was finished staring at him in disbelief, she turned her attention to people on the sidewalk below their porch. She spotted a pickup truck pulling into a parking spot in the small commercial district. Rick Teller climbed out from behind the steering wheel.

She nudged JC. His nose was buried in something on his laptop. He looked up at her and she turned his gaze downstairs toward Teller.

"Here's our chance," JC said.

They rose from their wicker couch on the porch, pulled on shoes and ran into the hallway and down the hotel stairs.

"Look nonchalant," JC said as they were both trying to catch their breath after the dash to the hotel door.

They peered out onto the sidewalk and saw Rick Teller emerging from a shop and walking toward his truck.

"Nonchalant," Robin repeated as they walked down the stairs of the hotel and onto the sidewalk.

"Rick," JC said in a raised voice. It stopped the man as he was putting a bag on the passenger seat.

"Hi guys," Rick Teller greeted them.

"What brings you here?" Robin asked.

"Toothpaste, deodorant, beer," he said. He looked into his bag as if to confirm it.

"Ah, you've been to Molly's," JC said. "Is there anything they don't sell?"

"Most of the stores up at the ski resort are closed for the summer," Rick replied. "This is where I come for my supplies."

JC tapped Robin as if they were going to continue walking nonchalantly. They took two steps and stopped.

"Hey," JC said, "have you bumped into that woman who we said is from your hometown? Altoona? Bobbi Chadwick?"

Rick Teller looked as though he was giving it some thought.

"No," he finally said. "I'll have to look her up, one of these days."

JC and Robin said their goodbyes and walked down the sidewalk, away from Rick Teller.

"Got him," JC said. "But what are they up to?"

# 19

"You never answered my question," Robin said.

He turned his head on the pillow to face her. He had an inquiring look on his face.

"Did you ever ask someone to marry you?" she asked.

"Yes."

"She turned you down?" she asked.

"No."

"You married her?"

"No," JC said. "She had the sense to break it off. She knew we'd be unhappy. She was right. It would have been a disaster."

The rising sun was shining through their lace curtains. It was Monday morning. Sunday had been what they sought, a day without work.

They had walked to the old Stonestead train station, where apples used to be shipped to Boston. The train station was first built before the Civil War. Then it burned down. This one was built after the Civil War.

They took a lazy ride on a scenic train that followed a loop deeper into Vermont before returning to Stonestead. They had dinner on the first-floor porch of the inn, overlooking the Town Green.

Now, there was pounding on their door. It was Bip, back from Lake Placid.

"Robin, I can't find JC. He doesn't answer his door," he blurted in mock panic. Then he started laughing.

"He's with me," Robin shouted through the door from bed. "I had a problem with my faucet. He's fixing it."

"He's working on your plumbing?" Bip asked, laughing.

"Funny," JC shouted. "Get a table at Molly's and we'll meet you there for breakfast."

First, JC wanted to return the envelope with photos and the study of Stonestead's fiery past to the Historical Society. He ran across the street but found the door to the Historical Society was locked. No lights were on in the building. He left, still holding the envelope.

"How is Patty?" JC asked Bip as he slipped into the booth at Molly's .

"Awesome," Bip replied with enthusiasm. "We had a blast. Thanks for letting me take the car."

"Is she any fonder of me?" JC asked.

"Funny," Bip said as he dropped his napkin into his lap. "She isn't." He started laughing. "She told me to say hi to Robin and the asshole."

Robin entered Molly's and sat next to JC.

"Patty says hi," Bip told her with a giggle.

"Did she say hi to JC?" she asked.

"In very clear terms," Bip said, laughing.

"Why doesn't she like me?" JC asked.

"You accused her boss of murder!" Bip reminded him.

"Oh sure," JC responded. "Kill the messenger. Why can't she be like every other American and hate her boss?"

"Yeah," Bip and Robin both said. They were looking at their boss.

Breakfast consisted of lots of coffee, some French toast and fruit.

"Well, let's make some phone calls and see who the lucky winners are," JC said as he pulled his phone out of a side pocket of his sports jacket.

First he called the office of the Vermont attorney general. He wanted an update on the investigation into the VSBB.

"No one is available to speak with you right now," he was told. "Would you like to leave a message?" he was asked.

He left a phone number and a message asking for a call back.

Next, he called Saratoga County Sheriff's Investigator John Foot. He had better luck.

"The district attorney only told half the story on Friday," JC told the investigator. "She said that you guys know when John Thurston last used his credit card and where. But the DA never said when and where it was used. Care to share that with us?"

"Yeah, there's no need to keep it a secret anymore, now that we have Gleichman," the investigator said. "It was last used on January fifteenth. It was used about five miles from where you're sitting, at the Mont Vert Ski Resort."

"Really?" JC's response was like an involuntary muscle movement. Like blinking an eye or swallowing. He looked at the two members of his crew.

"You said you were going to talk with Gleichman, after we got off the phone Friday," JC stated. "Did you?"

"Yeah," Foot replied.

"Did he admit using the credit card?" JC asked. "Did he say where he got it?"

"No, he didn't say anything really," the investigator said. "He had a public defender with him. That was fast. He just said that he didn't kill Thurston. He says he's never seen the guy in his life."

"What's Gleichman like?" JC asked. "He's homeless, right?"

"That's what he tells us. But he's not your typical homeless," Foot told him. "He's not dirty. His clothes are clean. His hair is cut."

"Can you place him ..." But before JC could ask another question, the investigator said that he had to go.

"I told you what I'm prepared to say," the law officer said. "I don't want to play fifty questions." And he hung up.

"How did that go?" Robin asked.

"Well, he's not much for long goodbyes. But he gave me some good stuff before that," JC told her.

Next, JC found the name of Larry Gleichman's public defender. As a journalist, he knew about the overload of cases piled on the desks of public defenders. It was a great way for a young lawyer to take a crash course in courtroom law, but it was about as rewarding as repeatedly driving a nail into your thumb. JC just hoped to catch her at a moment she wasn't in court.

"Faith Oaks," the voice said after picking up the phone.

"Wow, great name for a public defender," JC said. "You need a lot of one and the strength of the other."

"What may I do for you? I only have a moment," the woman said. It sounded like she had not heard an original remark about her name since pre-school.

"What is your defense going to be for Larry Gleichman?" JC asked.

"He didn't do it," Faith Oaks replied.

"Can you prove it?" JC asked.

"We've got a long way to go on this," she said. "But honestly, I don't think he did the murder."

"But he's not denying using the stolen credit card," JC said.

"We wouldn't get very far on that one. Look, he's scared crazy right now. He admits he's made some bad choices in life, but he's not a bad guy," she said. "He's never been arrested for a violent crime."

"Has he been arrested?" JC asked.

"Yes, but it's been for stealing. The credit card charge may stick," she said. "But he insists he didn't kill anyone, and the prosecution doesn't have any proof that he did."

"Where does he say that he got Mr. Thurston's credit card?"

"He says he found it," the defense attorney said with the deflating knowledge that everyone who gets caught with a stolen credit card says that they found it.

Usually, when the truth is learned, the accused beat some guy senseless and took the card. Or they grabbed a purse in a cart at the grocery store and made a run for it. Or they bought it from the guy who stole it. Rarely did they actually just "find" it.

"He says that he was staying warm inside a fast-food place and a lady at the next table left it there when she got up," the public defender said. "He says it was almost like she wanted him to take it. And he didn't need much convincing."

"Did you say a lady?" JC stopped her.

"That's right, a woman," she responded.

"Not Mr. Thurston?"

"Not Mr. Thurston. A lady," she repeated.

"What does Mr. Gleichman say he purchased with the card?"

"Well," the woman said, "this is his area of expertise. He knows how to steal. He quickly bought some food, short-term and long-term. He bought some new clothes, including a warmer jacket. And he bought a bus ticket to get out of town. He hoped he'd have a few days, halfway across the country, to use the card some more."

"Why did he pick Denver?" JC asked. "Does he have family there?"

"No, he says he liked to ski when he was growing up. He says he was on the high school ski racing team," she said. "And he always heard that Denver was a nice place."

"He'd never met John Thurston?"

"He swears that he never did. And I'm not sure there was much time that they even resided on the same side of the country," Oaks told him. "Thurston grew up in Colorado, but Larry was here in New York. Then Thurston moved here but my client was skipping around the country."

"Does he have family in New York?" JC asked.

"No, they're in Seattle," the public defender said. "But he says he's burned a lot of bridges. He really has nowhere to go."

"This woman who left the credit card on the table, almost begging your client to take it," JC began, "any idea who she is?"

"No," Oaks said. "We're going to look for security video. But this was eight months ago. Most of those security cameras tape over themselves well before eight months. I'm not hopeful."

"Does he say he could identify her?" JC asked.

"He doesn't sound very confident of that," she answered. "He's not an idiot and his brain is not fried like some of our homeless. He's clean and polite and he knows he's in a lot of trouble. I think he stole the credit card. I don't know how. But I don't think he killed this guy. They're going to have to prove it."

The public defender then explained that she had spent more time talking with JC than she should have. Court was about to convene and she had other cases to concern herself with.

"If you find anything, she said, "let me know." And the conversation ended.

"What did she say?" Robin asked.

"That he stole the card from a woman," JC told them.

"A woman?" Robin repeated. "How did she get it?"

# 20

"Y ou can't git the-ear from he-ear," Davey said.

"Did you just get back from the dentist?" JC asked over the phone. "I can barely understand what you're saying."

"That's my New England accent," Davey Kay laughed. "Needs work, huh?"

"I don't think work will help," JC remarked.

"Well, the place you're looking for is only about five miles from you," Davey said. "But it's five *New England* miles. It's Vermont. Not much is in a straight line."

JC thanked his friend for the new information. He slipped out of the booth at Molly's and left a generous tip for letting them sit there so long while they conducted the morning's business. Robin and Bip were waiting at the door to the store.

"Let's go to Mont Vert," JC told his crew. "But we have a detour."

"What's the detour?" Bip asked.

"Davey says that Ben Whitmore just bought a new house. Davey says that he paid a lot of money for it. It's up a winding road, but it will get us to Mont Vert, eventually."

"Mind if I tag along?" Robin asked. "I can call Denver from the backseat and fill them in on what we have for tonight's live shot."

"Tell them that I think it's going to be a story about the Thurston murder tonight," JC told her. "Gleichman's view of things, according to his public defender."

"I shot a ton of footage of Gleichman when the cops walked him across that courtyard," Bip informed his colleagues. That meant they wouldn't be using the same seven-second loop of video over and over again. It was a pet peeve of JC's when he saw that on the news.

Davey wasn't exaggerating. There wasn't fifty feet of straight road from the time they left Stonestead.

"These roads used to provide the straightest point from A to B," JC said. "But that was three hundred years ago. They used to lead to sawmills and grain mills that don't exist anymore. They used to go around farm fields that are now forests. Vermont law actually calls them "Ancient Roads.""

"This is a really cool state," Bip declared.

"It is," JC agreed. "Sometimes in the woods, you'll stumble across old postal roads. Low stone walls marked the path postal carriers would follow to deliver the mail on horseback, as far away as Boston. Now, you'll find them overgrown and in the middle of the forest."

"Wow." They heard Robin's voice from the backseat.

"Listen to this," she said. "There is an old law in Vermont that requires roads to be three rods wide. Do you know what a rod is?"

"Something you fish with?' Bip remarked.

"Yes, but not in this case," Robin said, reading from her phone. "Three rods is forty-nine and a half feet. This says that there are so many old lost roads in Vermont that some of them cut right through people's swimming pools and houses. The state is trying to get it all worked out. You can't even see some of them, but there are land ownership issues."

"We should be getting close to Whitmore's house," JC told them. "The address is 5-0-2-7."

"Uh, I don't think we're going to need the address," Bip said.

JC and Robin looked up the road. A copper roof was towering over the trees. There was a shiny remodeled colonial mansion beneath it. It had new stone pillars and window shutters. There were brick extensions on both sides of the original building. And there was a fountain in the middle of a circular drive.

A gate prevented them from pulling into the driveway. A wooden fence and landscaping prevented them from going around the gate. They stopped and gaped at the edifice.

"Wow," said Bip. "There's a lot more profit in non-profit than there used to be."

"Davey wasn't lying," JC said.

Bip got out of the car and shot some footage of the home. JC called the attorney general's office. There was still no one available to speak with him.

When Bip stowed his camera in the trunk, they proceeded to the ski resort. The road was winding, but it was well taken care of. They passed estates with planted flowers along the road. The fences all had fresh paint. JC would bet that in the winter, this was the first road to be plowed. This was Millionaires Row.

Arriving at the ski resort, Bip pulled the car into a spot near the ski lodge. Robin had called ahead and received permission to shoot inside the lodge. Any publicity was good publicity, in the management's view.

"The last time Thurston used his credit card, he used it here," JC said as Robin and Bip walked alongside him. "It was used to buy lunch. So, he still had the credit card. And as soon as the next morning, he was dead. When did he lose the credit card?"

"Someone probably stabbed him and took it," Bip suggested.

"That's probably exactly what happened," JC agreed. "Nine times out of ten, that's how it would have happened. We're probably wasting our time here."

JC led them to the cashier's station in the cafeteria. He asked a young man behind a cash register if there was a manager he could speak to. The young man got on the phone and passed along the request.

The cafeteria wasn't busy. It was still a little early for lunch.

"Do you have this job in the winter?" JC asked the bored young man sitting at the cash register. He looked to be of college age.

"I only work here in the summer," the young man said. "I go back to school in about three weeks."

"Do you know anyone who was a cashier last winter?" the reporter asked. The young man gave it some thought.

"Suzy was, I think." He put his fingers to his lips, as if he had doubt. He didn't seem to be used to this much responsibility. He seemed as though he liked to be invisible. "I think she did."

"And where can I find Suzy this morning?" JC asked.

"She works for the Birds and Bees charity," the young man said. He was gaining confidence because JC was asking questions that he could answer. "Just go out this door and take a left. Then, follow the stone path where all the shops are? It will be on your right."

"We know the way," JC assured him. "And her name is Suzy?"

"Right. Suzy," the cashier said. Now he was smiling. He thought he passed the test.

JC and the others walked past the resort's row of stores and into the VSBB office. There, he saw Scooter and Suzy.

"I'm sorry, Mr. Whitmore isn't here," Scooter said.

"How about Ms. Chadwick?" JC asked.

"No, I'm sorry," the young woman said. "She isn't."

JC wasn't there to see Whitmore or Bobbi Chadwick. He just liked to see the interns perform. He had a feeling they had a lot of practice saying, "Mr. Whitmore isn't here."

"You're Suzy, right?" JC asked. "We met the other day when we stopped by."

"Yes, I remember." Suzy said. She looked nervous but competent. She had Asian features. She was dressed sharp but professionally.

"You were a cashier in the cafeteria in the lodge last winter?" JC asked.

"Yes," said Suzy. "I go to college nearby. I do it to earn some spending money."

"What college?" Robin asked.

"Community College of Vermont, in Springfield," she said.

"What are you studying?" Robin asked.

"Early childhood education. I'll finish up at a four-year school," she said with a smile.

The conversation seemed to instantly relax Suzy. Robin had done it again, JC thought.

"Suzy, have police spoken to you about a man named John Thurston and a credit card he may have been using last January?" JC asked.

"Yes."

"Do you remember that day?" he asked.

"No, it was too long ago. And we're so busy during the lunch rush."

"I don't blame you. So, you didn't have anything to tell them," JC inquired.

"No, I'm sorry," she said.

"What did they tell you they were looking for?" he asked.

"They said they were wondering if I remembered a woman," Suzy said. "They said they think the credit card slip was signed by a woman."

# 21

"That guy's going to jail," JC told her.

Robin and JC were back at Molly's for breakfast the next day. They were watching Ben Whitmore and his executive assistant, sitting in a booth across the room. They were holding hands across the table. Bobbi had a smile on her face, displaying most of her brilliant white teeth. One of her feet rested on top of one of Whitmore's.

"They're practically undressing each other," Robin said.

"A pretty public display," JC observed.

"I'm almost certain that I saw Rick Teller with Bobbi Chadwick in the door last Friday night when we were at

MacLaomainn's. They looked like they were together. I mean *together*-together."

"They were probably seen by someone else too. And now, she's slobbering all over Whitmore during the breakfast rush in the busiest breakfast place in town," JC said. "It makes you wonder."

"Well, from what we see on display across the room," Robin said, "Whitmore and Bobbi are clearly 'a thing,' right?"

"It certainly is being orchestrated to make us think that," JC agreed. "But who is the orchestra conductor?"

"What do you mean?" Robin asked.

"Do you think Bobbi is cheating on Whitmore with Rick?"

"Maybe," Robin said as she stared at the couple in the restaurant.

"So, maybe Bobbi saw us Friday night, or saw someone else that knows her, and that's why she turned around in the door at MacLaomainn's and left," JC offered. "And maybe she's here this morning to cast doubt in anyone's mind who thinks she *isn't* Whitmore's girl."

"And maybe she's trying to clear up any doubt in Whitmore's mind," added Robin.

Bobbi Chadwick was wearing a form-fitting, low-cut dress. It was alluring and it looked expensive. She also had an expensive-looking bracelet around her wrist. It matched a diamond ring she had on her right hand.

"How much can an executive assistant at a non-profit earn?" JC wondered out loud.

"It depends on what she's doing to earn it," Robin responded.

"Our company should have benefits like that," JC snickered.

"It does," Robin said, looking at him with both a seductive look but also one suggesting he was overlooking the obvious.

"Oh yeah," JC said with an embarrassed laugh.

"So, where's my bracelet?"

"Here, let me pick up breakfast," he said with a smile. She rolled her eyes. "I wonder what they're up to?"

"Who?"

"Every one of them," JC told her.

Benjamin Whitmore approached the table.

"I understand you've been looking for me," Whitmore said to JC.

"Yeah, good morning. Would you like a seat?" JC responded.

"No, why don't we step outside," Whitmore said with a smile.

He was wearing a light-blue sport coat and yellow pants. His shoes shined. They were loafers. JC noticed that the glasses he wore were a different color than the ones he wore at the press conference. But like the others, these matched today's clothing. The frames had yellow in them. JC wondered if he had different glasses for each outfit.

"So, you were looking for me?" Whitmore asked again. "Or should I say looking *into* me?"

"Both," JC told him.

"You know," Whitmore said with a smug grin, "when someone spends that much money on a house, they don't do it without paying for security cameras."

"You saw us," JC said. "Outside your home."

"Yes," Whitmore acknowledged with a condescending grin.

"Nice house," JC told him. "How do you afford it?"

"That's not your affair, Mr. Snow."

"It kind of is," JC disagreed. "And just because it's buried deep in the woods doesn't mean the attorney general can't find it."

The smug smile fell from Whitmore's face. It telegraphed his concern about the investigation.

"Do you know what has been going on for the past decade?" Whitmore asked JC with some indignation. "Beekeepers in the United States and Europe have reported annual hive losses of thirty percent."

"That doesn't explain where your money is coming from," JC said bluntly. Ben Whitmore looked at the journalist without uttering a word for a moment.

"Josh Church was very good to me," he finally said. "And he was a wonderful benefactor for VSBB."

"Are you saying that he *gave* that money to you, in addition to the money he gave your group?"

"I'm saying," Whitmore emphasized, "Josh Church didn't fully understand the value of what he bequeathed to us. Josh didn't come close to maximizing his potential profits. Sometimes, Mr. Snow, someone who is a brilliant artist is bad at business. Sometimes, dying is the best thing they can do if they want to sell books."

JC's eyes widened. The blunt observation coming from Whitmore's mouth seemed to be done without remorse.

"I'm not guilty of whatever it is you think I'm guilty of, Mr. Snow."

"Then what are you guilty of?" JC asked.

Whitmore abruptly declared that he had to leave for a meeting, and he walked away down Main Street.

"Did you get what you're looking for?" inquired a velvety voice from behind JC. He turned to face Bobbi Chadwick.

Her smile was disarming. JC smiled back at her, knowing that any smile he could muster would lose in a mismatch.

"You know, I met someone from your hometown the other day," JC noted. He tried to sound like he was making small talk. "Altoona, isn't it?"

"You have a good memory," her perfect voice informed him. "I didn't know that anyone else from Altoona was here. Do you know his name?"

"No," JC lied.

"Hmm," she said. "I'll have to look for him."

With that, she told him to have a lovely day and walked down Main Street. JC noted that it was the same direction that Whitmore had walked. Bobbi, JC was certain, was smart enough to have observed where Whitmore went.

"Well, did you get her phone number?" Robin asked sarcastically, as she walked out of Molly's to join him.

"Funny," JC answered, with equal sarcasm.

"I paid the bill," Robin said with a condemning expression on her face.

"I guess those company benefits aren't what they're cracked up to be," he grinned.

"So, did they both confess?" she asked.

"No, but here's something interesting," JC said. "I told her that we ran into *someone* who was from Altoona. And she asked me what *his* name was and said she'd have to look for *him*. I didn't tell her it was a 'him.' What are they all up to?"

JC and Robin walked back toward the Flamstead Inn. JC was still carrying the manilla envelope with the pictures and report George Earl had loaned him.

"Let's sit on the porch for a second," JC suggested. "I want to make a call.

"Go ahead," she said. "I'll go upstairs and get Bip. Do we know where we're going next?"

"Yeah," he said. "I think so."

JC could hear the phone ringing as he held it to his ear. He was getting into the habit of putting phone calls on speaker. He was starting to be influenced by the unverified but unrelenting stories of cell phones slowly frying our brains.

But on the porch of the Flamstead Inn, where he could be overheard, JC held the phone to his ear. Sheriff's Investigator John Foot answered.

"So, you're looking for a *woman* who signed Thurston's name to his credit card slip?" JC heard a sigh coming from Foot's end of the phone.

"You've been talking with Faith Oaks," the investigator deduced.

"And you aren't dismissing the public defender's version of the facts," JC said. "You've been looking for a woman who signed that slip at Mont Vert?"

"Maybe," Foot responded.

"Maybe? That's a pretty bold statement," JC said.

"Maybe a woman signed that slip," the law officer elaborated. "We just thought the signature looked like a woman's handwriting. Do you think we have a laboratory test that tells us if a man or woman signed a piece of paper?"

"Sort of," JC shrugged. "Fingerprints."

"There are no fingerprints," John Foot disclosed. "It was one of those machines that you sign, not an actual piece of paper. And a thousand people may have signed that machine by the time we got our first look at it."

"I can't recognize my own signature on those things," JC said. "And you think it looked like a woman's signature?"

"Exactly," Foot agreed. "So maybe it was a woman and maybe it wasn't. We can't find any woman. If the attorney for Gleichman thinks there's a woman, she can go find her."

As Investigator Foot ended the call, JC looked up from his rocking chair on the hotel porch to see Bip and Robin standing there, waiting for him.

"Comfy?" Bip asked.

"So, let me ask you this," JC said to them. "If a woman signed Thurston's credit card slip at Mont Vert, and if Bobbi Chadwick makes a living seducing men, could Bobbi be the woman who signed Thurston's name on the credit card slip?"

"Our perfect Bobbi?" Bip exclaimed in fake horror. JC watched Robin roll her eyes, again.

"Don't start," JC said to his photographer.

# 22

The so-called "Stone House District," on the outskirts of Stonestead, uniformly looked like no other neighborhood JC had ever seen. Each two-story home had its own unique variation of gray granite, because they were all built by hand. The rock was pulled from the ground nearby, after resting there for millions of years.

Josh and Melody Church's front door was painted blue. The color exploded from the surrounding surface of muted grays. Their home was also unique from the others because it was quite a bit bigger. It had been expanded in three directions and a sweeping porch had been added to the front. The additions were wood-frame, containing two additional bedrooms and the large library in the back.

"Maybe we got away with it because you can't see our house from the road," Melody said with a sneaky smile. "I'm not sure what the rules of the historic district would say. We were afraid to ask. And the trees by the road always provided us with our privacy."

"And the long driveway," Robin added.

"Oh yes," Melody giggled. "I probably shouldn't say this, but sometimes Josh would walk out our front door without a stitch on. I'd scold him and he'd say, 'Who's watching?'"

They were standing in the gravel driveway. They could barely see the steeple of the stone church down the road. Otherwise, Josh and Melody Church couldn't see past their property line, and no one could see in.

"So, what's new?" the attractive host asked as she led them into the house.

"Oh, our TV station in Denver found more work for us to do," JC said. "The body of a murder victim found in New York belongs to a gentleman who grew up in Colorado. So now we're covering both stories."

"Where was the murder?" she asked.

"Saratoga County," JC told her.

"Lovely area," she responded. "Have they arrested anyone?"

"Yes, they have," she was told.

"What's his name?" she asked.

"Larry Gleichman," JC said. "Do you know him?"

"No," Melody replied.

"He's homeless," JC said. "He was just drifting through the area."

Melody nodded her head. "A shame. Would you like some tea?"

All three journalists accepted the offer.

"I like teatime," Robin said. "It feels so civilized. Does everyone in Vermont do this?"

"No," Melody laughed. "I'm afraid we have our share of uncivilized behavior too."

She reached for a teakettle on the shelf above the sink. She grabbed the one with a forest, a bear and deer on it.

"This was Josh's favorite," she said.

"I remember you telling us that," JC told her.

They took their tea in the library. The day was warm enough to open the French doors looking into the garden. A breeze brought in the fragrance of flowers in the garden.

"I love this," Robin said meekly. "Do you get wildlife in your yard?"

"Oh, yes," Melody laughed. "The deer eat my flowers in the spring and the rabbits eat the leftovers. After a while, Josh learned what they like to eat and what they don't. So, he planted the ones that would survive. I'm afraid I didn't do as good a job this spring. The deer have lunched on quite a few of the ones I planted."

"It's so green," Bip commented. "I grew up in Colorado. Our green season lasts about six weeks."

"Oh, I remember," Melody said. "I spent a number of years in Aspen. It's lovely, but it's not green like it is here."

They sipped their tea and admired the garden. JC also took an envious look at the books on Josh's library shelves. He was looking at an illustrated volume on the twenty thousand distinct bee species in the world. He turned to Melody.

"Do you have full trust in Ben Whitmore and the way he's spending your money?" He asked.

"My husband's money?"

"Yes, the donations you both gave to VSBB."

 читать

"I suppose so," she said. Her expression suggested that she hadn't given it much thought. "I know that Davey has told you that he thinks something is rotten in Denmark. And I love Davey, but I'm not so sure. I'll say that on camera, if you like."

"That would be nice," the TV reporter said.

Bip began to set up his camera, tripod and lights. Robin offered to help.

"Oh, I should check the mail," Melody said. "I'm expecting something. Do you want to walk with me to the end of the driveway?"

"I'd enjoy that," JC told her.

They took a slow walk up the driveway. JC inhaled the smell of the pine trees and listened to the crushed stone beneath his feet.

"Do you think you'd ever sell this place?" JC asked, making small talk.

"Oh, no," she said. "I love it here. I never want to leave."

Standing at the end of the driveway as Melody peered into her mailbox, JC spotted a witch window on the house across the street.

"Ha! A witch window," he said as he pointed it out. Of course, Melody knew it was there.

"Yes," she said with a scowl. "She watches everything that goes on in the neighborhood. A witch at her window."

"Who lives there?" JC asked.

"Deborah Sampson," Melody spewed the name. "If she ever smiled, her face would crack."

"The VSBB board member?" JC asked.

"Yes," Melody said without smiling. "That's actually how Josh first heard of the charity, I think, talking with her."

"But you don't get along with her?"

"I try to get along with everyone. That's how I was raised," Melody answered. "But every window she looks out of is a witch window, as far as I'm concerned. She's just weird."

They walked back up the driveway and inside the house.

"Did I miss anything?" Robin asked in a bouncy tone.

"Oh, I was telling JC about the neighborhood snoop," Melody said.

"Deborah Sampson," JC informed Robin.

"Oh, yeah, she's sort of weird," Robin said.

"See?" Melody said with a smile. "I told you." The woman's spirits were immediately lifted. Robin had a gift, JC thought to himself.

After the interview, Melody Church's phone rang. She excused herself. JC returned to browse more of the books in the library as Bip and Robin were wrapping up Bip's gear.

"You like books too," Melody said to JC when she returned to the room. "Josh would have liked you. That phone call was from a bookstore in Maine. They want me to come up for a book signing. I'd be signing Josh's books. I get requests from time to time. It seems to bring people joy, just telling me how happy Josh's books made them."

As they prepared to leave, JC thought he saw movement from the corner of his eye. It came from the garden. It was the image of a man. When the reporter turned to see who was standing there, there was no one. He had an image of the man in his head. It looked like Josh Church.

"This Vermont folklore has me seeing things," JC said to himself.


That evening, JC showed viewers in Denver the interview with Melody Church. It could be construed as an

156

endorsement for VSBB and Ben Whitmore, in the face of the attorney general's investigation.

JC also passed along Ben Whitmore's remarks, protesting his innocence. JC had phoned the attorney general's office for their response but had been told there was no one available to speak with him. He left his number.

Sam Brown was behind the anchor desk in Denver. But during Sam's toss to JC, who was listening through the IFB in his ear, Sam's voice sounded muffled. In fact, for *anyone* in the audience who was listening, it sounded as though Sam Brown was speaking with a pillow over his face.

Sam Brown, JC would later be told, had dashed to the bathroom during the commercial break. To avoid those in the control room hearing the sound of his urine hitting the porcelain, Sam unclipped his microphone from his tie and put the mic in his pants pocket.

But as Sam had rushed back to the set and took his seat in front of the camera before the commercial break ended, he forgot to place the microphone back on his tie. It was still in his pants pocket when he told the audience in Denver that they were going live to JC in Vermont.

The post-production meeting after the show spent a good deal of time analyzing Sam's blunder. The news director was angry, Sam was embarrassed, but the newsroom staff was thoroughly amused. It was a story that would be retold over drinks for years to come.

# 23

"Don't worry, it's history. It's not going to change a lot if you wait an extra day to look at it," George Earl told JC.

"Yeah, do you see us rushing around?" David Earl said, laughing.

JC had stopped by the Stonestead Historical Society to return the envelope with the photos and the eight-page study in it. He told them that he'd tried to return it on Monday, but no one seemed to be in the office.

"No, Monday was a holiday," George said.

"What holiday?" JC asked.

"We celebrate the day before Tuesday," George laughed. The executive committee all laughed too.

"What did you think of our work?" George asked.

"About the fires? It's interesting," JC said. "I'd like to do an interview with you. I think we want to air a story. Our viewers will eat it up. The TV station we're working with in Burlington will probably want to air it too."

"Okay," George agreed. "I'll tell you what we're doing now. We've narrowed our research to fires in Stonestead during the decade between 1880 and 1891. There's something interesting there. We just have to find it."

"There were a lot of them," David Earl agreed.

"Do you know what caused the fires?" JC asked.

"Lots of things," George said as he scratched his head. "At the time, they blamed some of them on lightning, some on hunters, some on cigarettes, some on a drought."

"Well, we took pictures of your pictures," JC said. "My photographer and producer are out right now taking video of some of the locations as they look today. Let's get together in the next day or two and shoot an interview. Does that work for you?"

"Do I have to get my hair cut?" George laughed.

"Not on my account," JC said.

"You might want to get a face-lift," one of the executive committee members laughed.

"And a tummy tuck," another said. They were all laughing now.

JC left the historical society and crossed the street in front of the Flamstead Inn. He recognized Deborah Sampson, the VSBB board member, walking past him.

"Hello, Ms. Sampson," JC said. She stopped and took only a moment to recognize him.

"Please, call me Deborah," she said with a straight face. "How is your work coming?"

"Oh, we have our hands full," he said.

"I see that you visited Melody Church yesterday," Deborah said. "I happened to glance out my window and saw you two by the mailbox."

"I hope we were behaving ourselves," JC joked.

"Oh, you were," she said. Her answer seemed to be quite serious, as though she had carefully considered it.

"And VSBB is getting all its ducks in a row to show the attorney general?" he asked.

"It's all fine," she said with stoicism. "They'll see. You should look at the last financial report. You'd see that everything is in its proper place."

"I'd like to do that," JC told her. "That's a good idea. Where can I get one?"

"I have one," the board member volunteered. "Come by my house. You can borrow it. I'm heading home now. I'll have it waiting for you."

"Thank you," JC said. "I can be there in a half hour. Is that okay?"

"That will be fine," Deborah Sampson said and turned abruptly to resume her walk down Main Street.

JC found himself with about fifteen minutes before he'd head to Sampson's home. That would give her time to tidy things up.

He called Robin and got a progress report on the locations they were shooting for the feature on Stonestead's old fires. He told her that George had agreed to an interview. He was sure another member of the executive committee would agree to go on camera too, just so they'd have more than one face delivering sound bites. Every member would know the story, after all.

"What I really need is the car," he told Robin.

"Oh sure, pretend you're my friend and then reveal the real reason for calling, like I won't notice," she giggled. "It's not a problem. We're nearby. We can drop off the car and walk to our last few locations."

JC pulled into Deborah Sampson's short driveway, to the side of her stone house. She opened the screen door before he was even out of the car. She was smiling. That was only the second time he'd seen her smile.

She was a plain-looking woman. Her hair was lifeless and dropped in that ponytail down her spine. The color and cut of her clothing were also dull. But it was her eyes that intrigued him. They never stopped looking at things. She didn't miss much, he thought. Far from it.

She had a kettle on for tea. Maybe it was a Vermont thing, he thought to himself.

Her kitchen and dining room were decorated with prints depicting old Vermont life. The kitchen had images of women washing clothes in a river and cooking over an outdoor fire in front of a tent. One picture in the dining room was of men on a fox hunt. Another was a print of a battle. She told him it was the Battle of Bennington.

They sat in the living room with their tea. The wallpaper wasn't faded, she had just picked a print with very little color. The antique furniture was dark, polished wood.

As he sipped his tea, he studied more art hung on the wall. But unlike the pictures in the kitchen and dining room, these were all nudes from the nineteenth century. There were prints of Goyas and works by Waterhouse and Collier.

JC looked at plain Deborah Sampson again. Was there a tiger in her tank?

"How did you become a board member of the VSBB?" asked JC. "If you don't mind my asking."

"No, not at all," she answered. "I've known Ben Whitmore for a long time." She paused and then gave JC a coy look. "We used to date."

"You dated Ben Whitmore?" JC said, trying to mask the shock.

"But that was a long time ago," she said with a small shy smile. She ran her hands across her dress to flatten a wrinkle that wasn't there. JC believed plain Deborah Sampson was actually having a naughty memory.

JC was speechless. He was struggling to say something to fill the awkward silence. Though, maybe it was just him feeling awkward.

"I saw something," Deborah said, breaking the silence.

"When?" JC asked, slightly mystified as to what she was talking about.

"Months ago. Before Josh died," she responded. "I saw Bobbi Chadwick kissing that man, Rick Teller."

"Rick Teller?" JC repeated. "The guy who works at the ski resort?"

Deborah nodded silently.

"It wasn't a peck on the cheek," she said. "It was passionate." JC saw her cheeks get red, and her eyes showed some fire. Wow, JC thought, you gotta watch the quiet ones.

"I saw them from the witch window," Deborah said as she looked up. It was as though she were looking through the ceiling to where the witch window looked out on the road.

"When Josh was still alive?" JC repeated.

"Yes," she said. "Bobbi was arriving for a meeting with Josh and Ben. I think Josh knew he was dying. He wanted to get things in order. Rick drove Bobbi to Melody's house. He dropped her off. But first, he got out of the car and they embraced, and they kissed. They were just about where you and Melody were at the mailbox yesterday."

"Could I see this witch window?" JC asked. "I don't think I've ever looked out of one."

"Certainly," she said.

She rose from her sofa and led JC up the kind of narrow staircase that all homes from that vintage have. At the top of the stairs, she turned in the direction of the road.

They walked into what looked to be a spare bedroom. On the far wall, there was a long rectangular window set at a forty-five-degree angle.

"You know why they call them witch windows, don't you?" she asked.

"Yes, I've heard," JC responded as he approached the window.

The first impression he had was that despite Deborah Sampson saying she just happened to glance out the window when he and Melody were at the mailbox, no one could just glance out the window. It was high on the wall. It provided needed light to the room but you had to make an effort to look out of it.

He looked out of it. Indeed, he had a view of Melody's mailbox and driveway. He could not see the house because of the tall trees along the road.

"So, you saw them from here?" JC asked.

"Yes, you can see that I have a clear view," she responded.

"I thought—" JC began. "Maybe it is just my imagination, but I thought Bobbi and Ben Whitmore were seeing each other."

"They are," Deborah said with a sad look. "I don't want Ben to get hurt by Bobbi. She, well you've seen her. She can have her pick."

"Really?" JC said. "You think so?" He was just amusing himself now. Deborah Sampson knew it too. She gave him a knowing chuckle.

A chuckle! JC noted the miracle and couldn't wait to tell his friends.

"So," JC said. "I don't want to hold you up. May I take your financial report for VSBB and take a look?"

Deborah didn't answer for a moment.

"You know," she started. "I gave our lawyers a call and they don't think it's a good idea. They said that everything should be cleared up soon, and now wouldn't be a good time to share that with the news media. You'll see it in good time. You'll see that it is all an innocent misunderstanding."

"Oh," JC said with surprise in his voice. "You don't want to disobey your attorney … unless you want to."

"I don't think I should," she said.

"Well, I'm sorry for wasting your time," JC told her. "I didn't know this would be an unnecessary use of your afternoon."

"Oh," she said without a smile. "It wasn't."

JC walked back down the narrow stairs, thanked her for the tea and left through the kitchen door.

He reminded himself not to underestimate Deborah Sampson.

# 24

"He was a John Doe, right?"

JC had called the police department in Niskayuna, New York. That was where John Thurston, allegedly stabbed to death by Larry Gleichman, had lived.

JC's call had been directed to Detective Ed London.

"That's a Saratoga County investigation," the detective said.

"Yeah, I know. And I'm talking with them," JC responded. "I'm just wondering how you figured out it was Thurston. You guys did that, right? And then you told Saratoga that you thought you knew who their John Doe was, right?"

"Yes," Detective London said. "That was us."

Niskayuna was an affluent suburb of the city of Schenectady. There wasn't a lot of trouble there. John Thurston lived in a big house in Niskayuna.

"He started as a missing person," the detective told JC. Actually, several days passed before he was reported missing. He was divorced and he was expected to drive to Red Bank, New Jersey, on Monday morning for a conference. The Molly Pitcher Inn says that he never checked in."

"He worked for a bank, right?" JC asked.

"Right," the detective confirmed.

"So, who reported him missing?" the reporter asked.

"His workplace," London replied. "They hadn't heard from him by Tuesday. He hadn't returned their calls, so they called us. We went to his house to check on him. We thought we'd find him deceased in bed."

"Was he suffering from an illness?" JC asked.

"Not that I'm aware of," Detective London explained. "That's just how a lot of these things end in Niskayuna. We get some overdoses and a few accidental deaths. We don't get a lot of murders here."

"So, you went to his house," JC said.

"Yes, we went to his house," the law officer continued. "We expected to find him inside, but we didn't. We did find his car parked inside his garage. And we found his wallet in the car."

"Was anything missing from his wallet?" JC asked. The detective hesitated before answering.

"You said that you're talking with the Saratoga County Sheriff's Office, didn't you?" the detective challenged. "So, you should know the answer to that question."

"One of his credit cards was missing," JC said.

"That's correct," the detective responded.

"Anything else missing from his wallet?" the reporter inquired.

"Well, if any cash was missing, we wouldn't know about that," the detective replied.

"Was the house robbed?"

"It did not appear as though that was the case."

"Neighbors have anything to say?" JC asked.

"Now, you might be getting into areas outside the limits of our conversation," Detective London told him. "You asked me how we identified the John Doe. And I told you."

"Okay," JC said. "So, he's no longer a John Doe, but he became a missing person in your jurisdiction, didn't he?"

"Yes," the detective confirmed. "We put out a 'missing persons bulletin' on him on January seventeenth."

"But there was no sign of him until his body was found across the river in Clifton Park on May seventeenth?"

"That's right," the detective told him.

"I know that you talked to neighbors," JC began. "Did they see or hear anything? Did they hear a car door slam? Hear the garage door open?"

"Again, you're crossing into an area that is part of the investigation," the detective advised. "And the investigation is being conducted by the Saratoga County Sheriff's Office. Those are questions they will have to answer, if they choose to do so."

"Did you have any role in identifying Mr. Thurston when they found his body?" the reporter asked.

"The usual things," the detective answered routinely. "We gathered some of his belongings from his home, like his hairbrush, and turned them over to Saratoga. That's how they identified him, with DNA and dental records. He'd been lying in that field for a long time."

JC thanked the detective and ended the conversation. He was sitting in a chair in his room at the Flamstead Inn. He called Robin but got a busy signal. So, he walked into the hallway. He could hear her on the phone.

He took a slow stroll down the hall, studying the pictures hanging on the wall. There was a covered bridge, waterfalls, lakes and snow-covered mountains. Through a window at the end of the hall, he could see an old barn of faded wood with a cupola on top. It looked old, perhaps the lone survivor of the most recent fire on the property.

It sounded like Robin had stopped talking on the phone, so he knocked on her door. She opened it and JC could smell her fragrance. He smiled without trying to, seeing her energetic blue eyes.

"Learn anything?" she asked.

"Yep," he said. "I can make stone giggle. I got Deborah Sampson to *chuckle!*"

"Seriously?" she blurted. "You got her to chuckle?"

"I have a gift," he said.

Then, he told her about his conversation with Niskayuna police.

"I got smarter too," she said when JC was done. "Let's go out on the porch."

The air tasted crisp and clean. But the afternoon sun seldom peeked out from behind the clouds. Vermont in September felt like it lost ten degrees when the sun passed behind a cloud.

"I've been on the phone with Altoona, Pennsylvania," she said as she tucked herself into the couch with a blanket.

"The whole city?" JC asked.

"Just about," she told him.

"I'll boil it down for you. Then, you can read the footnotes," she said, looking at her laptop.

"I don't know why they're denying it, but Rick Teller and Bobbi Chadwick *did* know each other in Altoona," Robin disclosed.

"Really? Interesting," JC said.

"Oh, but it gets more interesting," she said. "There's intrigue."

"My favorite flavor," he told her. She smiled.

"Remember that Bobbi told you that one of the reasons she left Altoona was to get away from a bad marriage?" Robin asked.

"And the end of the girls' basketball season," he said with a grin.

"Well, *she* had an affair!" Robin disclosed.

"That will ruin most marriages," JC muttered.

"And do you know who is named in the divorce papers as the recipient of her cheating affection?" she asked.

"Really?" JC said, anticipating the answer.

"Yep," Robin exclaimed. "Rick Teller."

"She could do better," JC muttered.

"Aw," Robin teased, "are you hurt because she didn't try to seduce you? She might be easy but she's not desperate."

"Luckily," JC concluded, "I found a knockout who has bad taste in men and must not see well."

"Lucky is right," she responded. "Anyway, the rest of her story checks out. Bobbi left Altoona, found VSBB and came here."

"And after some time," JC said, "Rick Teller came here too."

They sat on the wicker couch and looked at their laptop computers.

"Is it teatime?" JC asked.

"Yeah, I'm getting to like that too," Robin said.

"Hey, I got an email from Davey," JC said. He proceeded to read it to himself.

"Speaking of teatime," JC said while still looking at Davey's email. "Do you remember a copper teapot at Melody's house?"

"I don't remember a copper one. I remember one with a bear and a deer, I think, and a forest!" Robin responded. "That's the one she served tea from when I was there with you."

"Right," JC agreed. "But you don't remember one that looked like copper?"

"I don't think so," Robin said as she gazed at nothing, trying to picture their two visits.

"I do," JC said. "It was the first visit. I was trying to help prepare the tea. I grabbed a teakettle that was made of copper and I filled it with water. But Melody stopped me and grabbed another kettle, the one with the bear and deer, and said it was Josh's favorite. And she took the copper one out of my hands."

"So, Davey is talking about this copper teakettle?" Robin asked.

"Yeah, he's reminiscing or something," JC told her. "He specifically says that the copper one was Josh's favorite. He's very specific about it. He says Josh told him that it belonged to his great-grandparents."

"That's odd," Robin said. "I don't know what it means, but it's odd."

"Yeah, I'll give him a call and see what he makes of it," JC said.

JC thought more about their last visit with Melody.

"Do you believe in ghosts?" he asked Robin.

"That's random," she laughed. But then she gave it some thought. "Yes. I think I saw my father once, about a year after he died. It was when I was having a real hard time. I'd just broken up with my boyfriend because he was cheating on me. I was devastated."

"And you think you saw your father?" JC asked. He was serious because she was serious.

"Yeah. I saw my dad. It only lasted for a moment, but I think he was telling me that I would be alright."

They sat quietly. She was clearly thinking back to that episode, and he was respecting her silence.

"Do *you* believe in ghosts?" she asked him.

"I believe people I know to be good people," he said. "When they tell me that they saw a ghost, I believe them. Why would they lie about that?"

"Have *you* ever seen a ghost?" she asked.

"Outside of Vermont?" he said with a smile. "No."

"What about *inside* Vermont," she pursued.

"Not so sure," he told her. But he didn't say anything about the glimpse in Melody's garden of someone he thought, for a passing moment, was Josh Church.

# 25

"Mr. Snow. Who is your informant?"

JC had finally been allowed to speak to someone in the public information division of the State Attorney General's Office. Permission was granted after numerous failed attempts. And that was the greeting he received.

"What makes you think I have an informant?" the journalist asked innocently.

"Because you are reporting information that we haven't made public," the PIO responded.

"Is my information incorrect?" JC asked.

"That is not what I said," the AG's spokesperson answered.

The public information officer was a man who said he was named Reuben Tarbell. It was never JC's first choice to speak with a public information officer. He had learned long ago that their job wasn't necessarily to inform the public, but rather, keep the public from learning information the PIO's bosses didn't want the public to learn.

Certainly, JC believed, there were sometimes good reasons not to release the information he was seeking. Most of the time, he had learned, that was not the case. Of course, he acknowledged, that was the opinion of a journalist.

"I've had a hard time getting anyone at your office to talk," JC told him.

"Sorry about that. We're very busy," the man said. But JC didn't think the man sounded sorry at all.

"So, now you'll answer my question?" Mr. Tarbell asked. "Who are you speaking with about the VSBB case?"

"I'm sure you've heard how protective journalists are of their sources?" JC asked. "Sorry about that."

"Well then, Mr. Snow," Tarbell responded. "You can expect to learn less from us."

"How could that be possible?" JC asked. The next sound he heard on his phone was the call being disconnected.

JC's next call was the very one Reuben Tarbell was wondering about. JC called Davey Kay.

"They may be on to you," JC informed him lightly.

"I'm terrified," Davey said sarcastically. "You mean they may stop letting me spoon-feed them their case?" JC laughed.

JC told his old friend that he and his TV crew had been out to visit Melody Church.

"How is she holding up?" Davey asked. "Now that questions have surfaced about VSBB and the whole business?"

173

"She seems to be doing as well as any widow would be doing," JC said. "Eight months after the passing of her life partner."

"Yeah," Davey said in an understanding tone. "Did you just stop out there for tea?"

"We did have tea," JC laughed. "I'm getting to like this habit of taking a break to drink a cup of tea."

"It is rather civilized, isn't it?" Davey agreed. "Did she pull out Josh's favorite kettle? The copper one? The family heirloom?"

"No, she served from one with a forest scene with a bear and a deer," JC told him. "It's aluminum, I think."

"Oh, she won't let you drink from the good stuff," Davey joked. "Josh's favorite was definitely that copper kettle. It belonged to his great-grandparents. He pulled it out every single time we had tea together. That added up to only a few times a year, but he always told me it was his favorite."

JC proceeded to tell Davey about Bobbi Chadwick. He told him that her old flame, Rick Teller, had turned up in Stonestead.

"You know," Davey said, "I had the feeling that Bobbi was at the center of whatever was going on with the money. I mean, I looked for gambling debt. That's where people in my business often see guys blowing their money. But I didn't find Ben Whitmore anywhere near a casino or card game."

"What about a drug habit?" JC asked.

"Again, that's what accountants like me frequently see when a good amount of money starts to disappear," Davey agreed. "But there's absolutely no indication that Ben Whitmore is blowing the charity's money on drugs."

"So, you suspect it was the lure of a woman that was out of his league?" JC inquired.

"I have the feeling that Bobbi has very expensive tastes," Davey theorized. "And Ben Whitmore seemed to be spending a lot of money on things a high-maintenance girl might enjoy."

When he got off the phone, JC briefed Robin on what he had learned. She was on the wicker couch on the porch, wrapped in a blanket.

"Maybe we waste a lot of time when we actually go to crime scenes and meet people face-to-face," Robin said with a grin. "I've barely moved out from under my blanket all afternoon, and we're getting a lot accomplished."

"You make a good point," JC agreed.

"What do you want to do about dinner?" she asked. "I'm getting hungry. I'm going to call Bip and see where he is."

But JC was already back on his phone.

"I'm calling to request an interview with one of your inmates, Larry Gleichman," he said when someone picked up on the other end.

"I'll pass along your request," the jailer said, after taking down JC's identity, phone number and TV affiliation.

JC and Robin hadn't yet moved off the porch when his phone rang. He was a little surprised because it was after five p.m. Most businesses were closed and Happy Hour had begun.

It was Faith Oaks on the phone, Gleichman's attorney.

"What do you want to talk to him about?" she asked, without a greeting.

"I want to hear his side of the story," JC told her.

"You mean the truth," she asked. "Or something salacious for television?"

"If he says something salacious, I'll use it," JC told her. "But whatever he says, I'll use it. Police have him fingered for the guy who killed John Thurston. I just want to hear Gleichman's version of things."

"When?" she asked abruptly.

"Tomorrow?" JC offered.

"I can't be there tomorrow," the public defender said. "I'm starting a jury trial."

There was silence on both ends of the phone. JC knew how long jury trials could go. If Thursday wasn't going to be good, then Friday or next Monday, Tuesday or Wednesday might not be any good either. And maybe longer.

"I guess I don't have to be there," Faith Oaks said. "Just be on your best behavior, or you'll be the excuse I use to demand a mistrial."

JC hung up the phone. Bip was standing next to Robin, who still hadn't climbed out from under her blanket.

"Road trip tomorrow," JC told them.

"Yay," Bip said, doing his best to mimic a fifth-grader. "Are we going to the zoo?"

"Well, you're going to photograph someone held in captivity behind bars and you can't feed him," JC responded. "Yeah, I guess we are."

# 26

"They'd run out of games to play on the two-hour car ride. First, they'd looked for witch windows. The uniquely Vermont phenomenon wasn't that easy to find, even in Vermont. But they located one near the Stratton Ski Resort. Bip stopped the car and shot some video.

"You never know," he told JC and Robin, meaning that you never knew when you would need a specific image on short notice, like a witch window.

Then Robin suggested that they play the "alphabet game." She told them the scant rules.

"Start with the letter A and be the first one to get to Z," she instructed. "Names on signs or buildings or license plates are permissible. You cannot use things like a letter on a hat being worn by the guy sitting next to you."

"What about a hat being worn by a guy in the next car?" Bip asked.

"Fine, but don't drive me crazy," she said as she rolled her eyes.

That got them nearly to their destination in Ballston Spa. JC spotted a sign promoting the Zim Smith bicycle trail.

"Did you cheat?" Robin challenged him. "You're a local."

"Sort of," he admitted. "I've been waiting for that sign since Cohoes."


The county jail was a short ride from the Saratoga County Fairgrounds. It was a modern replacement to the older jail, downtown.

"Good-looking lady," Larry Gleichman told JC as Bip shot the interview. JC had asked the inmate to describe the woman he says left the credit card on a table at a fast-food restaurant in January. It was John Thurston's credit card.

"She had nice clothes on. She looked rich," the homeless man said.

Gleichman was wearing orange prison scrubs. He did not wear handcuffs or restraints. But a corrections officer stood by the door to make sure the inmate sat at the stainless-steel table across from JC and behaved himself.

Gleichman was heavy-set. He needed a shave and a comb pulled through his black hair. But he made eye contact most of the time and was polite.

JC thought that it was important to Gleichman to seem to be better than his colleagues under lock and key, and better than the homeless life he usually lived.

"I have a high school education," Gleichman said, "even a little community college. I've been to Europe. I've been up the Eiffel Tower and I've been in Buckingham Palace."

"Did you steal any of the Queen's silverware?" JC asked.

Gleichman stared at JC for a moment. Then he erupted in laughter. "Good one," he said.

"Then why are you homeless," JC asked. He thought that Gleichman wanted him to ask.

"Bad decisions," the inmate said. That's what he wanted to confess to, JC surmised.

"Let's get back to the woman with the credit card," JC suggested. "How did you end up with it?"

"I thought the whole thing was pretty strange," the inmate stated. He became more animated. "I mean, I'm homeless. I dress better than the other homeless people, I speak well and I find a way to get a shower. But most people figure out that I'm homeless. And most people don't choose to sit at a table next to a homeless guy. They think we're all crazy."

"But this didn't bother her?" JC asked.

"She sat down at the table next to me like that was exactly what she wanted to do. Also, this was a fast-food restaurant. She didn't look like the type that eats at a fast-food chain. I go in there to get warm. I see a lot of people who eat in fast-food restaurants," he laughed.

"People go to fast-food restaurants during work, on their lunch or dinner break," JC offered.

"I mean, sure, people who are well-off do eat at fast-food restaurants," he conceded. "But they usually are there with co-workers or they have kids with them. Mom or dad come there because their kids want to."

"And she was alone?" JC asked.

"All alone," Gleichman told him.

"What did she order?" the reporter inquired.

"A salad! See what I mean?" Gleichman blurted. "Who comes to a fast-food joint alone and orders a salad?"

"So, how did you get the credit card?" JC asked.

"So, she put the credit card down on the little table she's eating at, next to my table," Gleichman told him. "It was a foot from my hand, for heaven's sake." The accused man started laughing.

"But how did *you* get it?"

"She stood up and left!" the defendant exclaimed. "You see what I mean? She gets up, the card is right under her nose, but she walks away and out the door, leaving the card. I look to my left. I look to my right. No one is watching me and I palm the card. Opportunity knocked and I answered the door. What was I supposed to do?"

"And then what did you do?" JC asked.

"I walked calmly to the door on the other side of the building, in case she came back looking for her card, you know," Gleichman told the reporter. "And then I walked downtown and picked up a few necessities."

"Like what?"

"Like a warm jacket. The one I was wearing looked nice, but I was never warm," the inmate explained. "I got some other clothes, like new socks and tighty-whities. I bought some food, some to be eaten for dinner and plenty that would last for the next few days. And I walked to the bus station and bought a ticket. I thought I deserved to take a vacation."

"To Denver," JC suggested.

"Yeah," he said. "I heard it was nice. And it was warmer than here, even in the winter!"

"Did you kill John Thurston?" JC asked. The camera was still rolling. Gleichman snorted.

"I couldn't pick John what's-his-name out of a lineup,"
Gleichman insisted. "I mean, I saw the grisly pictures they
showed me, of a guy who had been dead in a field for a year.
That was not something I wanted to see. But they showed me
a picture from when he was alive. I've never seen him before."

"Could you identify the woman who left the card in the
fast-food restaurant?" JC asked.

"Oh yeah," the man in the orange scrubs responded. "I
would know her if I saw her again."

JC gave the corrections officer a look, indicating that the
interview was over.

"Let's go Larry," the guard said to the inmate. Gleichman
extended his hand and JC shook it.

"I hope this does me some good," the defendant said.
"They want to pin this murder on me."

"I don't see how this could hurt you," JC said. And the
man was led out the door and into the jail population.

Bip broke down his tripod, camera and lights. Two other
corrections officers had entered the room, by then, to escort
the three journalists out past the bars.

"Are you ready?" one corrections officer asked Robin. He
was good-looking and clearly spent a lot of time in the weight
room. He was flirting with Robin.

"Sure," she said, giving the man in uniform a smile.

As they walked past a common area for the inmates,
Robin, JC and Bip were separated from the prisoners only by
a single wall of bars. There were catcalls and hoots.

"Hey baby, I'm right here!" one inmate shouted.

"Tonight's my night for a conjugal visit!" another yelled.
The other inmates laughed and jeered.

Robin had been warned before she first entered the jail
area.

"Are you sure you want to do this?" a shift supervisor had politely asked her. "Some of these guys haven't seen a woman for nearly a year."

"Will I get some marriage proposals?" Robin smiled. The shift supervisor laughed.

"In so many words," he told her. "We'll protect you, but I've seen jail riots break out for less."

"You flatter me," Robin said with a smile.


The news crew climbed into their car and headed out of Ballston Spa.

"Abner Doubleday was born here," JC told them.

"The guy who invented baseball?" Bip asked.

"Yep, though he probably didn't invent baseball. Turn right here," JC advised.

In a matter of blocks, they stopped outside of a yellow, two-story, wood-frame home. A plaque outside stated that it was Abner Doubleday's home.

"He never claimed to have invented baseball," JC said. "It seems to have been a story that baseball thought it needed. Doubleday was a handsome hero after the Civil War. He had once lived in Cooperstown, where the Baseball Hall of Fame was built. Doubleday was the benefactor of corporate need."

"So, what do you think?" Robin asked.

"I don't think Doubleday invented baseball," JC told her.

"No, about Larry Gleichman?" she asked.

"Don't you want to talk about that corrections officer who had a crush on you?" Bip interrupted, teasing. "I think he was ready to do something with you that might have earned him those orange scrubs." They laughed. Robin blushed too.

"No, I want to know what you guys think of Larry Gleichman," she insisted.

"I don't think orange is his color," Bip told her. "It doesn't do his highlights justice." Robin gave him an amused but dismissive glance.

"That just leaves you," she said to JC.

"He's telling everyone the same story," JC said. "That's not as easy as it looks."

JC broke off his analysis to give Bip directions to get them pointed toward Vermont.

"I was also trying to see if it was Bobbi Chadwick who steered that credit card into Gleichman's hands, if he's telling the truth." JC said. "He said the woman was pretty and dressed well. That doesn't eliminate her."

"But what would be the point?" Robin asked. "Why would someone want to trick some homeless guy into being caught with Thurston's credit card?"

"To frame him for murder?" JC suggested.

# 27

"He admits he stole the credit card belonging to the murder victim, Colorado native John Thurston. But Larry Gleichman insists he didn't kill the man," JC told the television camera in front of him.

That was how JC wrapped up his live shot from downtown Stonestead that evening, reporting back to viewers in Denver.

He and Bip and Robin had returned from the Saratoga County jail in New York in time to edit and broadcast their story live. And it was "magic," their news director back in Denver told them.

"You've got the audience hooked," the news director, Pat Perilla, exclaimed.

After Bip and the live truck engineer wrapped up their gear, JC suggested dinner. The truck op/engineer said he would have to take a raincheck. He had been told to drive closer to Burlington to work with another crew for the eleven o'clock news. Bip, Robin and JC drove to the outskirts of nearby Chester for dinner at MacLaomainn's.

"What are we doing tomorrow?" Bip asked.

"Probably the feature about the fires in Stonestead over a century ago," JC said. He liked the story. He thought his viewers would too, even though it had nothing to do with the reason they were sent to Vermont.

"I like the fire story too," Robin said. "The next time we want to take a break and slip in another feature, we ought to do one on the witch windows."

"That's a good idea," JC agreed.

All three ordered scallops from MacLaomainn's menu. Robin ordered red wine and the two men ordered the Scottish beer called Old Engine Oil.

"The fire feature is almost done," JC said. "That should give us time to work on finding out what Bobbi and Rick are really up to."

"Where do we start?" Robin asked.

"I think Davey's instincts are accurate," JC offered. "Somehow, Bobbi is a major player in what's happening to Josh Church's money at VSBB. And if Bobbi is involved, I think Rick Teller is involved."

"Wanna stake out his apartment? We'll catch them in the act!" Robin said enthusiastically.

"I'm not sure that's the way to do it," JC said. "We could probably catch them in bed, but we're not trying to prove that Bobbi is cheating on Whitmore. The answer has to do with what drew Bobbi Chadwick here. And Rick Teller."

185

"Bobbi says she came here for the job," Robin said.

"And maybe she did," JC responded. "What brought Rick here? Was it just an attempt to win back her love?"

"Or was it something else?" Robin added.

"Exactly," JC said.

After dinner and another beer, they retired to their rooms at the Flamstead Inn.

JC was asleep. Robin was sitting up in bed, next to him, tapping at keys and staring at the screen on her laptop. She was wearing his Colorado State University tee shirt.

"I've got to create a password," she mumbled to herself. She grabbed a pen and pad of paper with "Flamstead Inn" printed across the top of it.

She struck more keys and her study of the computer screen intensified.

"JC, wake up," she said in a loud whisper.

JC ignored her. He finally stirred to a fist beating him on his back.

"Are you awake?" he heard Robin asking.

"Am I dead?" he asked.

"No," she told him.

"Then I must be awake," he mumbled. "I feel like I'm waking from the dead."

He rolled over and struggled to rise to an upright position. He had seen that she was on her laptop and presumed she wanted to have a discussion.

"It's dark out," he observed as he caught a glance at the window onto their porch. "It's not morning."

"I know," she said. "Sorry, but I knew I wouldn't sleep until I told you this."

"I'm listening," he muttered.

"Rick Teller is on probation!" she declared. She was pointing at her computer screen. "I signed on to the website for the Pennsylvania Department of Corrections. You can look up people who are inmates or still on probation and stuff."

"Probation for what?" JC asked. He was still sluggish. It required him to concentrate to keep up with Robin's wide-awake intensity.

"He was caught scamming people out of money," she said. "He had a room full of phones and hired people to pose as the electric company or social security office. They'd talk their victims into sharing their personal information and then Rick would withdraw money from the bank accounts of these poor people."

"Wow," JC said, slowly gaining his wits about him. "What a creep. Was Bobbi involved?"

"I looked for her," Robin told him. "She doesn't have an arrest record."

"Is he allowed to leave the state of Pennsylvania while he's on probation?" JC asked.

"I think he needs permission," she said. "But if he leaves without permission and drives back to Pennsylvania for his weekly conference with his probation office, how would they know the difference?"

"Nice work," he said. She smiled.

"And look at the dates," she said, pointing at the laptop. "Rick was still in prison when Bobbi says she moved here. So, Rick got released from prison later and he followed her up here."

"So, the pair of them may be in it together, scamming Whitmore," JC theorized. "Or Rick may have come here and recognized what was going on. Could he be blackmailing Whitmore without her help?"

"That sounds unlikely. Especially since we know Bobbi is two-timing Whitmore with Rick," she said.

"There's corruption at the heart of this love triangle," JC told her. "Whitmore is stealing from VSBB. Bobbi is probably the benefactor of the money Whitmore is stealing. Bobbi is cheating on Whitmore with Rick. And Rick is a professional con man. Is there any chance that they're not playing Whitmore?"

"It doesn't sound like it," Robin agreed.

"Let's talk with Bobbi Chadwick tomorrow," JC said. "Let's see if we can shake her confidence. We'll tell her that we know about her relationship with Rick. And we'll tell her we know about Rick's criminal record."

"Are you sure you want to put a frown on that pretty face?" Robin teased.

"She probably has a pretty frown too," JC said with a smile. And with that, he rolled back on his side to go back to sleep.

"JC, wake up."

JC had been sound asleep only seconds ago. He awakened to the now-familiar feeling of Robin's fist gently pounding his back.

"What now," he said. "Didn't we already do this? Is this Groundhog Day?" He still hadn't opened his eyes. "Go to sleep, babe, we'll talk in the morning."

"It *is* morning," he heard Robin say.

He opened his eyes and saw daylight bouncing off the walls of their room. Her room, technically. He rolled over and the early morning sun was pouring through the window overlooking the porch.

"I went down the street to get us some cappuccino, for a treat," Robin said. "There were a couple of sirens in the distance. Then, an EMT walked into the café. I asked him what was going on."

There was silence when JC thought he was about to be informed what the sirens were about. He rolled onto his back so he could look at Robin's face.

"They found a body," Robin said. She was wide awake, pumping slightly with adrenaline.

"It's Bobbi Chadwick," she told him. "She's dead."

# 28

"She even looks good dead," one emergency responder said to another as they strode down the pedestrian walk. Still only about seven in the morning, it was too early for any of the stores to be open. They passed JC, Bip and Robin without even looking up.

The journalists had parked their rental car on the side of a maintenance building at the Mont Vert Ski Resort. They had parked just short of where two volunteer firemen were posted. The firemen, wearing yellow reflective vests, had erected wooden barricades to block traffic. They told the news crew that they would be allowed no closer to the crime scene.

Now, concealed by the white stucco maintenance building, JC and his crew chose another path to get near the main chairlift at the base of Mont Vert. In the great outdoors, it was pretty difficult for police to seal off seven hundred acres from the news media.

Bip stopped about thirty yards short of the spot police were hovering over. JC had said that he didn't want to tread on the crime scene and risk spoiling evidence. The powerful lens on Bip's camera could close the remaining distance.

"Wow," Bip said. "That's her." He invited JC to take a look. Robin declined, when her turn came.

"Get some wide and medium-range shots that we can use," JC reminded Bip. "We won't be able to air any distinguishable shots of her body."

JC and other responsible television news organizations had learned that their audience didn't want to see video of dead souls on their TV screens at home. It made the audience cringe. It was too intrusive.

Focus groups made up of audience members made it clear that they would be interested in images of police at the murder scene, or even images of police leaning over a body. But the audience didn't want to see the actual body. That was crossing a line.

JC, Bip and Robin stood vigil next to their camera. Stonestead Police Chief Sipp Ives had seen them, but he hadn't chased them away. Nor did the journalists attempt to come any closer. The police were confident they could talk without being overheard.

After an hour had passed, Chief Ives walked across the grass to Bip's camera, mounted on a tripod. They were the only journalists there.

"Hey Chief," JC said. "Can we get a word?"

191

"Okay," Sipp told them. "But I've only got a minute."

Bip focused his camera, placing the police presence behind the chief, and pressed the record button.

"Tell me what you have, Chief?" JC said it as he held a microphone in front of Sipp Ives' mouth.

"We have a twenty-nine-year-old female," the chief began. "She has suffered a fatal stab wound. We are treating this as a homicide. The victim was discovered at the foot of The Granite chairlift. That's the name of it, The Granite. The victim has been identified as Roberta Chadwick. She was living locally."

"Do you know when this happened, Chief?" JC asked.

"We are still determining the time of death," the chief told JC. "Ms. Chadwick was discovered by a person walking her dog this morning. There is no one in custody. Anyone who might have information on the whereabouts of Ms. Chadwick last night, or circumstances surrounding her death, are asked to call the Stonestead Police Department or the Vermont State Police. That's all we have to say right now."

With that, Sipp Ives gave JC a nod and turned to walk back to the crime scene.

"Do you know she was in a love triangle?" JC called out to the chief.

Sipp Ives stopped in his tracks. He slowly turned and walked back to the reporter.

"Tell me what you know," the chief said with a serious look on his face.

JC proceeded to do just that. He told Ives things the chief already knew, like details of Whitmore's and Chadwick's romance. Everyone in town knew the two were sleeping together.

But JC also told Ives about what Deborah Sampson had seen from her witch window, Bobbi and Rick Teller sharing a passionate kiss. The reporter told of attempts by both Bobbi and Rick to disguise their history back in Altoona.

JC let Robin tell the law officer about what Bobbi's divorce papers said of Rick's role in the breakup of Bobbi's marriage.

Robin also informed Sipp of what she learned overnight, working from her laptop in bed: that Rick had done prison time for fraud.

The police chief looked at them for a moment, possibly waiting to see if they had anything else to share with him.

"Thank you," he finally said to the journalists. He gave JC a nod and then turned and joined other officers at the crime scene.


Robin was on the phone with a producer at their TV station in Denver. JC and Bip sat at the booth with her, eating breakfast at Molly's.

"We need to let things percolate now," JC told Bip. "In an hour or two, police will show their cards. They'll visit some people they think are important in the case and they might even bring someone in for questioning. We'll just track their movements and let the story tell itself."

"Okay," Robin said as she hung up the phone and turned her attention to her colleagues. "The feature about the fires in Stonestead has been put on hold. It's a cool story, but we can hold it for a slow day. Obviously, I told them that we're going to turn our attention to Bobbi's murder. That will be our live shot tonight."

"Where to?" Bip asked when they had finished their breakfast.

"Back to Mont Vert," JC told them. "We'll see if the police have wrapped things up there and we'll see who investigators are talking to."

"It's weird," Robin said before getting up from the seat at their booth in Molly's. "We just saw her here the other day. Bobbi and Whitmore in that booth across the room. She was full of life."

JC and Bip joined her, staring at the empty booth where the couple had been seated.

"It makes you wonder," Bip said. "None of us are going to live forever."

"Except me, you mean," JC said. It brought a grin back to the faces of his two friends.

Robin decided to return to the hotel and work from her computer in her room.

"I think I can help," she said.

"Alright," JC said. "But I'm going to call you from the car. I have a couple of things I want to run by you."

They walked out of Molly's together. JC's knee still wasn't entirely stable when he walked down the steps.

"I need to exercise this leg," he said to Robin. "I haven't been able to rehab from my knee surgery since we arrived here. I don't have a gym."

"You'll get caught up when we get home," she said. "Just take it easy."

JC and Bip drove toward Mont Vert. The reporter got on the phone to his producer.

"Remember, John Thurston was stabbed, too," Robin said. "And Mont Vert was possibly the last place he was seen alive."

"That's an interesting thought," JC said. "I'd not considered for a moment that the two cases could be connected."

"What if we showed Gleichman a picture of Bobbi," Robin suggested. "Maybe she was the woman who left the credit card behind."

"If it *was* her. She may have stabbed Thurston," JC said. "But it's unlikely that she stabbed herself."

"Then, was it Rick?" she proposed.

"Maybe," JC told her. "But what about Whitmore? He may have found out about Bobbi and Rick and gone berserk."

JC ended the call and Bip parked the rental car closer to the entrance of the ski resort's village. The volunteer firefighters were gone. They had taken their barricades with them.

JC led Bip through the door of the VSBB charitable organization.

"Mr. Whitmore is not here," Suzy told them automatically. Her eyes were rimmed by red. She had been crying.

"We're sorry for your loss," JC told the college intern. "Where might we find Mr. Whitmore?" he asked.

"He left with police," the young woman responded.

That meant Whitmore was on the list of suspects, JC thought. It made sense. He had a motive to kill Bobbi Chadwick, love and money.

"Are any board members here?" he inquired.

"No, I'm sorry," she said.

"Suzy, when did you last see Bobbi?" JC asked.

"We were the last two to leave, last night," Suzy sniffed. "I left at about five. She was still here, working."

JC asked Bip if he had any video with him of Rick Teller. Bip said that he did and proceeded to search in his bag. JC knew that Bip had the ability to rewind video in his camera and look at it through his viewfinder. He wanted Suzy to look at a picture of Rick Teller and see if she recognized him.

"No," Suzy said after looking at the image of the Altoona man. "Well, I mean yes."

"Which is it, Suzy?" JC looked at her.

"I've seen him around, but he doesn't come into the office. Sometimes, I see him outside the office. I see him through the window, just standing around."

"Did Bobbi ever go out to talk with him?" JC asked.

"Now that you ask it that way, sometimes Ms. Chadwick would tell me that she'd be back in a few minutes and she'd leave," Suzy told him. "Many times, it was around the time I'd see that man standing outside."

"And you're sure that it was *that* man?" JC asked.

"I think so. He looks like him," she said quietly.

"Have you seen him today?" he asked.

"No," the intern told him.

The news crew shot a quick interview with Suzy, mostly containing the young woman's description of Bobbi Chadwick as a nice person and Suzy's personal shock.

JC and Bip were heading out the door of VSBB when something else occurred to him. He stopped and turned back to the intern.

"Was it Bobbi who signed that credit card slip for John Thurston back in January, when you were working in the cafeteria?" JC asked.

"I don't know," Suzy said after wiping her nose with a tissue. "The police asked me the same thing this morning. It was eight months ago. It's always so busy at lunchtime. And I didn't know Ms. Chadwick then."

JC made a face. If Bobbi Chadwick used that credit card, it would be difficult to confirm. A lot of time had passed since that slip was signed. And at the moment, it seemed like an insignificant act.

"She was so pretty, though," Suzy said. "She was not someone you easily forget." She said it as she walked to a desk to pull another tissue out of the box.

# 29

As JC and Bip walked out of the VSBB offices, the sun had come out from behind the clouds. It was warming up. It was going to be another idyllic late-summer day in Vermont. Only, Bobbi Chadwick would miss it.

JC noticed a couple of uniformed police officers walking out of one store in the village and into the next. The sergeant was a woman. The patrol officer was a man. They were Sipp Ives' officers. They were making contact with business owners, now that they were open for the day.

The officers were doing the routine drudgery of police work that would, on occasion, end with a spectacular result. Most of the time, it just turned out to be drudgery. They would knock on every door and ask the merchant and staff if they knew anything about Bobbi Chadwick's murder.

There was a television crew from Burlington a few stores down, on the pedestrian walk. The photographer was on one knee, shooting footage of the police officers and the walkway and the base of the chairlift where, hours ago, the body had been discovered and removed.

Bip was shooting his own footage of the police officers. Bip and the other photographer had already introduced themselves. As a courtesy, they made sure they didn't block a shot being taken by the other photographer.

The crew was from the same TV station that was loaning JC the live truck. That made them allies in this particular event. JC approached the reporter and they shook hands.

"We just got here," the reporter said. "Do you have anything we might like to borrow from you?"

"It's your lucky day," JC told the reporter. His name was Rich Thompson. His dark hair had blond-frosted highlights and his teeth had been whitened. He was smoking a cigarette.

JC told Thompson that they'd give them a copy of the footage Bip had captured that morning, when police were still hovering over Bobbi's body.

"You'll be a hero in your newsroom," JC said.

"I was thinking the same thing," the reporter responded with a smile.

"Have you visited the VSBB offices yet?" JC asked. He recognized the distinct advantage he had over the other reporter, being in Stonestead for almost two weeks. And his particular good fortune that morning, when Robin heard the sirens.

"We haven't been to the charity's office yet," the reporter with frosted highlights said. "Will they talk to us?"

"A college intern is the only one there," JC said. "She might give you a generic description of the murder victim. Be nice. She's pretty shaken up."

"Aren't you the model of playing nice," Bip said to JC as they walked away from the Burlington crew.

"They're giving us a live truck every night," he said. "They can stop doing that any time they like."

"We'd have to fold our tents and go home if that happened," Bip said.

"Yep, It's worth our while to be nice," JC stated. "Besides, if I call that guy and ask him for a favor, two years from now, he'll remember me as the guy who made his job easier."

JC's phone rang. It was Robin.

"I am really good," she exclaimed when he put the phone to his ear. He agreed.

"First," she said, "I tracked down Faith Oaks, the public defender for Larry Gleichman. This was not easy because it's Saturday. She was not in her office. I found her getting ready for a barbeque with her boyfriend."

"Wow, that's impressive work," he said. That's right, JC thought to himself. It's Saturday.

"I emailed her Bobbi Chadwick's picture," Robin said. "She'll show it to Gleichman. But we'll have to wait until Monday. *We* may be working on Saturday, but she isn't planning to. Good for her."

"Monday will be fine," JC said. "Nice work finding her."

"Wait! I'm only getting started," Robin said. "So, get this, Bobbi may have been spending all of Whitmore's corrupt money, but she was also his partner in crime."

"Really?" JC said. "What have you uncovered?"

JC and Bip parked their car outside the Flamstead Inn. Robin was sitting on the granite steps, waiting for them. She was wearing a blue summer dress. The light fabric rippled in the breeze. Strands of her red hair danced in the wind.

"You look really great," he said. She smiled.

They headed down the sidewalk to Molly's. Robin had determined, with another wave of phone calls, that they would find the three local board members of VSBB there.

In the back of the diner/post office/general store, they saw Jerry Dean, Deborah Sampson and Tom Caryl.

"Hi folks," JC said. "I guess you have a quorum."

"Oh, we're just talking about the tragedy," Jerry Dean responded.

"The poor dear," Tom Caryl said. Deborah Sampson sat expressionless, casting her eyes on both men at the table with her.

"May we join you?" JC asked as he pulled two chairs to the table. Bip brought another.

"You are either victims or perpetrators," JC told them bluntly. "The police chief is expecting me to drop by as soon as we're through here."

"The police chief, why?" Jerry Dean asked nervously.

"I don't know what happened to Bobbi Chadwick yet," JC told the table. "But I don't intend to suffer the same fate."

"What are you talking about?" Tom Caryl inquired. His eyes were full of fear.

JC looked at the group. Deborah Sampson was cool. She looked at JC, waiting for the next shoe to drop.

The other two board members looked frightened. They lived in a remote small town. It had isolated them from the scary parts of the world. That had only now crossed their city limits.

"Robin, tell them what you've learned," JC commanded.

"There are *five* members on the VSBB board that Ben Whitmore has to answer to, right?" she said. "There are the three of you, who live locally. And there are two others who live in Pennsylvania. You've never seen them or even shared a telephone conversation with them, have you?"

The board members shifted in their seats.

"Well, no, come to think of it," said Dean quietly.

"I haven't," Caryl said softly.

Deborah Sampson said nothing. Her eyes remained on Robin.

"Bobbi was the other two," Robin said. "She was both of the other board members."

"How can that be?" Dean asked. He sounded like he was challenging Robin.

"What are the names of the other two board members?" Robin asked.

"One is Andrew Aiken and the other is Robert Jenkins," Dean answered.

"Jenkins was Bobbi Chadwick's name when she was married," Robin said. "Roberta Jenkins. Her divorce from Willie Jenkins was finalized a year ago, at about the time she accepted her position at VSBB as executive assistant. Only a few months after her arrival here, a new board member was named. Robert Jenkins."

"That can't be," Dean protested. "Robert Jenkins is a man!"

"Have you ever met him?" JC asked. "Have you ever seen a picture of him?"

Jerry Dean said nothing. He scratched at his temple.

"And the other board member, Andrew Aiken," Robin said. "He is Bobbi's stepfather. He'll not grasp the tragic loss of his stepdaughter. He's in a nursing home. He has advanced

Alzheimer's disease. We presume that Bobbi helped him cast his vote on VSBB matters."

The board members looked at Robin in stunned silence. But Deborah Sampson's expression seemed more calculating, JC thought.

"Both of your fellow board members are said to reside in Altoona, Pennsylvania," Robin informed them. "That's where Bobbi grew up."

"So, if Ben Whitmore wanted a spending item or a report to his board approved, he only needed to persuade one of you," JC told them. "The two other votes he needed for approval were in the bag."

"He seemed so fair," Tom Caryl said. "If one or two of us voted against him, he accepted it without quarrel. He was always so magnanimous about the whole thing."

"He couldn't lose," JC said.

# 30

"I don't want him to see you."

That was Police Chief Sipp Ives' explanation to JC, when the chief's administrative assistant was waiting for the reporter and his producer in the hallway of the town offices. They were guided through a door providing direct access to the chief's office.

"Our offices are so small," the chief explained, "you can see most of one end when you're standing on the other end."

The chief pulled a chair under him behind his desk and sat. He motioned to JC and Robin to do the same.

"Whitmore is in our interrogation room," the chief said, nodding in the direction of the room past another door to his office.

The chief leaned back in his chair and turned on the air conditioner in the window. It roared to life with a clank. The mechanical sound of the gush of air was loud.

"I don't want him to hear us either," he said.

"Has our information been helpful?" JC asked.

"You've nailed him on the fraud," the chief said as a smile came across his face. "He can't provide the same story twice, when we confront him with it. He's asked for a lawyer now. The only thing left to argue about is whether he'll get out on bail before he pleads guilty. And that's for the court to decide."

The police chief reached for his phone and hit a blinking light.

"I've taken the liberty to include the state attorney general on a conference call," Sipp Ives said. "Madam Attorney General, can you hear us?"

"Hi Sipp, I can. Hello, Mr. Snow. Nice work."

"Hello, Madam Attorney General," JC said. "I'm here with my producer, Robin Smith. She deserves most of the credit for this information."

"Well, congratulations, Ms. Smith," the AG said.

"Thank you," Robin said. She was blushing. People behind the scenes in television news don't normally get this kind of acclaim. It all goes to the faces who appear in front of the camera. JC was reminded of how underappreciated his off-camera colleagues are.

"And I'm joined by Reuben Tarbell," the attorney general said. "Mr. Snow, I think you two are acquainted."

"We are," JC said. Tarbell was the public information officer who had refused to return the reporter's phone calls. "It's lovely to hear your voice, Mr. Tarbell."

"JC, Robin, with your help, we're going to expose the fraud being perpetuated by Benjamin Whitmore," the attorney general said. She went on to detail how and how much money the executive director of Vermont Stands for the Birds and Bees had stolen.

"He spent his stolen proceeds on a lavish lifestyle, much of it with Ms. Chadwick," the AG continued. "Had Ms. Chadwick not met with her unfortunate end, she would also have been arrested and charged."

The AG went on to detail spending by Whitmore on a new mansion, on expensive vacations for two, dinner for two, resort stays for two, jewelry and expensive women's clothing.

"Only once," the attorney general said, "was there even a relevant business convention on the same Caribbean island that Mr. Whitmore and Ms. Chadwick repeatedly visited."

The AG said that they were already in the process of confirming all of Robin and JC's findings.

"So far, everything checks out," she said. "You've helped provide us with an airtight case against Mr. Whitmore."

She also informed the chief and the journalists that her investigators had not found evidence that the VSBB board was guilty of anything.

"They were playing against a stacked deck," the attorney general surmised. "They weren't going on the trips or receiving any extravagant gifts. We think Whitmore and Chadwick simply lied to them and controlled the votes."

Someone should probably inform them of that, JC thought. The last time he saw Jerry Dean and Tom Caryl, they looked like they were ready to sign a suicide pact.

"So, thank you, Mr. Snow and Ms. Smith," the AG concluded. Then, Reuben Tarbell spoke his only words.

"Mr. Snow, say 'Hi' to Davey Kay the next time you're back in your hometown."

It was a message to let JC know that Tarbell had figured out who was keeping the reporter informed about the attorney general's investigation.

It was a shame, JC thought, that Tarbell hadn't seemed as concerned with catching Whitmore as with plugging his "leak."

JC wasn't sure why the leak disturbed Tarbell so much. Maybe he was just a jerk. Or maybe a journalist reporting facts of the investigation so accurately had disturbed Tarbell's boss.

"I'll tell Davey that you owe him an expensive dinner," JC said before the phone call ended, "for spoon-feeding you your investigation."

When the phone call to the state capitol in Montpelier was disconnected, Sipp Ives leaned back in his chair and wiped his face with his hand.

"Now, we have the other matter to resolve," the chief said.

"The murder of Bobbi Chadwick," JC said.

"Whitmore says he didn't do it," Sipp Ives told them.

"Do you believe him?" JC asked.

"I'll let the evidence do the talking," Ives stated. "But he seemed truly crushed at the news that she was dead."

Muzzle-loading rifles sent shock waves through the air when they were fired. Smoke floated back into the riflemen's faces.

A Sunday crowd, gathered for Bennington Battle Day events, were delighted with the reenactment of combat during the Revolutionary War. Bennington Battle Day was an annual statewide holiday in Vermont to celebrate the American victory.

But this year, the actual anniversary of the bloodshed, August sixteenth, had suffered heavy rains and some flooding. Events had to be moved to a month later.

JC took Robin to the battlefield. The state park was actually just inside present-day New York State.

"The borders between states at the time were fuzzy," he told her. "New York and New Hampshire both claimed this part of Vermont."

"I remember reading that," Robin reminded him.

The replication of the battle included actors dressed in the uniforms of the British, the Americans, and First Natives who fought on both sides. The muzzle-loaders roared and cannons rumbled for the captivated spectators.

Sunday was a day off for JC, Bip and Robin. It came as a *command* from the accounting office at their television station. The director of accounting had told the news director what he would be spending in overtime, if they worked without halt through the weekend.

JC was paid an annual salary. His payday wouldn't change if he worked less or more than expected. But Bip and Robin were hourly employees. They were paid time-and-a-half and double time. It was immaterial that there was a breaking story to report and that they wanted to work.

Unofficially, they volunteered to work an extra day. Officially, they were voluntold.

# 31

"Luscious."

"Succulent."

"Yeah, succulent is pretty good," Bip said.

JC and Bip were seated in front of a computer screen when Robin walked into Bip's hotel room. They were looking through some of the footage Bip had been shooting in Vermont.

"What did I just walk in on?" Robin asked with a grimace.

"I'm writing my script," JC told her. "We were trying to come up with a word that describes Bobbi's lips." His smile widened.

"You are bookends of imbecility," Robin said as she stared at the pair.

"Don't pretend repugnance," JC teased her. "Piety doesn't befit you."

"Well, before you petition the governor to lower flags to half-staff," she grumbled, "I have been talking with Sipp Ives and the attorney general's office."

She pulled three coffees from a bag and placed them on a table. Then she pulled sweet rolls from the bag. That would be breakfast.

She pulled out a bag of ice, to place on JC's knee.

"Bless you," Bip said as he reached for a sweet roll. "JC made me say those things. I think you're much hotter than Bobbi."

"Oh, brother," Robin said, rolling her eyes.

"She's been doing that a lot," JC said to Bip.

"What?" he asked.

"Rolling her eyes at us," JC said.

"It's as though she's calling our character into question," Bip said with a grin.

"I don't have any questions about your character," Robin told them. "I have all my answers. I've rarely been apart from both of you for the last two weeks. It's like living with a pair of twelve-year-old brothers."

Bip and JC smiled. She smiled at them both.

"So, you spoke with the attorney general this morning?" JC asked.

"No, I spoke with Reuben Tarbell, in the public information office of the attorney general," she said.

"That jerk?" JC said. "What did he say, 'No comment?'"

"No, he was very nice," Robin responded. "He asked if he could take me out to dinner."

"What did you say?" JC asked. He found that he was a little nervous. He realized that his relationship with Robin could be mistaken for casual. He hadn't given her a ring. Their commitment to each other was largely an unspoken one.

"I told him that I had to babysit my two twelve-year-old brothers," she smiled.

JC and Robin shared a look. A look that lovers exchange.

"So, has anyone found Rick Teller?" JC asked.

"Nope," Robin said. "I just spoke with Sipp Ives. He says Rick has disappeared. But they're looking for him."

"Is he on the run or is he dead too?" Bip asked.

"That's a good question," JC said. "If Whitmore found out that Bobbi was cheating on him, then he was not going to be happy with Rick either."

"And what does the AG say?" JC asked.

"Well, it's what the AG and Sipp say," she answered. "It gives us a better idea of what's going on. Sipp says that Whitmore is spilling his guts. He's happy to plead guilty to the fraud charges if it means he isn't accused of Bobbi's murder."

"So, distill for us what you've learned this morning," JC said.

"The AG has the VSBB spending records, supplied by Davey Kay," Robin stated. "And both of them spotted more money missing from the charity. The *new* missing money seemed to go to expenses that have nothing to do with trips to the Caribbean or jewelry for Bobbi. There are periodic payments to a consultant who doesn't seem to exist."

"So, what do they suspect?" JC asked.

"They suspect a lot," Robin said. "First of all, they think they've got Whitmore on the fraud charges. They think that he got in over his head when he found himself dating a beautiful woman like Bobbi Chadwick. She had expensive tastes. He couldn't afford it, so he started 'borrowing' from the charity. But her tastes exceeded a desire for *nice* things. She wanted *spectacular* things. Whitmore kept taking from the charity's funds and passed the point of no return."

"That much, we sort of knew," JC said.

"Yes, But the attorney general also suspects that Whitmore was being blackmailed," Robin told him. "Bobbi may have been in on it. At first, maybe she was just enjoying dating Whitmore and collecting the gifts he showered her with."

"But then Rick shows up," JC interjected.

"Yes, Rick gets out of prison and comes looking for his old girlfriend," Robin said. "What I'm summarizing for you is still a blend of speculation by the AG and what Whitmore is telling Sipp."

"Okay, so how did Rick fit into this? Was he the blackmailer?" JC asked.

"Rick *and* Bobbi may have cooked up a scheme to blackmail Whitmore for even more money. Whitmore knew that Bobbi was above his pay grade. Say that Bobbi was sexually rewarding Whitmore every time he spent the charity's money on her. The bigger the gift, the bigger the reward. And all the while, Rick was recording it in some fashion, making some record that they could blackmail Whitmore with."

"Whitmore finds out, his heart is broken, he's furious and kills Bobbi," JC theorized.

"That's one scenario," Robin said.

"What's an alternative scenario?" JC asked.

"What if Rick killed Bobbi?" Robin asked. "What if Whitmore is telling the truth and he didn't do it? Maybe Rick did it."

"Why?"

"Because Rick may not have realized how, let's say, *committed* Bobbi was to the bait and hook," she said. "Sipp told me that, among other things, Whitmore vividly described his sexual exploits with Bobbi. If this was a scam, she was giving it everything she had."

"And maybe the sex was more than her boyfriend, Rick Teller, had agreed to or was aware of," JC suggested. "Maybe he got jealous."

"Yeah," Robin agreed. "Rick may have realized that Bobbi was sharing her—what do you call it—succulence? Maybe she was sharing more of it with Whitmore than Rick was comfortable with. And maybe Bobbi realized that she didn't even need Rick. If the plan was to get Whitmore to part with his money, she was doing all the work. What did she need Rick for?"

"Rick got jealous and thought he was being double-crossed and he killed her," JC offered.

"Right. Those seem to be the theories that Sipp and the AG are working with, as of this morning," Robin stated.

"And Rick?" JC began.

"Is nowhere to be found," Robin finished.

"So could Bobbi and Rick and their evil scheme have been involved in John Thurston's murder?" JC asked. "Again, Bobbi and Thurston were both stabbed."

"The investigation in New York is still hanging Thurston's murder on Larry Gleichman," she told them.

Her phone rang. Robin answered and held up a finger, asking JC and Bip to give her a moment. She walked to a window and stared out of it with the phone to her ear.

"Okay, thanks," she said into the phone and ended the call.

"That's a coincidence. That was Gleichman's public defender," Robin said. "She just told me that he didn't recognize the picture of Bobbi. He says she's not the woman who left the credit card on the table."

"He would have remembered her," JC said.

"He would have remembered her succulence," Bip said with a grin.

# 32

"I can't believe it," Melody Church said.

"You considered him a friend, didn't you?" JC asked.

"Yes! And Josh was closer to him than me," she said. JC and Melody were taking a walk on the gravel path in the garden of her stone house.

"Ben spent a lot of time here," she said. "He and Josh would drink tea here in the garden. They'd have long talks about the environment, Josh's books, travel."

They walked together along the flowers. Occasionally, Melody would stop, pull a set of snips out of the apron she was wearing and deadhead a flower.

"Did you know that a honeybee might make ten trips a day to a neighborhood flowerbed like this one?" she asked as they watched a honeybee make its rounds from one flower to the next. "He can pollinate fifty to one thousand flowers in each trip."

"Do you participate in 'No Mow May?'" JC asked. He was referring to a movement to persuade property owners to skip mowing their lawn for the month of May. The longer grass would become a haven for bees and encourage their population to grow.

"I love the concept. Yes!" Melody said. "VSBB is looking into some kind of official endorsement of the idea. Some cities and states are already implementing 'No Mow May' on a voluntary basis."

They walked toward the house and Melody opened the French doors. She asked if he'd like some tea and he accepted.

"You know, my mother loved this house," Melody told him. "It was a comfort on a day like this. I'd place her wheelchair at the open French doors and she could feel the breeze and gaze out at the garden."

Melody reached up to the shelf above the kitchen sink where all the teakettles were. She hesitated.

"I worked so hard to comfort her," Melody said. "That's why Josh and I moved back here from Colorado, so I could take care of my mother. But the last few years, she suffered a lingering death. She lost all the dignity she placed so much importance on. It was a mess. I had to clean up after her. She was terribly embarrassed."

Melody reached up to the teakettles again, bringing down the one with the deer and bear painted on it.

They took their cups of tea into the library and sat. Melody seemed lost in thought, perhaps in memories of her mother, Ben Whitmore and Josh.

"Give me just a moment, won't you?" she said. She rose and left the room.

JC spent his time alone scanning the titles of Josh's books on the shelves. One was on the history of granite in Vermont. Another was on local plants.

He pulled the book about plants off the shelf. When JC opened it, he formed the opinion that the book was produced on someone's printer at home. There were misspellings and grainy photos of the plants being described below.

But there were detailed descriptions of the flora and fauna surrounding Stonestead. One chapter was titled, "What's going on up there?" It was a description of the flowers and plants atop Mont Vert and other local peaks.

The spine of the book at that particular section seemed stressed, like it was opened to those pages more than the others.

Melody returned to the room and apologized for her absence. He told her that he was again admiring Josh's collection of reading materials.

"I don't think there's another library quite like it," she said. "I suppose I should think about donating his books somewhere appropriate."

"It would be treasured, locally," JC told her.

"But if I gave the books away," Melody said, "what would I put on the shelves in their place? I don't think they'll be going anywhere, soon."

"Did you know John Thurston?" JC asked her. It was a random departure from their discussion on books. But it had occurred to him that Thurston's bank had done work with VSBB.

The question seemed to startle Melody. She had been burrowed deep in memories of better times, JC thought.

"John Thurston?" Melody asked. "I suppose I did. A banker, wasn't he?"

"Right," JC confirmed. It seemed that Melody was grasping at some context she wanted to share.

"He was here for a cocktail party, I believe," she said. "It was for the Birds and the Bees. He worked with Ben on a loan, I think. Josh probably met him too. I didn't really talk to him much."

JC wasn't certain what to do with the connection. Melody had grown quiet. JC thought that all the death in his conversation was probably upsetting. He rose from his seat to leave.

"He died, didn't he?" Melody asked abruptly.

"John Thurston?" JC asked. "Yes, they think he was murdered."

"Did Ben do it?" she asked. "He killed Bobbi, didn't he?"

JC barely turned the steering wheel of his car when he pulled out of Melody Church's driveway. It was nearly a straight shot into the driveway of Deborah Sampson, across the street. He was making an unannounced visit.

The door to the kitchen opened on Sampson's stone house and she appeared through the screen. JC could see that her hair was down. It was the first time he had seen her when it wasn't pulled back. Her hair was thin, but it framed her plain face. She looked the slightest bit pretty.

She did not smile as JC approached, but her eyes, he thought, showed some kind of welcoming glint. He had already concluded that her eyes didn't miss much. Perhaps she also spoke with her eyes.

"Mr. Snow," was all she said and opened the screen door for him to enter her kitchen. He was surprised to see Jerry Dean standing there. He held a cup of coffee and his hair wasn't combed. He looked like he had just woken up.

Don't tell me! JC said to himself. Actually, he *shouted* the words to himself. He was afraid for a moment that the words might be heard escaping through his ears. Deborah Sampson and Jerry Dean were sleeping together!

JC attempted to appear oblivious to the obvious.

"We're all adults here," Deborah said, without showing any emotion. But her eyes were on JC. She can read minds, too, he thought.

The three of them stood in the kitchen without saying a word. It was to a point of being awkward when JC noticed it.

"Have you spoken to the attorney general's office?" JC blurted, to fill the silence.

"No," said Jerry Dean. "Should we have?"

"You're off the hook," JC informed them. "We've been speaking with the AG and other investigators. While they believe Ben is guilty of multiple felonies, as well as Bobbi Chadwick, they don't think you or any board member is responsible."

"Well, that's a relief," Dean said.

"They said that they wanted to do a conference call with us, this afternoon," Deborah stated. "That's probably what they want to tell us."

"They'll probably have more questions for you, also," JC said. "You're privy to a lot of VSBB secrets, even if you didn't know it at the time."

That made Jerry Dean look nervous. Deborah Sampson looked at JC with knowing eyes.

"Why don't I give Tom Caryl a call," Jerry said and walked out of the room. That left JC and Deborah alone in the kitchen.

"I saw something else," Deborah said. She was expressionless, watching JC.

"When? Where?" JC asked, a little mystified.

"I happened to look up and see a car pulling into Melody's driveway," Sampson replied.

"Today? Recently?" JC probed.

"A lot of times," she said.

"From the witch window?"

"Yes."

"The same car?" JC inquired.

"Yes, the same car," she told him. "It began when Josh was still alive. But it continued after he died."

"Was it Ben Whitmore's car?" JC offered. "Melody just told me that Ben used to visit Josh a lot. And he probably checked in on Melody after Josh died."

"No," Sampson said. "It wasn't Ben's car. He used to visit me too, though probably not as much. But I'd recognize Ben's car."

"Do you know whose car it was?" JC asked.

"No."

JC scheduled an "on camera" interview with the two board members for later that day. Then he took a circuitous route back to the Flamstead Inn, traveling some of Vermont's winding roads.

He had come to Melody Church's home alone. Robin was working from her room and Bip was editing the story about Stonestead's historic fires. JC had already laid down the soundtrack. When the day came that they could put it on the air, it would be ready to go.

JC recognized the road he was traveling down as the one Benjamin Whitmore lived on. Within minutes, JC was parked outside the gated mansion belonging to the embattled executive director.

The gate was padlocked and the fountain was turned off. There was a "For Sale" sign with the face of a smiling Realtor next to his phone number.

"That was fast," JC said to himself. He turned the key in the car's ignition and continued down the road. Ben Whitmore's bright future was in foreclosure.

# 33

Robin was still asleep. The sun was starting to creep through the window of her room. JC was awake next to her. She was cradled in his arms.

He was thinking more about his relationship with Robin. He was thinking about his reaction when she told him that Reuben Tarbell had asked her out to dinner.

JC didn't know how to put words to his coupling with Robin. She wasn't his wife or fiancée. She was his girlfriend. And even that label was used little between them. He didn't think it was necessary. He knew that she was more than a girlfriend. But would *she* like to hear that from him?

They enjoyed each other's company and they enjoyed each other's bodies. He'd given her a key to his apartment and didn't ever think about being with another woman. But he had never told her that he loved her. There was a time in the past when he told Shara that he loved her.

And look how that turned out.

When Robin awakened, he gave her a kiss. He was happy just to be at her side. He knew that she was his, for at least another day.

They rose from bed and met Bip for breakfast.

"What are we doing today?" JC asked his crew. Robin sat next to him. Bip sat across the table.

"I'm running away with your photographer," Robin said with a smile.

"What took you so long?" JC asked. "He's almost as pretty as Bobbi."

"Oh boy," Robin said. "Another day of hearing how succulent Bobbi was." There was silence from JC and Bip. They realized that they had been insensitive.

"I'm just not used to covering felons who are only slightly less beautiful than you are." JC recovered, looking at Robin.

She looked back without expression. It was like she was thinking.

"Smooth," she finally said.

Bip exhaled and cheered, raising his hand to solicit a high five from JC. Robin leaned over and placed her head on JC's shoulder.

"But *I'm* still the prettiest one at the table, right?" Bip said with a smile.

"She makes you look like an ogre," JC said.

Bip and Robin pushed themselves out of the booth at Molly's.

"We are going to shoot a feature about fall foliage in Vermont," Robin informed JC. "Our producers back in

Denver want to see maple syrup being made and autumn leaves that aren't aspens."

"I've noticed some buses carrying early leaf peepers," JC said.

"I've been asking around," she said. "There are some spots near here where the leaves turn early. Anyway, Bip will shoot it and I'll write it. Then, you can record the voice track."

"You should voice it," JC said. "If it's your work, you should get the credit."

"That is a radical concept that our fearless leaders in Denver cannot envision," she said. "Anyway, tonight we'll run the story about the Stonestead fires in the 1880s, since it's already cut. That will give us some time to write and edit the story about autumn in Vermont."

"What are you going to do?" Bip asked, looking at JC.

"I promise to use my time wisely," he responded. At the moment, he didn't have a clue.

"Where's Rick Teller?" JC asked Police Chief Sipp Ives, over the phone.

"Your guess is as good as mine," the chief said. "We're out looking for him. We've alerted Pennsylvania too. Sometimes, suspects just want to go home when they get in big trouble."

"So, you think he did it?" JC asked.

"We don't know that," the chief said. "But disappearing doesn't make him look any more innocent."

"What about Whitmore?" the reporter inquired.

"Mr. Whitmore is in custody and headed for Burlington in handcuffs today," the chief said. "The worst of the crimes he committed, assuming he did not commit murder, were crimes against the state. The paperwork for the charity called 'Vermont Stands for the Birds and Bees' is filed in Burlington. So, the case against him will probably be pursued there."

"And if he did murder Bobbi Chadwick?" JC asked.

"Oh, we'll know where to find him," the sheriff said, laughing a bit.

JC decided to call an Uber and ride out to the Williams River Hose Company. He remembered that Rick liked to sit at the bar there. Maybe he could find some people to interview about the suspect.

Pulling the door open and stopping at the spot where the hostess would check him in, he noticed that the dining room was empty and dimly lit. It was early for lunch.

He waited for a hostess to come out while he gazed at old firefighting equipment decorating the walls.

After standing alone for a few minutes, he was drawn into the next room. The lights were out in the waiting area, just like the last time he was there.

He checked the seat in the corner to see if Frederick Earle was sitting there quietly. He was not.

JC looked at the sofa. He stared at the spot where Frederick told him the spirit of a young woman was seated. The sofa looked empty. He still gave the spot a little wave.

His ghost hunting was interrupted by the sound of crashing dishes. The racket came from behind a door into the kitchen.

There was a small glass window on the door, which JC peered through from the waiting room.

He saw a lot of broken dinner plates on the floor. But the lights to the kitchen were mostly turned off. There were no cooks. It was dawning on JC that the restaurant was not open for lunch today. Why the front door was open was a mystery to him.

He turned to go. But before he could take a step, the door he had been looking through opened. It slapped him in the back.

"I'm sorry," JC said before turning. "I'm in your way."

JC turned and what he saw was not a cook in his white smock. He was staring at Rick Teller.

They stood there and stared at each other. They were both surprised by their encounter.

"They're looking for you, Rick," JC finally said.

Teller looked disheveled, like he had slept in the woods. His hair was uncombed, his clothes were dirty and he smelled of alcohol. That was probably what brought him to the restaurant, to hide and drink when he knew the establishment was closed.

"I know where they keep an extra key outside," Rick said. "I told you, I know where the bar is and where the bathrooms are. Maybe I know a little more than that."

"You might as well call police and give yourself up," JC said. "I mean, now that you've been found."

Rick took two steps back, pushed in the two-way door and reached for something on the counter. His hand re-emerged holding a sizable chef's knife.

"*They* haven't found me," Rick said. "*You* have."

JC reached to his side and toppled an antique end table in Teller's way. But running wasn't an option. JC's knee was still weak. He knew that he couldn't outrun his assailant.

So, he ducked behind a large round oak table. It was heavy. Rick tried to push it out of his way but he couldn't, not with one hand. The other hand held the eight-inch knife.

"Do you really think you're going to keep this table between you and me until the dinner staff arrives?" Rick sneered.

"You could just put the knife down. But I guess this removes any doubt that you killed Bobbi," JC said.

"That bitch cheated on me!" Rick shouted. He was spitting the words out. "I did prison time for her! Do you know why I was arrested in Altoona? She was in on it with me! She was as guilty as I was. I never told police about her role in it! I went to prison for her! She owed me her loyalty!"

Teller was only getting more agitated. JC thought that he should keep him talking, to buy time, but couldn't see how this would end well. No one even knew where he was.

"A jury would see it your way," JC told him. "They'd understand what you've been through. She should have been grateful to you."

"Do you think I'm a moron?" Rick asked. "Of course, she should have been grateful. She's all I thought about in prison. I appreciate your sympathy and all. But do you think I'm going to let you go? Nothing personal, newsman, but you've got to go. Say 'Hi' to Bobbi when you see her."

Rick lunged around the table. JC knew he couldn't avoid the knife. Then he heard a growl.

"Yoouuuuch!" Teller screamed.

The assailant dropped the knife and grabbed his hand. His face was twisted in pain.

"Fuck!" he bellowed, clutching his wounded hand.

JC seized the advantage. There was a heavy antique table lamp within reach. He raised it above his head and it came crashing down on Rick Teller's skull.

Teller dropped to the floor and didn't move. JC stood above him for a moment, breathing heavily. He watched for

Teller to stir, ready to hit his assailant again. But the attacker lay still.

At the same time, JC reached into his pocket and dialed 9-1-1.


"You alright?" The question came from Sipp Ives.

"Yeah. It was just a close call," JC told him, sitting on the edge of an open ambulance door.

"What did you do to him?" the police chief asked.

"I hit him over the head with a big antique," JC laughed.

"No, his hand," Sipp asked.

"The one holding the knife?" JC asked.

"Yes, that one."

"I avoided it," JC told him. "Like my life depended on it."

"You didn't just avoid it," the chief told him. "His hand is mangled. It's broken and he bled quite a bit."

"His hand?" JC asked.

"Yes," the chief said. "You don't remember?"

JC thought about it. He did everything he could to avoid the hand Rick was holding the knife with. He remembered Rick lunging. He heard a growl. Rick screamed and stopped his advance. And JC hit him with the heaviest blunt instrument that he could reach.

"It looks like a dog bit him," the chief said. "I've seen a number of dog maulings in my time. That's what it looks like. Did you see a dog?"

"No," JC told him. But he heard a growl, he thought. Picabo.

# 34

"H ere we go again," Bip said with a smile.

Robin and Bip rushed to the restaurant in the old firehouse after being pulled over by a green and yellow patrol cruiser belonging to the Vermont State Police. At the request of Sipp Ives, the trooper informed the journalists of the incident at the restaurant involving their reporter. Robin embraced JC when she arrived. She held him as though she would never let him go. He heard her crying.

"I'm okay, babe," JC said.

When she pulled away, Bip shook his hand.

"Glad you're alright, man," he said. Robin still wasn't letting go of JC's arm.

"Should I get my camera and shoot some of this?" Bip asked.

"I think you'd better," JC told him.

"What were you doing?" Robin asked in a weak voice. "How did you know where he was?"

"I was very good at hide-and-seek when I was little," JC smiled. "Apparently, he wasn't."

Rick Teller was taken to a hospital in Bennington in police custody. He would be under guard at the hospital and then taken to jail until he was arraigned.

With JC's testimony, detailing Teller's ranting confession while holding an eight-inch knife, Bobbi's ex-boyfriend would be charged with her murder.

JC was prepared for what came for the rest of the afternoon. So were Bip and Robin. JC had been caught in the middle of a sensational story before. *He* had become the story.

He was uncomfortable with the notion of *being* a story instead of *covering* one as a journalist. But when a man is trying to plunge a knife into your torso, it's too late to inform him that you prefer playing the role of "a fly on the wall."

The trajectory of their day had been changed. JC now would be interviewed by his own television station, live via satellite. He was told to be available for the next three newscasts that night and then again in the morning.

Bip would shoot the interview and Robin would be the field producer.

JC was also told by the management at his television station in Denver that he would need to be available to speak with other television stations across the country that wanted to interview him. And there would be phone calls from newspapers. The story of a reporter capturing a man suspected of murder was compelling television.

"It is television magic," JC's news director told him over the phone. "It's fucking magic! I'm glad you're okay, JC."

The interview requests came from this country and others.

"I was just trying not to get killed," JC would tell them. "I wasn't trying to capture him. I was trying to avoid him."

"You are very humble," interviewers would say back to him.

"Did Mr. Teller kill that poor woman?" many of them asked.

"He pretty much confessed to that," JC told them. "That was the sum of his statement while he was waving that knife around."

"What can you tell us about Bobbi Chadwick? What will you remember about her?" many of the interviewers asked.

That caused Bip, behind the camera, to laugh every time. And it left JC at a loss for words each time. That made Bip laugh harder. If he heard the word "succulent," he would be on the ground.

"She could capture the attention of an entire room," JC would finally come up with. "She was a very resourceful woman."

He would leave it to the attorney general in Vermont to tell the rest of the news media that had Chadwick lived, she would have been indicted for many of the same crimes as Ben Whitmore.

JC was seated on the porch of the Flamstead Inn for the interviews. That way, he and Bip and Robin could order food when they were hungry and enjoy the warm evening breeze.

A crowd of Stonestead residents gathered on the sidewalk to watch. It was not something that happened every day in Stonestead. Some of them would applaud when JC ended each five-minute interview. The onlookers could only hear JC's answers. They couldn't hear the questions coming from Chicago, San Francisco, Montreal, London and the other television newscasts. But they could watch a small monitor provided for JC. It was like seeing the interview on TV, only without sound.

One interviewer asked JC where he was speaking from. He said that he was perched on the porch of the historic Flamstead Inn in beautiful Stonestead, Vermont. That triggered the biggest cheer of the night from his new fans standing on the sidewalk.

And when all the interviews were over, a dead dog named Picabo had never come up in the conversation. JC wondered what he would have said, if someone had asked.

It had been a long day. When the camera was turned off and the light kit was packed up, the inn's bar began passing beers through a window to the porch. It was a local beer called Snow Republic, brewed in West Dover.

JC, Robin and Bip remained on the porch for quite some time, long after the satellite truck had driven away and onlookers had approached JC to share a word with the celebrity.

"You're lucky you're not dead," Bip said, tipping a beer in JC's direction.

"You don't know how true those words are," JC told them, taking a sip of his own Snow Republic. "I don't even know what happened. I thought I was a dead man."

"You hit him over the head with a twenty-pound lamp," Bip laughed. "That's what happened."

JC took another slug from his bottle of beer and thought about it.

"Yeah, but that knife should have gone through my front and come out my back, by then," he said solemnly.


"What happened?" Robin asked when they finally laid down next to each other in bed. JC didn't answer for a long time.

"I heard a growl," he finally told her, softly. She didn't understand what that meant.

"You remember that I told you old Frederick Earle said that a dog was following me? A ghost dog?"

"I do," she said. She was not going to question his sanity after what he had been through.

"He described Picabo," he said. "She was a dog that, when she was alive, would have done exactly that if she thought I was in danger. She was that kind of dog."

Robin looked at JC with believing eyes. She didn't say anything. She was grateful that he was alive and lying in her bed.

"Do you want to go steady?" he asked.

"Do I what?" she asked softly and smiled. "That's a big commitment. Are you going to give me your letter jacket to wear?"

"I don't know what to do with you," he said. "I love you and I don't want to lose you. I don't want you to think that I don't take you seriously."

"You what?" she asked softly, not daring to move a muscle.

He stared at her. He knew that anything else he said wouldn't be heard, now.

"I love you," he said.

She rolled toward him and kissed him. She stroked his hair and kissed him again.

"I love you," she said, brushing his hair off of his forehead.

"So, you didn't answer me," he said.

"What?" she asked.

"Will you go steady?"

"You didn't answer *me*," she told him.

"What?"

"Do I get to wear your letter jacket?" she said and smiled.

"Wow," he said. "That's a big commitment."

# 35

"You're not as dumb as you look," JC told Davey Kay over the phone. "You were right about your hunch that someone was stealing from Josh Church's charitable donation."

"The numbers don't lie," Davey responded. "Have you caught Josh's killer yet?"

"You're still convinced that he was murdered?" JC asked.

"You have more suspects than when we started," Davey said. "If Josh figured out that someone was stealing that kind of money, you have a list of people that would have killed him. There's Whitmore, that Rick Teller, even the radiant Bobbi Chadwick."

"Fair enough," JC said. "But how did they do it? He wasn't stabbed, he wasn't shot. He suffered a long, lingering death. It looks like some awful ailment that doctors just couldn't put their finger on. Maybe it was Lyme disease. We have no shortage of that around here, and it can be hard to diagnose."

"I was right about the corruption in VSBB, wasn't I?" Davey asserted.

"Alright, I'll give it another look," JC told his old friend. "But I'm not promising anything. You may be wrong about this."


"You are a hot ticket!"

That's what JC was told by his assignment editor back in Denver. JC and Robin were awakened by his phone call.

They were told to do a follow-up story that day on yesterday's near-deadly clash between JC and Rick Teller.

The more management wanted to hear about his heroics, the less JC wanted to talk about it. He didn't like being the center of attention. He liked to report on others who were the center of attention. But ultimately, he was paid to do what he was told to do.

"When can we wrap things up and bring you home?" the assignment editor, Rocky Baumann, said he was told to ask.

"We still have work to do," JC told him. "Thurston's murder. He's a Colorado story. And I'm not sure that there isn't more to the Josh Church story."

"Like what?" Baumann asked.

"Remember the first thing we were told, before all this other drama?" JC asked. "We were told that Josh Church was murdered."

"Do you have any evidence of that?" Rocky asked.

"Not a sliver of evidence," the reporter responded.

JC and Robin met Bip at Molly's an hour later than usual, because they'd had a long night. Their day would be filled with interviewing those they hadn't interviewed the day before, who could also provide reaction to the capture of Rick Teller.

JC would also be required to have a live conversation with the anchor, telling them something about his struggle with Teller that he hadn't told the day before. At the moment, he was at a loss as to what that would be, but he'd think of something.

JC, Bip and Robin felt like they would be rehashing news that they had already reported. But it was what the bosses wanted. And they knew that it might be what viewers wanted too.

They planned their day and made some phone calls while still sitting at their booth at Molly's. The occasional Stonestead resident would stop by the table and tell them how exciting it was to watch JC do his string of live interviews from the porch of the Flamstead Inn the night before.

"I've got two good interviews lined up," Robin said as she got off the phone. "You look tired," she said to JC. "Would you like Bip and me to go get the interviews? You can look at the tape when we get back."

"I wouldn't mind that at all," JC said. "Thanks."

The producer and photographer pushed themselves out of the booth and went to perform their duties. JC stayed behind and paid the check. She was right, he thought, he was emotionally and physically drained.

There was something about surviving an attempt on your life, he thought. Your body rallies in the face of the threat. It's "All Hands on Deck." And when it's over, every muscle and every organ needs a little rest. From your brain to your heart to your quadriceps. They had all risen to the occasion.

JC walked down the stairs of Molly's to the sidewalk. He was limping a little. His knee throbbed.

He saw a light shining through the door at the Historical Society across the street and he walked there.

Inside the building, four men sat on their folding chairs at folding tables, including Town Historian George Earl.

"Glad to see that you're still with us," George said. "Otherwise, the only one you'd have to talk with in town would be my daddy." He was alluding to Frederick, the one who could see ghosts.

"I'm sorry that we haven't been able to get your story about the fires on the air yet," JC told them. "It's been bumped twice by more pressing stories. Yesterday and today, our story is about an idiot who nearly got stabbed by a ski resort employee."

"That would be you," George said. The men laughed. "When the fire story finally does get on TV, you'll get us a copy, won't you? We won't be able to see it in Denver."

"I promise," JC said.

The men showed JC a map they had made, marking the fires between 1880 and 1891. The buildings were all plotted on a map. They were color coded to distinguish which fire scene was a home, a barn or a business. They also had dates next to them, dates of the fires.

Some of the fires were in the village of Stonestead and some were near the village, in places with names like Crockers Camp and Popple Dungeon. They were all within ten miles of each other.

JC studied the map. Nearly every property outside of the village, and many in the village, had burned over the span of eleven years. Of course, there were far fewer buildings in the town in the 1880s.

"If you stand in this spot," JC said, holding his finger to a place on the map, "just about every fire is a five-mile walk, at the most."

He picked up a red pen off the table and put a small dot where his finger had been. Then, he drew a circle around it, making five miles in any direction.

"Five miles wasn't much of a walk for people in those days, was it?" JC asked.

"That was about like walking a hundred yards to people today," George responded. "They were strong."

"Who lived here?" JC asked, pointing at a spot on the map.

"That was the Hall family farm," George told him. "Richard and his wife, Lucia, and their daughter Melatiah."

"And who lived here?" JC asked, pointing to the spot in the middle that he had marked with a red dot.

"That's the Davis farm," George said. "Joseph, his wife Berenice and their son, Tace."

"I read about all these people," JC said. "They were in the notes you loaned me."

"Yep, they were," George answered.

JC silently stared at the map. During the long pause, the four members of the historic society resumed doing what they were doing before JC walked in. JC just stared at the map.

"You've got a Firestarter," he finally said. "A pyromaniac."

The eight eyes of the four members of the Stonestead Historical Society Executive Committee all looked up from what they were doing and peered at the map. They stood and moved in for a closer look.

"The Hall child and the Davis child," JC said. "Were they about the same age?"

"About," David Earl said. "We divided the map and all studied our portion of it. We learned as much as we could about the families who lived there or the businesses they owned. That was in the study you read."

"Did the Davis boy fancy the Hall girl?" JC asked.

"It's possible," David Earl said. "We don't have a lot of personal information. We have some letters and short biographies if they belonged to the Masons or if they appeared in the newspaper. But from what we have, I sort of wondered the same thing, if he had a crush on the Hall girl."

"Just a crush?" JC asked.

"Well, he didn't end up with her," David said. "She married another boy."

"When?" JC asked.

"That would be around 1889," the man stated. "That's when she married another young man from town."

"Tace Davis was the arsonist," JC declared as he looked back at the map for assurance. "He started most of these fires."

The members of the historical society reacted with a collective gasp. They exchanged surprised looks and small remarks with each other.

They pressed closer to the map. They looked at the mark for the Davis farm and the marks of the other fires.

"Through 1890," JC told them. "The Hall farm and the Davis farm were the only two properties inside that circle that hadn't suffered a fire. All the fires were within a walkable distance for Tace. The Hall farm was barely two miles away."

"Tace Davis? Why would he do it?" one member of the executive committee asked. "No one said anything about an arsonist in that day."

"The last thing they wanted to think was that someone in their small community, someone they went to church with on Sunday, would do such a horrid thing," JC said. "Real pyromaniacs have a sort of mental illness. They almost can't help themselves. They love to see fire. Tace was probably doing it for his own amusement and to feed his sickness."

"It doesn't make sense," another executive member said. The others told him to shush.

"But Tace was sweet on Melatiah Hall," JC said. "He wasn't going to burn down her family's farm. Of course, he wasn't going to set fire on his own family's farm either. After over a decade, they were the only untouched properties left. They never caught him?"

"No," George said. "You're the first one to ever suggest there was an arsonist."

"So, what happened to Tace?" the reporter asked them. The historical society members looked amongst each other, not saying much.

"He died a hero," George said. "We have a plaque here at the museum. It used to hang at the old hose company on the Williams River."

"The one you almost got killed at," another member laughed. The others laughed too.

"In 1891," George explained, "the Hall farm caught fire. It burned ferociously. Everyone got out except Melatiah. She was living there with her husband. They'd just had a baby. People thought that maybe Melatiah couldn't get to her baby and she wouldn't leave without the little one."

"It was awful," an executive committee member said.

"Tace ran into the burning building," George continued. "He never came out. Neither did Melatiah or the baby. They all died in the fire."

"Oh boy," another executive committee member muttered. "Maybe we ought to take that plaque down."

"The plaque honored Tace Davis for his heroics," George said. "Everyone thought he gave his life trying to save Melatiah and her child. No one thought that he set the fire in the first place."

"I suspect," JC said, "that Tace couldn't stand that the woman he loved married another man. Maybe the baby just pushed him over the edge. He sought revenge and set the Hall farm on fire. It was the last fire he set. The only place that hadn't had some sort of fire, aside from his own family's home."

"But he still loved her, deep down," David Earl speculated. "He couldn't let her die and went in after her."

"Probably," JC agreed.

"Love triumphed over evil," another member said. "Just too late."

"The fires ended," another member said solemnly. "That's why we ended the study there. The Hall fire was the last one for a number of years.

The Stonestead Historical Society Executive Committee went silent. They stared at the map with reverence.

"We should take down the plaque," one finally said quietly.

# 36

"It's a better story." JC said.

He described his discovery of the historic arsonist to Robin and Bip when they returned from shooting their interviews.

"We can't leave you alone for a minute," Bip joked. "You'll just walk across the street and solve a hundred-and-thirty-year-old crime."

"We'll have to re-edit the fire story that we already cut," JC said. "But the story has a more interesting ending now, doesn't it?" Both of his colleagues agreed.

"We were thinking that we should go see Melody Church," Robin told JC. "We should get her whole take on Bobbi's murder and Rick's arrest."

JC agreed and said that he would come with them.

The paved road leading to the Stone District was intersected countless times by dirt roads. Vermont seemed to prefer dirt, if at all possible. It was cheaper to maintain than pavement, even if you took into account how many times more dirt had to be brought in to replace the dirt that washed away in a storm.

Dirt was preferred even if the school buses couldn't get up the hill during mud season. It also assured many Vermont residents of perpetually dirty cars and the occasional cracked windshield from a thrown stone.

Most Vermonters would say, "Other than that, the road is fine."

Bip pulled into Melody's gravel driveway. JC instinctively looked up over his shoulder to see if Deborah Sampson was looking out of the witch window. He couldn't tell.

Robin had called ahead and Melody prepared tea. She served them at an old table in the garden.

"This is beautiful," Robin said of the setting.

"Thank you," Melody said. She was eyeing the garden. "My tomato plants are drooping. That won't do."

"I love your flowers," Robin said. "And you grow your own food too?"

"I enjoy growing something that I'll be able to add to my dinner plate," Melody told her. "My tomatoes are my great success this summer. But there are so many, it's pulling the plants over."

Their hostess rose from her chair and walked to the plants, trying to straighten them up.

"JC, would you be a dear and go in the shed?" she asked. "I have some tall green sticks in there on one of the shelves. Could you bring me a few?"

"Of course," he said. He walked to the faded wooden shed in the corner of the garden and opened the door. It squeaked as it allowed him passage.

He scanned the shelves on the wall to the right. The only light was provided by a dust-covered window.

He saw garden gloves and he saw the small snips that Melody used to behead dying flower stems the last time he visited her.

He thought that he saw some green sticks sprawled across the back of a shelf, behind some other things. He moved a few empty planting pots out of the way and he picked up a white cylinder to safely set it aside. It was about the size of a to-go cup.

He looked inside to make sure he wasn't going to spill anything. The inside of it was stained a deep purple and lined with dried flower petals. Maybe she had created some natural clothing dye. The cup needed a good cleaning. He set it on a small dusty table.

JC pulled out four of the long green sticks. She had requested three. He'd bring one extra.

"Perfect," Melody smiled and turned her attention to her tomato plants. She looked happy working in her garden, he thought. She really was lovely. She looked much younger than her forty-eight years.

"What else do you grow in your garden?" Robin asked.

"Oh, I'll try anything," Melody said. "I've tried growing hemp to make rope for my hanging pots. Not the kind that you smoke," she laughed. "Though I've grown that too." She laughed some more.

"What did I see in the shed?" JC asked. "Did you try to make clothing dye?" Melody looked puzzled.

"Oh, I probably did," she said. "I can't keep track of all my failed experiments in the garden."

Clouds had been moving in. A slight drizzle began to drop. JC, Robin and Bip scrambled to pick up the cups and kettle and accompany Melody inside. In a short time, it began to pour outside.

"I enjoy the rain," Melody said. "Just smell it. Listen to it."

"We'd better move the interview inside," Bip said. Melody told him to set up his equipment in the library.

JC and Robin helped their hostess carry everything into the kitchen.

"Just leave it there," Melody said, pointing next to the sink. "I'll wash it after you leave. I don't have anything else to do."

"Did you get my mess cleaned up?" JC said as he opened the cabinet under the sink. He peered in, remembering the water that sprayed when he used the wrong faucet.

"I've still got to get that filter repaired," she said. "No, you didn't do any damage," she told him as she gently closed the cabinet door.

They shot their interview and Bip packed up his gear.

"It has really been lovely," Robin said as they prepared to leave the stone house. "I can't believe that I get paid to have tea in the garden of a beautiful home," she laughed. Then her phone pinged.

JC and Bip said goodbye and walked to their car. Robin hadn't moved from the doorway, looking at her phone.

"Hmm, do you recognize this car?" she asked Melody. Robin was in a festive spirit. She really didn't believe Melody would have any reason to recognize the car in the picture.

"No, I don't," Melody smiled and said after looking at the picture.

The journalists climbed into their car and gave Melody one last wave.

"What did you get on your phone?" JC asked Robin.

"I had asked Detective London in Niskayuna for a picture of John Thurston's car," she said. "I'm not sure why, but I thought it would be good to have. He just sent it to me."

"Did you think Melody Church was going to recognize it?" JC asked.

"No," Robin responded. "And she didn't."

They drove back toward the center of town.

"Do you want to see it?" Robin asked from the backseat.

"See what?" JC asked.

"The car, silly."

"Sure."

She handed her phone to JC in the front passenger seat. He took a look. It was a police photo. A silver car was parked in a garage. JC presumed the garage belonged to John Thurston.

"Some kind of Mercedes," he said.

"Let me see," Bip asked. He knew something about cars.

"It's a C-Class," Bip said. "It's a nice car. This one is a few years old. Maybe a 2015."

"Turn around," JC said. Bip looked at him.

"I want to go to Deborah Sampson's house," JC said. "Deborah Sampson said that she had seen a car pulling into Melody's driveway, before and after Josh died. Actually, she said she saw it a lot after Josh died. She didn't know whose car it was. I'd like to show her this picture."

Deborah Sampson appeared at her screen door when their car pulled up. Her hair was pulled back. Jerry Dean was not there.

She gave JC a friendly look with her eyes, but her mouth just sat there. Not a smile to be found.

"You said that you happened to glance up and see a car pulling into Melody's driveway?" JC asked.

"Yes," Sampson replied.

"Would you recognize it?" he asked.

"I haven't seen it for a while," she said. "But I think I'd recognize it. It was a nice car. Silver."

Robin showed her the picture of John Thurston's Mercedes.

"That's it," Deborah said. "I saw it a lot, for a while."

# 37

"L et's send another picture to Gleichman."

JC's request came as they sat in their rental car, parked in front of the Flamstead Inn. It was time to edit their story for the news that night.

They had already sent a picture of Bobbi Chadwick to Larry Gleichman. He remained in jail in Saratoga County, New York. Prosecutors were asking a grand jury to indict Gleichman in the murder of John Thurston, after Gleichman was caught with the murder victim's credit card.

Gleichman, through his public defender, said that he'd never seen the beautiful Bobbi before.

"Whose picture should we send to Gleichman, now?"

"Melody's," JC said.

"You've got to be kidding," Robin said.

"I don't think it will go anywhere, either," he protested. "But Deborah Sampson says that she saw John Thurston's car pulling into Melody's driveway a lot. Maybe it was a mix-up. Maybe he gave her the card and she dropped it somewhere."

"I'll give Faith Oaks a call," Robin said with little enthusiasm. "But I think you're going to be disappointed."

"I hope so," JC said, "if that means that Gleichman doesn't recognize Melody."

They locked the car and climbed the stairs up to their second-floor rooms at the Flamstead Inn. JC told Bip that he'd report to his photographer's room momentarily and they could record the reporter's voice track.

JC stepped into his room and emptied unnecessary items from his pockets. He unlocked the door to the porch and opened it. The wooden screen door, on the porch he shared with Robin's room, would allow a fresh breeze to blow into his quarters.

He went to use the bathroom. When he emerged and ran his hands under the running water, he heard scratching on the screen door to the porch. He turned and saw Robin there.

"My room is broken," she whimpered.

"How broken?" he asked.

"There's water on the floor," she said. "I think the sink is leaking."

JC went to look. A thin but steady stream of water was running from the cabinet below the sink and onto the floor. The rug was starting to soak up the water.

He dropped to his knees and located a shut-off valve. Twisting it, he thought that would stop the flow of water, but it wouldn't clean up the mess.

"I'll call the desk and we'll move your stuff into my room," he said. "Is this just a cheap trick to get into my bed?"

"Yes, I was sick of finding you in *my* bed," she said, grinning.

JC made the call to the desk. Then he walked down the hall to Bip's room to record the soundtrack for their follow-up stories about his scrape with Rick Teller. It would be as the newsroom's management requested.

The news photographer's setup in his room was something he called "road-trip chic." Instead of an elaborate collection of editing technology and speakers like those found in the suites with glass doors at their television station, this editing facility involved his laptop. There was nothing else. It sat on the desk next to a lamp and a travel guide to Vermont. There was a microphone that JC could speak into.

After recording his script, JC was back in his room, tying his tie. He had hair spray and a makeup bag on a small shelf next to the bathroom sink. It was a routine he followed before going on the air each evening.

"It's not Melody, you know," Robin said. She was leaning against the doorway of the bathroom.

"I hope not," JC answered.

"She was happily married, right?" Robin asked.

"That's what Davey tells me," JC said.

"So why would she kill Thurston?" she thought out loud.

"She's not even on the cops' radar," he said agreeably. "She said she barely knew him."

"So, you agree?" she asked as she drew close, pressed her body against his and straightened his collar.

"I never disagreed," he said.

His collar straightened, his tie knotted and his light layer of makeup applied, JC washed his hands and walked toward the screen door leading to the porch.

"I'm going to check on the plumber and see how he's doing in your room," he told Robin.

"I'll go down to Bip's room and see if he's done editing," she said.

"Hi," JC said as he walked through the door into Robin's room. There was a man lying on his back under the sink.

"This your room?" The plumber asked. He looked up at JC from the floor for just a moment.

"It's one of my team's rooms," JC said. "We're in town on business."

"You're the news guy," the plumber said, looking up again from under the sink. "I was with my family watching you the other night, when you were doing TV interviews all over the country from the porch here. My kids had never seen a real TV newscast. They thought it was pretty exciting."

"I'm glad they enjoyed it. Did you know Rick Teller?" JC asked.

"No, I didn't know any of that bunch. I didn't know the girl he killed, either," the plumber said. "Funny. You'd think you would know everyone in such a small town, wouldn't you?"

"I guess they hadn't been here that long," JC said. "What happened here?"

"The sink?" the plumber asked. "The filter for the drinking water sprang a leak. It's just a hard plastic container with a filter in it. I replaced it. I'm just tightening up all the connections."

The plumber pulled his head out of the cabinet and sat up, leaning against the cabinet frame.

"It's all fixed," he said, "though the rug is going to have to dry out. I'll bring up a fan. That will dry it out overnight."

"So, just a crack in a piece of plastic?" JC asked.

"Yeah, I use these water filters on all my sinks," the plumber said. "They don't cost too much and they're easy to replace. I'll bet seventy-five percent of the sinks in Stonestead have these water filters under them. That's because they're all my customers."

"Wow, you do a good business," JC said.

"Thank the Lord," the plumber said. "I do whatever it takes to keep a customer like the Flamstead Inn happy. They bring me a lot of business. And they say I'd be surprised how many people calling to make a reservation ask about the drinking water. They're worried more about contaminants in the water than people used to be, I guess. Anyway, the innkeeper says, when they tell those customers that they have filtered water coming from the tap in their room, it seals the deal."

"Do all the hotels use the filters?" JC asked.

"There aren't that many hotels in Stonestead, as you might have noticed," the plumber told him. "But I'll bet all the nice homes have them. Just about every one of them."

JC thought about that. He looked at the cracked plastic container the plumber was putting in his bag. It looked like a beer cup.

"Did you put a filter under Josh Church's sink?" JC asked. The plumber stopped what he was doing. He looked like he was thinking over the question.

"I believe that I did," he said, looking up with a smile. "They have a nice house."

"You should pay her a service call," JC said. "She told me that hers is broken."

# 38

"What are you, nuts?" Robin asked.

"I'd rather you asked me if I was crazy," JC told her.

"What are you, crazy?" Robin asked.

"Crazy like a fox," JC responded with a smile, as he perched a coffee cup at his lips.

They were having breakfast at Molly's with Bip. The news photographer had just asked what they were going to do that day.

"We should take the day off," JC had said. "We should go have some fun."

Bip was surprised by his answer. Robin was perplexed. She was the producer. She was the conduit to their superiors back in Denver. She was the one who would get the flak when she told them that JC wanted to have a "play day."

"They're going to say 'no,'" Bip said.

"We could finally air the story about the historic fires here in Stonestead," Robin suggested. "It's a really good story since you identified the arsonist."

"Then we'd have the day to do what we need to do," JC said. "And we'd be back to front the live shot about the fires."

"But what am I going to tell them the real reason is for taking the day off?" she asked.

"Just tell them that I have an idea," he said. "I have to see if I'm right."

From Molly's, they climbed into their car and headed for nearby Chester. They stopped at a store called *Blair Books and More*. Most of it was books, but there was great chai tea and latte sold in the back.

JC spent the remainder of the ride to Mont Vert flipping through a book about flowers and plants that grow wild in Vermont's mountains.

He looked up, from time to time, to see runners and bike riders challenging themselves on the rising elevation leading to the ski resort. There were more leaves changing color, he noticed.


"Sweet!" Bip exclaimed as a mountain bike was rolled in his direction.

"Right?" said Robin, delighted when she received her bike from the rental.

JC also had a smile on his face. It was a great day to be paid to go mountain biking, he thought.

It was the first day of autumn. The spread of red and gold leaves was underway at higher elevations on Mont Vert. The ski area's summer season was coming to a close.

A poster on the shack where they rented their bikes announced Octoberfest was approaching, the annual beer party at the ski resort. Another poster set the date for the annual used-ski swap in the large cafeteria inside the ski lodge.

There were other bikers at the mountain. Like the three journalists, they paid thirty-five dollars to ride the chairlift to the top. Then, they were allowed to make the wild ride down.

"What about your knee?" asked Robin with concern.

"I took my Advil," JC told her with a smile.

Unlike the other riders, JC and his colleagues were going to ride *up* the mountain. He wanted to see things at ground level.

"Let's go," he told the others, and they pedaled their rental bikes up a dirt road, gradually leading to the top of the ski runs.

"Are you ready to tell us what we're doing?" Robin asked.

"That's broadleaf plantain," JC told them. He raised his voice so they could hear him. He was pointing at a green weed alongside the trail. "If one of us falls off our bike today, we'll chew that up and place it on the scraped skin. It will feel better."

"You really think that I'm going to let you spit chewed-up leaves on my knee?" Robin asked.

"You've let him do grosser things to you," Bip laughed as he accelerated past her.

"Pig!" she yelled at him as she picked up her own pace.

The ride became a steeper climb. Mostly it followed service roads cut to maintain the mountain during the summer. They sometimes crossed paved roads that led to slope-side homes and condominiums.

JC was enjoying the exertion. It was the first time he'd been on a bike since hurting his knee. That leg was weaker, but not enough to dampen his enthusiasm.

"That's wild mint!" he exclaimed as they rode by the green bush.

Bip and Robin looked at each other. They had never known JC to be an expert on plants and herbal remedies.

"Seriously, are you going to tell us what's going on?" Robin shouted ahead to him.

"Sure," JC said, "if you can catch me." He smiled as he pedaled past them.

"Why do I suspect that we're not taking the day off, at all?" Robin shouted at him.

"Because you'd be right," he said after pulling his bike to a stop. The other two pulled up to him. They were all breathing hard and pulled water bottles off of their bikes and took a drink.

"You look tired. You should have some of that," JC said to Robin. He was pointing at a plant with large leaves. "It's called coltsfoot. It can relieve lung congestion."

Bip and Robin gave JC a bewildered look.

"I've been doing my homework," JC told them. "Beginning in Josh Church's library. All those books about plants."

They took in the view. They were looking down a grassy ski run to the ski lodge below. A wooden sign intended to tell winter skiers that the run was called Athena.

"What are we doing?" Robin asked.

JC pulled a small backpack off from around his shoulders. He pulled out the book he had just purchased in Chester.

"I don't completely understand what happened to Josh. But I have an idea of what I'm looking for," JC told them.

"It dawned on me when I was talking to the plumber in your room," JC said, looking at Robin. "There's something going on with Melody's faucet at her house. Remember how I sprayed water in the cabinet under her sink when I used the wrong faucet?"

"The first time we were at her house," Bip said. "You made a mess." He laughed.

"Right," JC said. "It made the same kind of mess that the cracked water filter just made in your room, Robin. It was almost identical. I spoke with the plumber. He said that he installed the same water filter in the home of Melody and Josh Church."

"That's quite a coincidence," Robin agreed.

"I happened to look under Melody's sink," JC continued. "There was no filter in place. There were three small hoses hanging there loosely. That's why water sprayed out in the cabinet. The hoses weren't connected."

"She said herself that it was broken," Robin told him. "Maybe it cracked too. She just hasn't gotten around to replacing it."

"Maybe," JC said. "But remember when she asked me to go into her shed and find those sticks to prop up her tomato plants? I found the cup and the filter in there on a shelf. The filter wasn't cracked. I took a pretty good look at it. I didn't know what I was looking at, but I looked it over."

Robin and Bip watched JC. They knew there was more to come.

"The container with the filter was full of old plant matter," JC told them. "Purple flower petals, for lack of a more precise term."

"So, what was it?" Robin asked.

"I don't know," JC said. "But I think we're going to find it up here."

"Up here is big," Robin said, looking around her.

"Yeah," JC agreed. "There's a lot of acreage. Maybe I'm crazy."

"You think she was poisoning Josh?" Bip blurted.

JC gave him a look. He didn't say yes and he didn't say no. But now they knew what they were looking for.

"Why here?" Robin asked.

"Remember when we bumped into Melody here one morning?" JC asked. "She was getting ready to hike up the entire mountain. She said she did it once or twice a week. She said Josh used to do it with her. This is the logical place to look."

They continued to ride up the mountain. They passed a bright orange fireball lily. Its bloom, JC had read, announces that autumn is approaching.

They brushed past black-eyed Susans and oxeye daisies. But JC didn't see what he was looking for.

They arrived at the top. They climbed off their bicycles. The grass was tall and the breeze felt cool and clean.

They shared some food, slices of apples and dried oranges.

"Are you ready to ride down?" Bip asked with anticipation. "We are going to rip!"

"Is this going to get scary?" Robin asked. "I'm brave but I'm not stupid, like you two."

"The best fun is scary fun," JC said.

His words were brave but Robin sensed that JC's heart was heavy.

Bip picked up his bike and pushed toward the downhill slope.

"You didn't find it," Robin said quietly, so only he could hear it.

"No," he said back, also at a whisper. She knew that he was disappointed.

"Do you think you're wrong about Melody?" she asked gently.

"I might be," he said. "I'm looking for the wrong thing or I'm looking in the wrong place."

# 39

"Doing something stupid twice," JC told her, "just makes it twice as stupid."

Robin had rolled over the next morning and saw that he was awake. JC was staring at the ceiling. She looked at the ceiling too.

"It isn't a very interesting ceiling, Jean Claude," she said. He laughed a little.

"I can go downstairs and get us some coffee," he told her.

"I love the sound of that," she said.

He pulled on some shorts and a tee shirt and ventured down the hall. It was Saturday. They had the day off, whether they wanted it or not.

Bip took the car to Lake Placid to see Patty MacIntyre.

"She's expecting me," Bip said the night before, with a grin and beaming eyes. He would be back Sunday night.

It meant that for the next forty-eight hours, JC and Robin could only go somewhere within walking distance.

"What do you mean, 'doing something stupid twice is twice as stupid?'" Robin asked when JC returned to bed with two coffees.

"I've thought about it all night," he told her. "Trying to prove Melody killed Josh is a reach. His death hasn't even been ruled a murder."

"It sounds like you're beating yourself up about it," Robin told him softly. "You took an intelligent look at it and it didn't work out. I remember you told me that sometimes the people you think are guilty, just aren't."

"Yeah, I might have been looking at it backwards," he said. "I was assuming he was murdered, and I just considered who had opportunity to murder him. Melody's name came to the top of the list. But she doesn't even have a motive."

"So, what are you going to do?" Robin asked.

"All night I was thinking of another way to prove Melody was guilty," he said. "I think I need to put it down. I need to pick up another book."

"Like?" she asked.

"Who killed John Thurston," he said.

A weekend without work evolved in slow motion. For a time, Saturday morning, they resisted. Sitting on their porch at the Flamstead Inn, they tried to work.

JC called the Saratoga County Sheriff's Office in New York and asked to speak with Investigator John Foot. He was told that the investigator had the weekend off unless this was an emergency. JC acknowledged that it was not. The best he could do was leave a message asking the investigator to give him a call on Monday.

He called Detective Ed London of the Niskayuna Police Force. He too would be unavailable for the weekend unless crime broke out.

Robin tried to collect more background information on Thurston. Offices were closed and people unavailable.

They sat on their porch. They had neither a car, a camera nor a photographer. JC recognized the sound of a whistle blowing from afar.

"Do you want to go to a high school football game?" he asked her.

"I haven't been to one of those since," she thought for a moment, "since high school. Sure."

They walked toward Stonestead High School's football field. The sound of the referee's whistle was joined by the sound of a marching band.

"You haven't given me your high school letter jacket," she said. "Maybe I can get the quarterback to give me his."

"I don't see a problem with that plan," JC told her. "I can't wait to see him introduce mom to his new thirty-five-year-old girlfriend."

"There's probably a law against that, huh?" she giggled.

"Yep," he said. "Sadly, I'm about as good as you're going to do in this town."

"Did you play college football?" Robin asked.

"I played college rugby," he said. "That's what high school football players in the United States do if they're not good enough to play college football. In other countries, they probably play American football if they're not good enough to play rugby."

"I don't think I know the rules for rugby," she said.

"It's a little rough around the edges in the U.S.," he said. "Someone brings their balls, a bunch of guys fight to touch them, and then we all have drinks together."

"That sounds dirty," she said.

"You get very dirty," he told her.

"No, I mean that sounded dirty," she repeated.

"That's what I said," he repeated, laughing.


On Monday, JC and Robin sat at breakfast with their exhausted news photographer.

"I really had fun," Bip said, pawing at his eyes. "What did you guys do?"

"Robin tried to pick up the Stonestead High School quarterback," JC said.

"I was just thinking about it," she protested. "Excuse me for sharing my feelings."

A phone rang and all three reached for theirs. It was JC's phone. Saratoga County Investigator John Foot was on the other end.

"I understand you swing a mean blunt instrument," the investigator laughed. "We could use you on our force. Sipp says it was a pretty good takedown on your part."

"Where's a cop when you need one?" JC said.

"What can I do for you?" the investigator asked.

"John Thurston," JC said. "How can we find the spot where his body was discovered?"

"It's marked by a yellow ribbon staked in the ground," Foot told him. "I wouldn't normally share this with a member of the news media, but Sipp thinks you're alright. I can text you directions."

"He was found with his ski boots on, right?" the reporter asked.

"Left," the investigator said. JC was a little baffled.

"It was on his left foot," the deputy replied. "He was found with only one ski boot on. A gray ski boot."

"Puzzling," JC said.

"Tell me about it," the investigator responded.

"How did he get to the field where he was found dead?" JC inquired. "Did he walk there with one ski boot on?"

"You are asking questions that keep me awake at night."

"You are working on the belief that he was dressed to go skiing because he died during ski season?" JC asked.

"That is our working theory," the law officer told him.

"He wasn't dressed for Halloween?" JC asked.

"He was last seen in mid-January," Foot said. "His body was found in mid-May. Halloween doesn't fall between those two dates."

"Did you ever find a lift ticket on Thurston's body?" JC asked. "Or an RFID card?"

"I personally looked over all of his belongings, after our last talk. No lift ticket and no RFID card," Foot answered. "RFID is the lift ticket with a little computer chip in it, right? They just put it in their pocket and a scanner can read it?"

"You've been doing your homework," JC said. "You have designs on becoming sheriff?"

"That is a headache I don't need," Foot responded. "I prefer criminals to politicians."

"You're in New York," JC said. "I thought they were the same thing."

"Funny," Foot replied. "Not all the time."

"The coroner found a stab wound," JC asked. "Did he find anything else?"

"Did he find anything else that I want you to know about?" said the investigator. "There were cuts and contusions. I'll leave it at that."

"Like he was dragged?" JC asked.

"I'll leave it at that," the investigator said. "Alright? I should wrap this up. Nice work fracturing that killer's skull. Say Hi to Sipp."

"Did you know that the wicket, to hold lift tickets on your ski jacket, was invented in Vermont?"

Robin was showing off some of the info she was gathering on her laptop, as she rode with JC and Bip to the Mont Vert Ski Resort.

"Those are the little metal things that loop through your zipper thingy that you stick your lift ticket to," she told them. "I know that zip ties are used more these days. But ski areas *used* to use wickets."

"My zipper thingy?" Bip asked.

"Technically," Robin said, sounding like a scientist. "The zipper thingy is called a 'pull tab' or 'slider.' And wickets were invented at the Killington Ski Resort in Vermont in the early 1960s."

The parking lot at Mont Vert was half full. There were a lot more cars than they were used to seeing. There was a line of people extending down the pedestrian walk lined by shops.

At the front of the line, the human resources office of the ski resort was taking job applications for the coming ski season. They were looking for everything from cooks to waiters to ski instructors to chairlift operators. Stonestead's population would soon be fully employed.

JC was playing a hunch.

"Why would someone wear their ski boots for a moment longer than they had to?" he asked. "Why not take them off in the lodge and put on more comfortable shoes?"

"Someone stole his shoes?" Robin suggested.

"Something like that," JC responded.

"Maybe he just couldn't find them. Maybe he ended his day at the bar," she smirked. "Maybe someone took them by mistake, thinking they were theirs. Maybe they were at the bar, too."

They approached a desk under a sign saying "Guest Services." A pleasant woman with short gray hair greeted them.

"Can we look at the lost and found?" JC asked.

"Of course," she said. "What did you lose?"

"Some shoes. Last January," he told her. She gave him a surprised look.

"Size nine," Robin said. JC had asked her to call the coroner and ask what shoe size Thurston probably wore. The fact that his feet were smaller than the average American male would narrow the field.

"The coroner said that Thurston was six-foot-two," Robin had told JC. "The average foot size for a man of that height is eleven or twelve. Nine is unusually small."

"Come with me," the woman told them. They followed her into a hallway off a cafeteria. The hallway was lined with shelves where skiers and snowboarders placed their belongings during winter. Then she led them through a metal door.

"You're not alone. People leave everything here," the woman told them with a grin. She stopped at a tall set of heavy-duty shelves. "They leave their jackets, their wallets, their cell phones. You won't find any wallets or cell phones in these boxes. We take special care of them."

She pulled two large cardboard boxes out and placed them on the floor. She looked in a third box and pulled that out too.

"Here you go. Good luck," she said and walked back through the door.

The boxes were full of single mittens, scarves and hats. There was a middle-school math book and three sets of eyeglasses.

"Dude, check it out," Bip told them. He was wearing a baseball hat with a popular cartoon character standing on the bill.

"The kid probably had lice," Robin said. Bip hastily pulled the hat off of his head and ran his hand through his spiked hair.

"Size nine?" JC said, pulling a pair of black slip-on boots out of a box. They had slip-resistant, grippy soles.

"Let me see," Robin said. He handed her one. She had her phone in the other hand. She started searching for a match. He was always impressed with her mastery of internet searches.

"They sell for two hundred and twenty-five dollars," she said, looking at the match she found on the phone. "So, they didn't belong to a kid. Kids outgrow their shoes every six months. No parent is going to pay two hundred and twenty-five dollars on that kid's shoes."

"A bank executive could pay that kind of money for shoes that will get ruined in the snow," Bip said.

She looked inside the shoe. Then she looked up with a smile on her face.

"There's a stamp on the insole. It has the name of a shoe store in Niskayuna."

The gray-haired woman from the guest-services desk pushed through the metal door with paperwork in her hand.

"I was looking through lost-and-found claims," she said. "People will call and ask us to keep an eye out if they lost something of value. There's one here for a pair of shoes."

"Does it have a date?" Robin asked.

"January fifteenth," the woman said. "He said he was calling from his car. He couldn't find his shoes. It's from a John Thurston from Niskayuna, New York. Is that you?"

# 40

"So, we know that he drove away from Mont Vert without his shoes," JC said. "If he was driving, he just pulled his ski boots off and drove in his stocking feet."

"And if he had to get out of the car," Bip added, "he just slipped his ski boots back on."

"But he probably didn't buckle them," JC said. "Who buckles their ski boots if they don't have to? That's probably how he lost one."

"Unless he was kidnapped from the lodge," Bip said. "Maybe that's why he didn't get his shoes."

"Kidnapping someone with literally thousands of witnesses?" JC said. "Not likely. Besides, Thurston called from his car and said that he'd lost his shoes. So, we know that he made it away from the ski lodge safely."

"He must have been mighty distracted to leave without his shoes," Bip said. "Or maybe the mountain has a strict policy against leaving your stuff under the cafeteria table. Cafeteria employees will take the shoes away and you have to ask to get them back, the point being made."

"How did you know to look for his shoes?" Robin asked.

"It was a guess," JC said. "But we knew he was here on January fifteenth because of that credit card expense at lunchtime. If we hadn't found his shoes, we would have found something else."

The morning after they had found the murder victim's shoes, they were driving into New York.

JC wanted to see the spot where John Thurston's body was discovered. They also had plans to drive into Niskayuna and look at Thurston's house. They would knock on the doors of neighbors to see if they could add anything.

JC had phoned Niskayuna Police Detective Ed London. The detective told JC that Thurston's car had been scrubbed clean before police found it. So had Thurston's house. Both, presumably, by the killer.

"Whoever killed Thurston," Detective London said, "knew that his DNA was all over the car and house. He worked hard to pick up after himself."

"What does that tell you?" JC asked.

"That the killer was in Thurston's car," the detective told him. "Otherwise, why wipe it clean? And the fact that he was in Thurston's house suggests they may have known each other. It was someone Thurston probably invited into his home. There wasn't a break-in."

"What about a kidnapping and robbery?" JC asked. "A situation where someone overpowers Thurston, maybe after hiding in his garage or something."

"Nothing was taken," the detective said. "It was only cleaned. This guy can break into my house if he just wants to clean it."

"Was Thurston killed inside his house?" the reporter probed.

"It's possible," the law officer stated. "But personally, I doubt it. We looked for blood spatter. There was nothing. A killer usually misses something when he tries to clean up blood. It's not easy to get everything.

"All this cleaning up also means that the killer knew he had time to do it," the detective surmised. "That's another indicator, I believe, that he knew the victim. The killer knew that a wife or a child wouldn't be coming home."

"Did Thurston have a girlfriend or boyfriend?" JC asked.

"Not that we're aware of," London responded.

The call ended and JC returned the phone to his pocket. He directed Bip off the highway at Exit 8 and into Clifton Park. They drove down Crescent Road through a commercial district and then through residential neighborhoods. They turned down Van Vranken Road, named after an old colonial family, and parked at the bottom of the hill.

The preserve where Thurston's body was found was old fertile farmland, stretched across the north bank of the Mohawk River. The land was once owned by a handful of wealthy families. JC had read that they were slave owners.

"Some believe that the awful institution of slavery was the sole propriety of the Deep South. But affluent families in the

Northeast also owned slaves," JC said as they walked to the top of an old truss bridge over a canal.

"But slavery in New York and most of the North ended much sooner than the South, well before the Civil War," he added. "Vermont was the first of the states to abolish slavery."

"How far are we from where you grew up?" Robin asked.

"Pretty close. Maybe twenty-five minutes," JC told her. "I mountain-biked down here a couple of times. I moved back home for a short time after graduating from Colorado State. I got a job in radio in Albany. Then, I got the job in Colorado that I really wanted and went back."

"This is the famous Erie Canal?" Bip asked in wonderment.

"Yep, the original," JC said. They had stopped on the bridge and peered down at a stagnant body of water. It was choked by green pondweed and water chestnut.

"I can't believe that I'm looking at the real Erie Canal," Bip said. "I thought it was long gone."

"Most people think that. The water is relatively clear for about three weeks each spring," he told his friends. "That's when it's fun to kayak here."

They followed a dirt path on the other side of the bridge. It had marshy water on both sides. Cattails and tall swamp plants provided a natural fence between the water and the path.

At the end of the marsh, they turned right and followed a trail entirely carpeted by grass. The way was still bordered on both sides by tall reeds, high grass and wildflowers.

"It's beautiful," Robin said. "We don't have anything this green back home."

She swatted at her neck, causing a small burst of blood as she crushed a mosquito.

"Oh yeah, there's that too," JC said. "This place is full of mosquitos."

They walked and waved bugs away for a short time longer. Then, they found the spot Investigator Foot had directed them to. It was marked by a small yellow ribbon staked into the ground.

"We've been talking about John Thurston," Bip said. "It's kind of weird to finally stand where the poor guy was found."

"His soul is long gone," JC said.

"Do you think he could be here, watching us?" Robin asked. "His spirit, I mean."

"We could find out," Bip answered. "Did you bring a Ouija board?"

"Ha, ha," Robin responded, knowing she was being mocked.

JC looked over the lay of the land. He gazed at the groves of trees that had grown since the last days that it was used as farmland.

He looked north. The Erie Canal was just beyond those trees. He looked south. The Mohawk River was close, just over a grassy bank and some wetlands.

"I want to walk this way, a little bit," JC said.

Bip remained behind to shoot footage of the spot where John Thurston's body was found. He said he would catch up. Robin walked with JC.

"What do you have in mind?" she asked.

"I'm testing a theory," he said as he followed a less-traveled path. It would lead to the Mohawk.

On each side of them, there were stumps and fallen trees tangled in the tall grass and plants. But the grass was short on the path they followed.

"The grass path is mowed by the town," JC told Robin. "Including this one leading to the river. Most of the town's underground aquifer is right under our feet. Town crews mow the paths to keep certain points accessible. You notice the paths are about as wide as a pickup truck?"

The ground was getting moist as they approached the river. The tall grass off the path was matted down.

"That tall grass has been underwater," he said as he swatted at a mosquito. He stopped and looked back where Bip was collecting images for the night's story.

"And it leads right to the body," JC muttered.

"You've figured it out?" Robin asked.

"Part of it," he told her with a smile creasing his face. "He floated here. I worked in radio news for a short time when I came back here after college. At the end of winter, the Mohawk River often flooded over its banks. It was not a rare occurrence."

He led Robin back toward Bip. They wanted to inform him of the shots they'd need.

"All the attention when the Mohawk floods is on Schenectady, which is just upriver and on the other side," JC told her. "There's a colonial-era neighborhood there called The Stockade that frequently floods. People live there. The flood threatens their old homes.

"But the flood also pours water into this preserve," he said. "The soil is barely above the river's water level to begin with. And this part of the preserve is submerged every spring. Most people don't even know, because there are no houses down here. It doesn't get any news coverage."

"And you think John Thurston floated here?" Robin asked.

"I'm sure of it," JC told her. "He didn't walk here with one ski boot on and he wasn't carried here. There would be no reason for his killer to carry him this far to hide his body. That would be too much work."

JC and Robin reached Bip and he followed them to the Mohawk, to shoot footage there.

"Thurston was last seen alive on January fifteenth," JC told them. "Someone killed him, probably that night. Then he was thrown into the river. He probably didn't fall into the river and die, because the autopsy would have found water in his lungs and they would have known he floated here. He was thrown into the river after he died. But he floated here. He followed the path of least resistance, including that grass path leading from the river to this very spot."

# 41

"This is a new bridge since I lived here," JC said.

They drove over the bridge from Clifton Park into Niskayuna.

"What's that?" Bip asked, pointing to a wall made of masoned stones.

"That's more of the Erie Canal," JC told him.

"This is a really cool place," Bip marveled.

"And your tour guide is a complete history nerd," Robin said with a smile.

They pulled their rental car up to a house on a tree-shaded street. The house was wide and two stories tall, made of red brick with white window trim. It was John Thurston's house.

279

"Detective London told me that it's empty," JC said. "Thurston's kids inherited the house but they haven't decided what to do with it."

They rang the doorbell anyway. No answer.

They peered in the windows. The grass needed cutting and there were small branches on the driveway from the last windstorm.

Bip collected his camera from the trunk of the car and began shooting pictures.

"Are you going to buy it?" a voice came from next door.

JC looked to see a man in a button-down white shirt and khakis. He looked like he had just returned home from a white-collar job. His hands rested on his hips.

"We're just looking," JC said. He approached the man and introduced himself. He told the neighbor that they were a news team from Denver. He informed the man that Thurston was a Denver native.

"He was a nice guy," the man said, and introduced himself as Tom Morford. "It came as a shock to learn that he was murdered."

"When did you last speak with him?" JC inquired.

"Our driveways are next to each other," Morford stated. "We had small conversations often. We must have spoken a few days before he passed away. He asked me about Red Bank in New Jersey. He had a conference coming up there. I grew up near Red Bank. I told him about the Molly Pitcher Inn, a really nice old hotel where his conference was being held."

"The police spoke with you?" JC asked.

"Yeah," the man said. "I didn't have anything to tell him, though. I didn't see anything unusual. I guess they don't think that he was murdered in his house."

"No, they don't," JC confirmed.

"He was going to join the yacht club," the neighbor said.

"Excuse my ignorance," JC said. "I haven't lived here for a long time. What yacht club?"

"Oh, that makes it sound fancier than it is," Morford smiled. "We own regular boats. None would be considered a yacht. We have ski boats, pontoon boats, pleasure boats, a few nice old Chris-Crafts. It's on the Mohawk River, a few miles from here. John wanted to buy a boat and I invited him to join the yacht club."

"Did I see it?" Robin asked. "I saw a lot of boats moored on the river by that bridge we went over."

"Yes," the man said. "Rexford Bridge. Like I say, it's only about three miles from here. I think he was going to join. It's kind of coincidental. The police looked at our surveillance video at the club and I thought I saw his car. Maybe he was looking over the club."

"You saw his car on the surveillance video?" JC repeated.

"Well, a piece of what might have been his car," the neighbor clarified. "See, we have surveillance cameras at the club, but most are trained on the boats. They're the most valuable things on the property, get it?"

"Makes sense," JC confirmed.

"Right," Morford said. "So police looked at all the surveillance video, I'm told. I wasn't there. But one weekend, the club executives let us sit down and look at the surveillance video. It's not often you're involved in a murder investigation. We were just curious."

"And you saw John Thurston's Mercedes parked at the club?" JC asked.

"Not exactly," the man said with a grin. "We watched the video, and like the police said, it didn't seem to show much. But I noticed that there was a car parked on a stretch of gravel on the land next to the yacht club. You could barely see the car, only the nose of it really. But later, I got to thinking. The nose had a Mercedes logo on it like those cars do, don't they?"

"They do," JC agreed. "You told the police about this?"

"No, I didn't," the neighbor said. He smiled and looked at the ground. "I thought about it, but I figured it was just my imagination getting away with me. I didn't want to waste their time."

Bip joined them and told JC that he had all the shots of Thurston's house that they would need. JC asked the man for directions to the gravel patch where he might have seen Thurston's car.

"And you didn't hear or see anything at Mr. Thurston's house on the night of January fifteenth?" JC asked.

"Not a thing," Morford told him. "The police asked me that. I would have told them if I'd seen anything."

Bip drove the rental car, reversing the directions they had followed to Thurston's house. But they pulled off of a traffic circle on the near side of the bridge and into a small asphalt parking lot.

A short dirt path led them onto an old stone pier reaching one hundred feet into, and thirty feet above, the Mohawk River. The pier was fenced-in so no one would fall into the river.

"What is this?" Bip asked.

"It's part of an aqueduct for the old Erie Canal," JC told him. "The canal was so busy, they had overpasses like modern highways do. This one took barges over the Mohawk River from Niskayuna into Clifton Park."

"This is so cool," Bip said, and started shooting footage.

"Are we on the right side?" Robin asked JC.

"I don't think so," he said. "The killer would have had to lift him over the fence. It's a tall fence. I think he must have been parked over there." JC pointed across the river to another towering stone structure standing in the water at the edge of the riverbank. Next to it was the yacht club.

They climbed back into their car and crossed Rexford Bridge. Following the directions of John Thurston's neighbor, they took their first right. There was a gravel lot just short of the entrance to the yacht club.

Climbing out of their car, they followed a path on foot. It was composed of dirt and broken gray asphalt and led to the river. At the end of the path, only a rusty guardrail separated them from the water.

"They call that a prism support," Robin said, pointing to a massive limestone ruin in the water, only twenty yards from shore.

JC was surprised by her command of old canal construction. But then he saw she was on her phone searching the internet.

"I think it held a timber canal bed that held the water and carried the barges over the river," she added.

"That makes sense," JC agreed. "Timber would be a lot more forgiving on the side of a barge than limestone."

JC looked to his left. He could see a section of floating pier belonging to the yacht club. Otherwise, the spot was secluded by an overgrown stone wall. It was the east side of the canal. It once held water.

Bip started shooting. JC and Robin stepped over the guardrail and sat on a containing wall. Their feet dangled above the river water.

They admired the craftsmanship of the towering masonry arches that remained.

"Built in 1828, they tore it down in 1918," she read out loud.

"Otherwise, it would still be here," JC speculated. "They built it to last."

"It's a good spot for fishing," JC said.

"Or a romantic picnic," Robin said with a smile.

She rose, slapped the dirt off of her jeans and walked to the overgrowth, bent over and emerged with a bottle. She came back to JC and sat down next to him.

"It's a wine bottle," she said. "I'll share it if there's anything left."

"Gross," he said.

"I told you this was a picnic spot," she told him. She looked at the faded label on the dark bottle.

"It's cabernet," she said. "I can barely read it."

JC smiled and glanced at her treasure. Something stirred his memory.

"Can you read what kind of wine it is?" he asked.

"C-A-R," she struggled to see the print on the black label. The letters were printed in faded gold or yellow. She held the bottle at different angles to the sun, to see it better. "Something-something-N-E-T. Reserve. It's Car-something-net Reserve."

"Does it have a year?" he asked.

"Something-16?" she read.

"2016. A good year," he said. "One of Melody Church's favorites. It's Carmenet Reserve. She has a shelf full of them back at her house."

"You're shitting me," Robin said. Her shocked eyes were steadied on JC.

"It's about a ten-foot drop from here," JC said, peering from his seat of stone to the water below. "She could roll him."

"But why?" Robin pleaded.

"I don't know, but it's her," JC said solemnly. "Deborah Sampson said she saw Thurston's car entering Melody's driveway many times. Not only before the death of Josh, who Thurston might have had business with, but after."

"Do you think she was having an affair with Thurston?" Robin asked.

"It's possible," JC told her. "And I remember when I told Melody about the murder investigation in New York, when we were first told to cover it. She asked me who had been arrested. I told her it was Larry Gleichman. But she never asked me who had been murdered. It was John Thurston. But it was like she already knew."

"Because she killed him," Robin said, still shocked.

JC pulled the phone from his pocket and gave Investigator John Foot a call.

"Did the coroner find water in Thurston's lungs?" JC asked.

"He did not," Foot answered.

JC told the detective everything they had learned and surmised that day. The investigator listened intently.

"We're going to want that bottle," the investigator said. "I suppose you touched it. Just put it down. We're going to want to test it for DNA. I'm coming to you right now. I want to see this for myself."

It took Foot about an hour to arrive at the Erie Canal aqueduct on the Clifton Park side. That gave Robin time to make some calls.

She called Josh Church's literary agent. The woman told Robin that Melody had informed her of their presence in Stonestead.

"Melody tells me that she does some book signings," Robin said into the phone.

"Yes," the agent said. "Readers loved Josh's books and love to talk to Melody. She's the closest they can get to Josh any longer."

"Did Melody have a book signing on January fifteenth or sixteenth?" Robin asked.

The agent asked Robin to be patient and she would pull out an older calendar. She said that Melody kept her informed of her personal appearances, just so they could stay on the same page. Everything was written down.

"She did!" the agent said after looking at a calendar. "She had one in Schenectady on the sixteenth. It was at the Open Door Bookstore on Jay Street. Are you familiar with it?"

"That was the day after Thurston was last seen," Robin told JC.

"So, she wasn't in Stonestead," JC said. "She was here."

"Maybe even having a picnic the night before with Thurston," Robin said. "Right here."

"But why would she kill him?" JC asked aloud.

While Robin was on the phone, JC called Detective London in Niskayuna and told him of their scenario.

"What color hair does Melody Church have?" the detective asked.

"Blonde," JC told him.

"I didn't tell you this," the detective informed him, "but as well as Thurston's house was scrubbed, we found some long blonde hairs. They were between the mattress and the headboard in the master bedroom. We've never found a match. They do not match Thurston's ex-wife."

Investigator Foot arrived and looked over JC's findings.

"I'm going to call in divers," the investigator said.

# 42

"Eat Bigfoot Here," a sign said. "We Already Caught Him, You Might As Well Eat Him."

JC, Robin and Bip were driving back to Stonestead. They passed through an area that said it was home to the East Coast's version of Bigfoot. They stopped to pick up sandwiches at the Bigfoot Subway Shop.

They ate in the car as they drove for home. The forested roadside provided a pleasing backdrop. And plenty of places for Bigfoot to hide.

"I do not feel so well," JC said after finishing his sandwich.

"You're vaccinated and boostered. Is that what it feels like?" asked Robin with concern.

"The gourmet Bigfoot liverwurst sandwich didn't agree with you?" Bip laughed.

"If they actually did catch Bigfoot, would they really just throw him on a spit and eat him?" Robin asked.

"You mean, that wasn't really Bigfoot?" Bip asked and laughed some more.

They were racing home to meet the live truck on loan from the TV station in Burlington. JC was writing his script. A number of times, he asked Robin how to phrase something he wanted to report.

"What are you doing?" Robin blurted. "You never ask anyone to help write your story. We collaborate on the story but, I don't mean to be rude, you treat your copy like it's your private domain."

"They're my words. They're sacred," JC said with a smile. "Regardless, I'm asking you how *you* would say it."

They talked over the story and what they could and would report.

"Here," he said handing the notebook to Robin in the backseat. "You write it. I don't feel well."

Robin voiced protest as JC took off a fleece vest he was wearing. He rolled it up, placed it under his head and leaned against the car door. He closed his eyes.

The drive would get them back to the inn about an hour before their live broadcast. They'd need to work quickly. JC could record his finished script as soon as they got up to Bip's room. That would give Bip about a half hour to edit the piece. He would still need to feed the finished work to the station in Denver and place JC in front of the camera.

"We found a knife," the voice on the other end of JC's phone told him.

The voice belonged to Saratoga County Investigator John Foot. JC waved at Robin, behind him, to return his notebook. He wanted to take notes.

"Divers found it in about an hour," he said. "The water isn't very deep, there's so much silt there. It also allows a lot of sun to shine on the shallow bottom. You guys did nice work."

"Do you think you'll find any fingerprints or DNA from the killer?" JC asked.

"Doubtful," the investigator replied. "But we'll take a look. Just by the look of the knife, I'd bet it fits into Thurston's wound."

JC asked the investigator if he could put the call on speakerphone, so his producer could hear this. John Foot agreed and they discussed other aspects of the case.

"Something else you'll find interesting," the investigator informed them. "We found a gray ski boot. It was only about fifteen yards downriver. We'll check, but it's going to be Thurston's. The divers tell me it's the first time they've ever found a ski boot in a river."

JC thanked Foot for the call and mutual congratulations were exchanged.

"Again, you guys did a great job," the investigator told them. "We appreciate the tip."

With the call over, JC handed the notebook back to Robin in the backseat.

"Add the discovery of the knife to the script where you think it belongs," he told her. And he rolled over to go to sleep.

When the rental car was about fifteen minutes outside of Stonestead, JC woke up from his nap.

"Someone else has to do the live shot," he said.

He could see the sudden snap in Bip's neck as he swung his head toward him. JC could only hear Robin's panicked wail from the backseat.

"What are you talking about?" she screeched.

JC spoke quietly. He used his words efficiently, as though one word too many might cause his Bigfoot liverwurst to make a return appearance.

"Well, if you don't," Robin said, invoking all of her producer might, "who will?"

"It has to be one of you two," JC whispered.

"Well then it's going to be Bip," snapped Robin.

"Do you know how to work my camera?" Bip said and turned to give her a smile.

"Then, it's you," JC declared, closing his eyes after the decision was made.

"C'mon, JC! You've been through tougher things," she cried. "A guy tried to kill you just the other day."

"Shhh," he said. "I need to sleep or I'm going spew in Bip's car, probably on Bip."

Bip cast a frightening look over his shoulder at Robin and put a finger over his lips, signaling her to be quiet.

"Look over the story that I wrote," JC said softly without opening his eyes. "Make the changes that you think are appropriate and familiarize yourself with it. In about five minutes, you're going up to Bip's room to record your soundtrack. Bip doesn't have time for you to do ten takes. Get it right on the first one."

He looked back toward her and smiled, to take the sting out of that last part. Then he settled back into his car seat and closed his eyes.

"Shit!" he heard a terrified voice say behind him.

JC trailed them up the stairs of the Flamstead Inn. He dragged his feet into Bip's room and told them that he was going to bed.

"You got this?" he said, grasping Robin's elbow and looking into her eyes.

"Yeah," she said, sounding both deflated and terrified.

"Give yourself a few minutes to use my makeup kit to get the shine off your nose and forehead," he said.

"Gee thanks," she said. "Now I look hideous?"

"No, you look beautiful. But the camera can be your friend or your enemy," JC told her. "It sees a little makeup like we see chocolate chip cookies. Yummy."

"JC," she whined, "Please do this."

"After you put on your makeup, go down on the porch where you're going to do the live shot and stand where you'll be when you do your report. Get accustomed to your surroundings, then nothing will distract or surprise you when you're trying to concentrate and you're actually on TV."

He put his head down like he had exhausted himself by giving her those instructions. He stopped at the door.

"You're going to be magnificent," he croaked.

Robin had informed the TV station back in Denver of the change. They were alarmed but assured that JC could not go on the air that night.

Robin had no choice. She reviewed her script, applied her makeup and took her position in front of Bip's camera. When he gave Robin the cue to begin talking, her name appeared below her on the TV screen and she flawlessly introduced the package of material they had recorded.

The story revealed the answer to the mystery of how John Thurston's body reached Vischer Ferry Preserve, downriver from where he was murdered. She also reported that the murder weapon had been found by sheriff's divers, only a few hours before.

But Robin did not report, as she agreed with JC, that Melody Church was a suspect. That would have to wait until Melody's arrest or at least until she was summoned by police to be questioned.

JC had slipped down the stairs and stood by the hotel's entrance, watching Robin's broadcast. She sounded smart and she looked beautiful. He knew that at that moment, back home in Colorado, she was in full ownership of television screens in thousands of homes. The audience would be captivated.

When her live shot was over and Bip informed her that she was "clear," she stuck her tongue out and nearly fell into the chair next to her. Then a smile grew on her face.

"It's kind of an adrenaline rush, the first time." The voice came from behind her. She turned and saw JC holding three beer bottles in one hand. He was beaming at her. The smile fell from her face.

"You faked!" she said accusingly. "You were never sick!"

"I recovered," he said. "I'm quite resilient."

"You lied," she told him.

"Yes, I lied about the Bigfoot liverwurst sandwich," he told her. "It was delicious."

She approached him and punched him in the chest. He softly grabbed her waist with his free arm.

"You were magnificent," he said.

"You jerk," she said, hitting him again, gently. Then she kissed him.

The bottles of beer that JC distributed to his friends were from Weird Window Brewing in South Burlington.

"A star is born," Bip said as he proposed a toast to Robin.

"Uh, oh," Bip then uttered.

JC and Robin looked at him and then looked in the direction of his gaze. They saw Melody Church leaving a restaurant a few doors down.

They made eye contact. She gave them a small wave and a smile. They waved back. She had been at dinner with friends while Robin had broadcast their findings to their audience in Denver.

She had no idea that they had uncovered her misdeeds. But she gave JC a long look as she walked to her car.

Robin's phone rang.

"Hi Faith," Robin said. JC's head turned, hearing that the call was from the public defender for Larry Gleichman.

"Yes, he's here. I'll tell him. Thank you, Faith. He always likes a new fan. We'll just watch his head swell a little more," Robin said, giggling into the phone. Then she hung up.

"She says that she has grown mighty fond of you," Robin told JC after taking a sip from her beer. "She says that you may have just won her case. She showed Larry Gleichman the picture of Melody Church. And he says *that* is the woman at the fast-food place who left the credit card on the table."

# 43

"S o, are we done?" Rocky asked JC.

"I don't think so," the reporter told his assignment editor back in Denver. "I know that sounds crazy, and I've already been proven wrong once. But I think there is something more."

"How long is this going to take?" Rocky asked. "What I mean is, how much is this going to cost us?"

"I think we're close to something no one else is even looking for," JC said. "I'll know in a day or two. You can bring us home by the end of the weekend."

"So, how are you feeling?" the assignment editor inquired.

"I'm fine," JC told him. "It was just some food poisoning. Robin was great though, wasn't she?"

Robin was sitting across from him at Molly's. She was on another call, but she'd heard JC and gave him a face, wrinkling her nose. He had not seen that face before. He thought it was pretty cute.

"She was fantastic," Rocky replied. "We all took notice. So, what will you have for us tonight?"

"It's not even ten in the morning," JC told his insatiable assignment editor. "Over seven thousand people die in this country every day. Only one of them has to be worthy of a headline story. The odds are in your favor."

"You make me out to be a ghoul," Rocky laughed. "But I'm going to take that as a promise."

JC disconnected the call. Robin was off the phone too. He joined her conversation with Bip.

"You've become a movie star back in Colorado," JC told Robin. She rolled her eyes.

"I have news," Robin said proudly. "There is going to be a discreet conversation conducted in about an hour between investigators from New York and Melody Church. John Foot is on his way."

"Where is this going to be?" JC asked.

"They have a conference room reserved at Mont Vert," Robin told them. "Her attorney insisted that this be low-key, otherwise they weren't going to cooperate."

"In an hour?" JC repeated.

"Yes," she said.

"Well, that may work to our advantage," the reporter told her. "You two can stake out Mont Vert and get some footage of everyone's arrival for the police interview."

"And what will you be doing?" she asked. "Are you going back to bed?"

"Nope," he told her. "I'll be committing a felony."

"Oh, I hope it's one of my favorites," she answered sarcastically.

"Breaking and entering," he told her.

They departed from Molly's. Bip and Robin collected gear the news photographer would need for the stakeout at Mont Vert.

The three of them drove to Mont Vert and selected a spot in the parking lot where they could keep an eye on the two preferred entrances to the resort village.

It was a typical journalist stakeout. JC had done it a hundred times over his career.

They waited inside their rental car so they didn't attract unwanted attention. Bip had his camera at his side. All three heads were on swivels, inspecting each car that pulled into the lot and the people who climbed out of those cars.

After about a half hour, their patience paid off.

"I think that's her," Robin said, watching a car that passed behind them.

They followed the vehicle with their eyes to the spot where it parked. Bip leaped out of the car and approached. His camera was on his shoulder and he was already rolling when Melody Church emerged with another woman, presumably her lawyer.

"I'll be back as soon as I can," JC told Robin as she got out of the car.

"I'll call you if she leaves before you're back," she said.

He pulled out of the lot, casting a glance at Bip and Robin as they walked ahead of Melody, gathering their footage. Melody Church walked with her head down. Her attorney tried to walk between her client and the news photographer, but Bip easily eluded her.

JC drove back toward Stonestead. He took a turn into the Stone District and pulled into Melody Church's driveway.

The car kicked up gravel as he pulled up in front of her house and got out of the car. He tried the doorknob on the front entrance but it was locked. He walked around the back to the garden.

He tried the handle on the French doors and it gave way, allowing him access to the library. He looked both ways, but knew the home was secluded. There was no one to witness his crime.

"Hello?" he called out just in case. "Melody?" There was no answer.

The neat stack of papers sat on the desk of Josh Church. But JC walked to a set of shelves loaded with books.

He scanned the titles. He found the book he was looking for and pulled it away from the others.

It was the home-printed journal describing the flowers and plants of Stonestead and its surrounding mountains. It fell open to the page he was looking for. It must have been opened there many times. The page floated free from the spine of the book.

JC placed the page on Josh's desk and pulled out his phone.

He photographed the page, turned it over and photographed that side too. He confirmed that he could read the page when he enlarged the image on his phone.

Placing the floating page back into the book, he delivered it back to the spot on the shelf where he had found it.

Exiting the home, JC pulled the French doors closed behind him. He was glad to be leaving the scene of his crime.

He took a few steps but then stopped. He looked across the garden.

"She might destroy it," he muttered to himself.

He began walking toward the shed.

Opening the door, he allowed his eyes to adjust to the darkness and took a step toward the shelves. There, he found the white container that looked like a beer cup. The filter was still inside, as were the dried purple petals.

He pulled an empty oversized sandwich bag from his pocket, the kind he often carried. He placed the container in the bag and zipped it shut.

Emerging from the shed, he closed the door and walked toward his car at a hurried pace. Again, he looked in every direction to assure himself that he hadn't been seen.

In his car, he placed the bagged container in a beverage holder on the console between the front seats. He backed the car up, again hearing the gravel under his tires, and pulled out of the driveway.

He breathed a sigh of relief when he'd escaped without detection.

Except for a pair of eyes watching from a witch window.

# 44

"Their lives can never be restored. But one hundred and thirty years later, the mystery surrounding their murders has been solved. I'm JC Snow, in Stonestead, Vermont."

"Phew," George Earl said.

Bip leaned back from his laptop where he had just replayed their story about Stonestead's historic fires. The news crew had promised a showing for the town historian. They did so in Bip's room at the Flamstead Inn.

Bip handed Earl a thumb drive.

"That's your copy," JC told him. "You can dub it or do anything you want with it. We appreciate all your help."

"We're going to show it at the next historical society meeting," George told them. "The whole town will come to see it, I venture."

"You mind taking a look at something else before you go?" JC asked him.

He pulled out his phone, hit the icon with a camera on it and sorted through pictures.

"Have you ever heard of this place?" JC asked. He handed the town historian his camera. It displayed a portion of a page he had photographed at Melody Church's house.

"Where did you get this?" George asked. "I've never seen this before."

"I was thumbing through a book," JC answered vaguely.

"It sounds like Reindeer Peak," George said after reading and thinking for a moment. "It's an old ski area near here. It closed about thirty years ago. The lodge burned down about fifteen years ago."

"Can you tell me how to get there?" JC asked.


"George tells me that all you have to worry about is Lyme ticks, poison ivy, snakes, falling in a hole that you are not likely to see, and tetanus, maybe," JC told them. "There are probably a lot of old rusty nails and cables."

"Did you say snakes?" Robin asked.

"You had me at tetanus!" Bip laughed. "Count me in."

"I hate boys," Robin said. "You always want to get dirty and infected. Fine, I'll go."

They drove out of Stonestead in a direction opposite of Mont Vert. It was a winding, two-lane road. At a turnoff, the road became dirt.

They passed homes, occasionally. They were old ski chalets. Some were A-frames and some had lace moldings. The structures looked like they belonged in a Bavarian alpine village.

The homes appeared to be inhabited, though their location was no longer ideal. It reminded JC of a ski resort ghost town.

Their car approached a road marked by two stone pillars. A rusty steel cable looked as though it used to stretch between the two pillars, but it lay down on the hard dirt.

They advanced over a hill and past a pond. The ruins of a small building stood by the road. In faded wood, large letters spelling E-I-N-D-E remained on the side of the structure.

"Reindeer," JC supposed out loud.

They drove as far as they could drive on the dirt and stone path. It ended in a circular turnaround in front of a stone foundation and some charred timbers.

"That must be the old lodge," Robin said.

They parked and JC was climbing on the ruins while Bip and Robin were still considering what they should bring for the hike.

"I love this stuff!" JC cried out to them.

He looked over the stone and burned wood that remained of the site. He considered where the cafeteria was and where the kitchen should have been.

It hadn't been a large lodge. The only portion of the structure that remained intact was the stone fireplace and its tall chimney.

JC pictured weary skiers who used to crowd around the fire, clutching cups of hot chocolate.

"It opened as a ski area in 1938," Robin read from her phone. "It closed in the 1980s. It wasn't very big. It had one chairlift and a Poma lift."

Bip was busy shooting footage of the ruins of the lodge. He loved this stuff too.

"I'll bet they never had a snowboarder," Bip said.

"I'll bet they used them for human sacrifices," JC replied with a laugh.

The ski runs leading down to the lodge were now thick with plants and young maple and birch trees.

When Bip told them he was finished shooting the lodge, they turned their attention to the hike to the top.

"Hopefully," JC said after pushing through only about twenty yards of thick brush, "we'll find a deer trail to follow."

They didn't. They proceeded slowly up the hillside. Tall grass and horseweed was chest-high.

JC brought the book on plants and flowers that he'd purchased at the bookstore in Chester. He pointed out oxeye daisies and joe pye weed.

"That's gross!" Robin cried. She cringed at a collection of tall plants with spit covering the leaves.

"That's from a spittlebug," JC told her, holding his book above the tall growth.

Their feet were buried beneath the thick cover of plants and grass.

"Luckily, it's not that far to the peak," JC told them. "The ski area only had seven hundred feet vertical."

"What's that?" Robin asked, pointing uphill.

"Cool," Bip proclaimed and aimed his camera in that direction.

Rusty cables hung a few feet off the ground. Ahead, they saw a structure leaning over toward the pull of the cables. It narrowed at the top.

"It's an old Poma lift," JC told them.

They stopped to allow Bip to shoot his images.

"You said snakes, didn't you?" Robin asked, looking down at her feet. They were unseeable through all the ground cover.

"Here," JC said, offering a hand and pulling her up on top of a log. They looked down on the lodge that was growing smaller as they climbed.

They hiked above the skeleton of the Poma lift, pushing through goldenrod and something JC identified as obedient plant. They could see no sign of the chairlift.

After an hour of hiking, the slope leveled off. There was a small body of water.

"It must be the glacier pond they used for snowmaking," Robin said, reading from her phone.

JC approached the glacier pond, with its moist shoreline feeding a different set of plants and flowers.

He stared at them. The only thing moving was his eyes. There were yellows, the occasional orange. Lots of blues. He recognized fireweed.

His eyes stopped on a flower he had never seen. It was a beautiful shape, something he couldn't imagine was sculpted without the aid of human hands.

A slight breeze was blowing. It made the tall grass and the flowers dance in the sun.

"What is it," Robin asked as she walked to JC's side.

"It's called devil's helmet," he told her. He spoke softly and pointed to it. "The purple one."

"It does look like a helmet," she said.

"There are other names," he told her. "Like friar's cap and monk's hood. It needs water. And for some reason, it only wants to grow at elevation, around here."

"It's poison?" she asked quietly.

"Yep," he told her. "In Alaska, the Aleuts would grind it up and use it when they hunted for whales. They'd soak the tips of their spears. The poison would paralyze the whale and it would drown."

JC was speaking reverently. Robin supposed it was because his quest had brought him to the answer he had been seeking. It was an awful end, wrapped in a beautiful package.

"Its real name is Aconite. The root is most toxic," he said. "He must have suffered a terrible lingering death."

# 45

They caught John Foot before he left town. When Robin called his number, he was visiting with Sipp Ives.

"JC says that you'll both want to hear this," she told them. "We're on our way."

As they entered Sipp's office, JC placed three of the purple specimens of devil's helmet on a piece of paper on the police chief's desk. Next to it, he placed the plastic bag containing a beer cup-sized container. It was the water filter from under Melody's sink. It was stained purple and, he suspected, held more than enough deadly residue from the plant's root to be used as evidence.

JC told the law officers where the items had been. And he told them of his findings.

"Melody and Josh Church hiked a lot," JC told the men. "They must have found this at the top of Reindeer Peak. A book in Josh's library fell open to the page about devil's helmet."

"She ground it up and put it in the water filter," JC told them. "There are two faucets on the kitchen sink. She was careful to avoid using the smaller faucet for *herself*. But she was just as careful to train *him* to *use* it.

She told him that he wanted to use the faucet with the filter. That's a portion of the filter in front of you. I have the name of a plumber who will identify it."

The two officers looked at the container with the black filter at the bottom. It looked like a small hockey puck.

"Josh drank tea all day and every day," JC continued. "Davey Kay told me that, as did Melody. But she wouldn't always be there to prepare it for him. The filter was the perfect vehicle for the poison. She'd grind up the root, some flower petals seemed to get mixed in, place it in the filter and he'd unknowingly be preparing his own deadly mix."

"When we were at her house," Robin explained, "she was careful to stop JC from filling a teakettle from the poisoned faucet. You should also inspect a copper teakettle on a shelf above the sink. We believe you'll find it contaminated with the poison, too."

"The symptoms of Aconite poisoning include weakness, nausea, diarrhea, breathing problems, numbness and eventually heart problems," JC continued. "It wouldn't happen all at once. It was a slow, inexplicable death."

"Josh's doctor told me an hour ago that Josh showed up at his office with all of those symptoms," Robin said. "He would get nauseous in the morning and then appear to improve during the day. But the symptoms always returned. It must have been awful. The doctor told me that they could never arrive at a diagnosis that proved helpful in treating Mr. Church. His official cause of death was a heart attack."

The two law officers looked at each other.

"Is that it?" Chief Ives asked.

"I think so," JC said. "For now. May we do a quick interview on camera? Something we can use for the news this evening?"

"Let's hold off on that for right now," Sipp Ives told them. "But I'd remain available, if I were you."

As JC, Robin and Bip walked out of the chief's office and past the security glass protecting the administrative assistant/receptionist, they heard Sipp Ives call her with a request.

"Would you please call the sergeant out on patrol and ask him to bring in Melody Church," he asked her. "I believe she may be found at her home in the Stone District."

The television news crew did better than remain available. Their car never left the small parking lot at the side of the police station.

When Melody Church was escorted back to the police station, she was not handcuffed. She wasn't the type who would dart into the woods and lead law officers on a two-week manhunt.

She looked at JC as she was walked past Bip's camera. Her face had a small smile on it, confused between greeting her friend and her captor. She disappeared through a white door on the side of the building used only by police officers.

It was less than two hours before she emerged from that white door again. This time, she was wearing handcuffs and was escorted toward the back of the police car.

Bip started his camera rolling. Robin pointed a microphone toward the suspect.

"I meant what I said the first time we met," she told JC. "I told you that I loved him. I just couldn't stand watching him decay like my mother did. He would have hated it and so would I. He was a wonderful man."

The police officer covered her head with his hand so that she wouldn't hit the roof as she was seated in the car.

"I have a long life ahead of me," she told JC as she pulled her legs into the vehicle. "I have time to start over. I was so young when I married Josh."

The law officer closed the rear door of the car. JC could still see her through the window. She looked at him. He thought she was looking for understanding.

As the police car pulled away, Sipp Ives walked out on the stoop of the side door to the police station.

"I've got a minute now," he said to the news crew. They followed him through the white door and into his office.

"She's in handcuffs," JC said as he took his seat and Bip began recording.

"She's confessed to everything," the police chief informed them. Saratoga County Investigator John Foot was seated next to the police chief.

"She was confronted with the evidence in the death of her husband, Josh Church, and told us she was responsible," the chief said into the camera. "We'll complete the investigation, but we're confident that the water filter and a teakettle will produce evidence of a poison and the remains of Mr. Church will show evidence of the same poison."

Sipp looked toward the investigator from Upstate New York.

"We have also notified Ms. Church that she will be arraigned on charges in the murder of John Thurston of Niskayuna, New York," Investigator Foot announced.

"Ms. Church has confessed to killing Mr. Thurston," Foot disclosed. "We believe that Mr. Thurston and Ms. Church had been having an affair for some time before Mr. Church's death.

"At a picnic on the night of January fifteenth," the investigator continued, "Mr. Thurston became aware of Ms. Church's role in the death of Mr. Church. Mr. Thurston was not in agreeance on her methods. They had an argument and Ms. Church stabbed Thurston, fatally."

"She threw him into the river?" JC asked.

"That would appear to be the case," John Foot replied. "The recovery of the murder weapon and an article of Mr. Thurston's clothing, namely one ski boot, places the crime at the Erie Canal aqueduct in Clifton Park. We believe that Mr. Thurston's body floated down the Mohawk River, including over a sizable dam, and came to rest in the Vischer Ferry Preserve in Clifton Park during spring floods."

"And Mr. Gleichman?" JC asked.

"Mr. Gleichman remains in custody for using a stolen credit card," Foot continued. "He has informed us, through his attorney, that he will testify that Ms. Church is the individual who left the Thurston credit card at a business in Niskayuna. The investigation into Mr. Gleichman's connection to the murder of John Thurston has been closed and will not be prosecuted."

Bip was wrapping up his gear and JC continued to talk with the two law officers.

"How did Thurston's car get back in his garage and Melody get back to Stonestead without anyone noticing?" JC asked.

"It had been their plan, Thurston's and Melody Church's, all along to take two cars to his house that night," Foot told him. "They had been skiing here at Mont Vert that day. He had to drive to New Jersey the next day for a business meeting, but they wanted to spend the night together. She had a book signing in Schenectady the next day. So they each drove their own cars to that picnic site."

Investigator Foot stopped speaking. He asked the chief if there was something to drink available.

"Two doors down the hall," Sipp told him. "There's a refrigerator with water and soda. Take anything you need."

The investigator left after asking if anyone else wanted something.

"I can finish answering your question," the chief told the news crew. "They drove two cars to the picnic site, which was supposed to be a romantic surprise on Mr. Thurston's part. Anyway, after Thurston's demise, she drove his car to his house. It was only a three-mile walk and you said yourself that she was an avid hiker. So she walked back to the picnic site and drove her own car to Thurston's house and put it in the garage unseen. She spent the night scrubbing away all the evidence, in the house and in Thurston's car. She left before daylight and the neighbors say they never saw a thing."

"She was never seen with Thurston skiing at Mont Vert?" JC asked.

"She probably was," Sipp responded. "But they were both probably wrapped up in cold-weather gear. And no one knew who Thurston was. They didn't give it much thought, I guess."

"I showed her a picture of Thurston's car," JC told the chief. "She said she didn't recognize it."

"She told us the same thing," Chief Ives responded. "She was lying."

Investigator Foot returned to the room.

"I don't know if I mentioned this," he told JC and Robin, "Melody even acknowledged that she lured Gleichman to that credit card. She found it in her wallet after leaving Thurston's house and did everything she could to get him to steal it. She just wanted it out of her possession."

JC and his crew rose from their seats to leave.

"Nice work, guys," Investigator Foot told them. "Sipp wasn't wrong about you."

"That was a pretty good hunch," Sipp said to JC. "You remember what you asked me?"

JC remained silent.

"You asked me," Sipp repeated, "should I harbor any suspicions about the death of Joshua Church."

# 46

"You were having that dream again," Robin told him.

"The medieval one. The knight carried out of the woods on his shield," he said. "How did you know?"

"You were huffing and puffing," she told him. "I woke you up."

"Sorry," he said. "I wish I knew what it means."

"I believe that our ancestors pass things along in our DNA," she said. "It's like the little kid who sat down and played a concerto on a piano, when he didn't even know how to play the piano. I think he was born with a hyperdose of DNA from an ancestor who could play the piano."

"So, you think I can play the piano?" he asked with a grin.

"You can't even cook," she told him. "You must come from a long line of people who just pulled plants from the ground and shoved them in their mouths."

The digital clock on JC's phone told them that the time was approaching noon. It had been a late night, celebrating a job well done.

"Let's get up," JC said to her. "We have to go home tomorrow. We have a lot to do."

They ate a late breakfast at Molly's. Bip had told them to go without him. He said that he had a lot of sleep to catch up on.

A number of townspeople stopped by JC and Robin's table at Molly's. The news team had broadcast from Stonestead to Denver for the last time, the previous night. The community was still stirring about the arrest of Melody Church.

JC's phone rang. It was Davey Kay.

"I couldn't do what you do," Davey said. "I never saw that coming."

"I didn't see it coming either," JC told him. "Not Melody. But it was your hunch that something was wrong. No one else would have caught it."

"Well, it doesn't bring Josh back," Davey said.

"No, it never does," JC agreed.

Robin was already on her own phone when JC said goodbye to his old high school friend.

She whispered that she was speaking to their news director, Pat Perilla. She received his permission to put him on speakerphone.

"You did a great job out there. You all did," Perilla said. "We've booked you flights out of Albany tomorrow at eleven in the morning. We'll email you the particulars."

"Thank you," they both said.

"Robin," the news director added. "We were all impressed with the job you did filling in, on camera, for JC."

"Thanks, Pat," she said and beamed.

"When you get back," Perilla said, "we should talk about elevating you to a reporting position. Wouldn't you agree, JC?"

"I do, Pat," JC said. "Once you make her a reporter and take her away as my producer, you'll see that I actually stink at doing this."

"I doubt that," the news director said. He bid them a safe trip home to Denver and hung up.

JC looked at her. She had a broad smile on her face.

"You're going to be a TV star," he said. "And rich!"

"I've seen where you take me to dinner," she laughed. "Rich must not be part of the deal."

He laughed. "Well, you'll be debt-reduced."

"I'd like that," she told him. "I hope I don't let it give me a big head," she said.

"Do you know anyone like that?" he asked. She smiled at him.

"Thank you," she said as she reached for his hand.

"I have someone I want to visit," JC told her. "Will you come?"

She agreed and they climbed into their rental car. They drove to the edge of town, following the Williams River Middle Branch. They waited for a busload of leaf peepers to pass and then pulled into the parking lot for the Williams River Hose Company restaurant.

Getting out of the car, fallen leaves blew across the road. The wind was picking up and the days were getting colder.

"How many for lunch?" the hostess asked them when they walked inside.

"I'm sorry," JC told her. "We're here to see someone."

He led Robin into the next room. It was dark. It wasn't being used as a waiting room until the dinner shift.

He stood there in the dark, feeling a little foolish. He was as unsure about what he was supposed to do, as he was sure that he had to do it.

"You're back," an old voice said behind them. They turned and saw Frederick Earle, the town historian's father. "I was having a late breakfast and saw you come in."

"We're leaving tomorrow," JC said.

"My son told me about the story you did on the fires," Frederick said. "We're all going to get to see it next week at the historical society meeting. I look forward to it."

"I know who she is," JC blurted. Frederick gave him a look. Then he looked at the sofa where he said that she sat.

"Is she there?" JC asked.

"No, she is not," the old man told them.

"It's Melatiah Hall," JC said.

Frederick looked at JC silently. Then he walked to the chair where JC had first met him and sat down. He waved them over to sit on the sofa.

"She's not using it, presently," Frederick said.

"You said that she was a young woman. You said that sometimes she appears to you holding a small baby," JC reminded him. "The baby who died in the fire with her."

"She felt safe here, at the firehouse," Frederick told them softly, looking down at the floor.

"Am I right?" JC asked.

"I think so," the old man stated. "I don't think she'll be back. I think maybe she feels better after you figured out the fires."

JC and Robin stood. They still had things to do elsewhere.

"I don't think your dog will be back either," Frederick stated. "I was wondering where she went to. I think she's done everything she can for you."

JC looked around the room and at the space beside his leg.

"Bye, Picabo," he said.

JC and Robin returned to the Flamstead Inn. JC told her that they still had another spot to visit, but they should get some coats.

They walked up the granite steps to the hotel and up to the second-floor room they shared.

"I've got something for you," he said.

He handed her a large box and she looked at him with a surprised face.

"I asked Milt to send it," he said. "It finally got here."

She opened the box and saw a jacket made of blue wool. It had leather sleeves and a large white "S" on the left breast. She gasped as she pulled out JC's old high school letter jacket.

"A deal's a deal," he said. "Now you have to go steady with me."

"Oh, Jean Claude."

The letter jacket kept Robin warm as they walked over the ruins of the Hall farm, the place where Melatiah and her baby lost their lives.

The site consisted of little more than a stone foundation now. Tall maples grew out of the ground in what might have been the living room. The Hall farm had been rebuilt after the fire. But it had burned down again, later.

It was a quiet spot above town. Remote. They spied a doe and her two fawns, feasting on some evergreens.

JC and Robin looked at the land, a place where entire lives had been lived and lost. It was a drama that played itself out a long time ago.

The air was damp, and the sky was growing dark.

Leaves on the trees were taking on the autumnal colors of yellow and orange and red. It would not be long before they would drop like snow. They would swarm in the wind below the oaks and the maples. And the people of Stonestead would be in their yards, raking.

JC and Robin reached for each other's hand just as small snowflakes began to fall.

The snow continued to fall as they drove back into town.

As they climbed out of the car, JC's phone rang.

"Hi JC," said Pat Perilla, their news director. "I wanted this to wait until you got back, but word got out. I figured that I should give you a call."

"Whatever you think is best," JC said.

"There's no easy way to say this, and I may not even be making the right decision," the news director said. "I'm going to give the anchor job to Sam Brown."

It didn't come as a surprise to JC. It had probably been a week since he even thought about the anchor position he was competing for.

"You're a hell of a journalist, JC," the news director said. "Sam is not in your caliber, in that regard. Hell, I even told him that when I told him that he got the job. I told you, JC, I sleep a lot better when I know that a story is in your hands."

"Thanks, Pat," JC said.

"We can talk more when you get back home," his boss said. "Maybe I can find some money to make you feel a little better about the whole thing."

"That rarely makes me feel worse," JC told him. Their conversation ended cordially.

"What did he say?" Robin asked, already knowing the answer.

"That I lost the job to the guy who forgot he had a microphone down his pants," JC smiled.

The accumulating snow was generating excitement in Stonestead. In the winter, it was a ski town. And nothing advertised the ski season like a fresh layer of snow.

People passing JC and Robin were having animated conversations about the coming ski and snowboard season. There were new adventures ahead. Stores, restaurants and bars would get crowded again. There would be a little more money in everyone's pockets.

"I *thought* there was something going on between you two."

The voice belonged to Deborah Sampson. She was coming down the sidewalk, behind them.

She looked at JC and Robin holding hands. Sampson had a smile on her face, as well as in her eyes.

"The ends justify the means, I suppose," she said, as she pulled her jacket closer to deflect the falling snow.

JC was bewildered by the statement.

"That visit you made to Melody's house helped figure out what she did to Josh," the plain-faced woman said.

JC wondered how she knew about his clandestine visit to Melody's house. But the likely answer dawned on him just before she said it.

"The witch window," she told him.

# The Names

There are twenty characters in this novel who are named after men and women who fought in the Revolutionary War.

Eleven of them came from Chester, Vermont, my unofficial inspiration while writing much of this book.

They are: Pvt. Richard Thompson, Reuben Tarbell, Frederick Earle, Pvt. Richard Hall, Thomas Caryl, Joshua Church, Jeremiah Dean, David Earl, George Earl, John Thurston and Benjamin Whitmore.

There are three characters named after women who fought alongside the men during the Revolutionary War: Deborah Sampson, Margaret Corbin and Mary McCauley.

Molly Ockett was an Abenaki woman who was well known for her medicine.

Two characters are named after German soldiers who fought alongside the British: Lawrence Gleichman was captured at Bennington and when he was done with his war, settled in Berne, New York.

Johannes Caspar Fuss was a Hessian and was captured at Saratoga. He agreed to fight for the American Continental Army after that, changing his name to John Foot. He also settled in New York after the war.

There is a character named after a Black New Yorker who fought at the Battle of Saratoga: Pvt. Edom London.

Two characters are named for men who came from New Hampshire to fight for the American side in the Battle of Bennington, Pvt. Andrew Aiken and Pvt. Samuel Brown.

And one character takes the name of a man from Massachusetts who fought at the Battle of Bennington. The Black soldier belonged to Seth Warner's Continental Army regiment. Sipp Ives was wounded at Bennington and died a day later.

# Acknowledgements

Thank you to the lovely people of Chester, Vermont. Thanks to Allie O'Neill, a part-time resident who gave me the idea of looking into witch windows. And Becca Garner, her co-worker at Salvatore Dental, who also had some great ghost stories.

Thank you to Alan Brown, owner of MacLaomainn's Scottish Pub in Chester. The owners and staff of the Fullerton Inn in Chester always aimed to please. Thanks to members of the Chester Police Department for their insights.

Ron Patch is the Town Historian in Chester and has wonderful stories to tell in his newspaper columns and in person about real places like Popple Dungeon and Crockers Camp.

*The Forensic Sciences Research Journal* was one of many contributors to my education regarding poisons found in wildflowers. Special thanks to Doctors Xincai Zhang, Vuanyi Zuo, Yun Wang and Shaohua Zhu.

Picabo, the ghost dog, was once a real dog and did a wonderful job of keeping me company for ten years. Her full name was Picabo Street, named after the remarkable ski racer. I'm a great admirer.

My wife, Carolyn, has become indispensable in the path to publishing these books. She has been, at one time or another, a photographer, videographer, cover designer, marketing director, confidant and much more.

Deirdre Stoelzle is my wonderful editor. She gets me. And thanks to Debbi Wraga, who performs the formatting and feats that are beyond me.

And Robert Burns penned *Such a Parcel of Rogues in a Nation*, in 1791. Slainte!

# About the Author

**Phil Bayly** was a television and radio journalist for over four decades. He lived and worked in Denver, Fort Collins, the Eastern Plains and the Western Slope of Colorado, as well as Wyoming, Pennsylvania and New York.

He was a reporter and anchor for WNYT-TV in New York's state capital, Albany.

He attended the University of Denver and is a graduate of Colorado State University.

He's been a ski racer and a ski bum. It's too late to stop.

He was born and raised in Evanston, Illinois, and now resides in Saratoga County, New York.

Visit Phil at murderonskis.com.

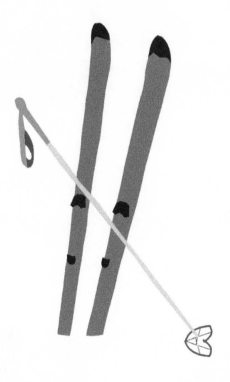

CPSIA information can be obtained
at www.ICGtesting.com
Printed in the USA
BVHW031719100123
656009BV00004B/232

9 781605 716343